STRANGE HIDING PLACE

Also by Graham Marks published by Catnip

Faultline
Takedown

STRANGE HIDING PLACE

GRAHAM MARKS

To Janet and Phil

With many thanks to Robert, Andrea
and Martin for bringing this story back to life

CATNIP BOOKS
Published by Catnip Publishing Ltd.
14 Greville Street
London EC1N 8SB

First published 2008
1 3 5 7 9 10 8 6 4 2

Originally published in 1995 as three books under the titles *Hard Drive, System Crash* and *Download*

A CIP catalogue record for this book is available from the British Library

ISBN: 978-1-84647-033-2

Printed in Poland

www.catnippublishing.co.uk

Chapter 1

Whispers in the air. Scrambled messages on an unknown frequency. Invisible commands to silent watchers ...

'Scanners tracking the southern quadrant have a pick-up. Do you read?' they said.

'Reading,' came the reply.

'Confirm distance.'

'Two kliks and closing.'

'Units in place?'

'Yes.'

'All systems operational?'

'All systems operational.'

'Estimate time to final countdown.'

'Four minutes. The accident is waiting to happen.'

* * *

It had been a long day and Dez was getting fed up. He was stuck in the back of the car, watching countryside that his mother kept describing as 'wonderful' but which he was thoroughly sick of.

His father was fed up as well. Fed up with Dez for getting himself lost in the little town they'd stopped at for lunch. Their timetable was now, according to his dad, shot to pieces – though why they had to have a timetable at all Dez couldn't understand. They were on holiday, driving around somewhere in France called the Dordogne (which sounded to Dez more like a medical condition than a place), and timetables were for school – somewhere he wouldn't be for at least another six weeks.

As his dad grumbled away in the front, mostly ignored by his mum, Dez got his phone and, with the sound muted, let his mind wander as he played one of the games. When they got back to England it would be to a new house and the slightly worrying prospect of a new school.

New school, new teachers, new boys – friends or enemies, who could tell? – and only his dog, Rufus, to help him through the inevitable bad times. Dez was not looking forward to the first few weeks of September, but he was determined to enjoy this holiday – timetable or no timetable – even if it was supposed to help him with his French.

He paused the game and looked up from the phone's tiny glowing screen; it was properly dark now. The car's headlights were on, but the road twisted and turned so much you couldn't see a lot. On the side of the road nearest the car the jagged silhouettes of fir trees made an almost impenetrable wall as they zipped by; on the opposite side low, scraggy bushes led off to yet more trees. It had been like that for the past half hour. At this rate, surely they'd be at their hotel soon. He'd just started playing again when he heard his mother gasp. He sat up straight and leant over to peer between the seats at what she'd seen.

'Ted!' she shouted, pointing at the approaching bend in the road. 'Ted – slow down!'

Dez could just make out the dark shape his mother had spotted first because she was sitting where the driver should be. It looked like a brick wall, and the thought flashed through his mind that it must be a broken-down lorry.

'The brakes aren't working, Mary!'

Dez looked at his father, mouth open, face lit up by the soft green light of the dashboard. His arms were rigid in front of him, as if he was trying to force himself through his seat and into the back of the car.

'We're going faster!'

Right then time seemed to slow, stretch, e-x-p-a-n-d.

Dez watched, fascinated, as the huge black shape in the road grew even bigger. He watched his father fight with the steering wheel and gear stick. He watched his mother twist slowly round to look at him, her left hand reaching between the seats, the diamonds in her engagement ring glinting. The last thing he remembered thinking was that he hadn't put his seat belt on …

Chapter 2

Dez woke up.

Had he been dreaming? He opened his eyes and made out a strange orange light somewhere in front of him. He was lying on his side, and everything he owned seemed to ache as he moved his left hand down to help push himself up. If he was in bed it was a bed covered in dust and small stones … then it all came tumbling back. Their car had crashed! The orange light was fire – his parents could still be trapped!

Dez tried to stand, his feet scrabbling in the dirt. Suddenly he felt a hand on his shoulder, pushing him gently down and pulling him back at the same time. He froze. And then he heard a man's voice.

'Stay still,' it whispered. 'You are in great danger – move away from the road.'

There was something odd about the way the man spoke, but his voice had an edge that made Dez do what he was told. He glanced over his shoulder to look at the speaker just as the light from the road intensified and he could make out the man's face and the fact that he was wearing what appeared to be black mechanic's overalls.

The car – it was burning! He couldn't just lie there if his parents were inside, injured and unable to get out. Breaking free from the man's grip, Dez lurched forward, only to be thrown back, punched by the force of a huge explosion.

For a moment the night sky was lit up by a vivid gout of flame that reached up five, ten metres. Dez's ears felt as if someone had boxed them and his head seemed to be looser than it should be on his shoulders. Gasping for breath he peered through the tangle of bushes towards the burning car and was stunned to see what appeared to be men in uniform gathering round it for a second or two. One then gave an order, gesturing with a gun, and they ran off.

The night was strangely silent after the dragon's roar of the explosion, and then in the silence Dez could hear a high-pitched whine in his ears, like you do after a big bang. He felt something wet on his face and realized that he was crying.

'There's nothing we can do,' said the man's voice. Dez had forgotten all about him and whirled round in a panic. Crouched right next to him, the stranger's face had an odd, wax-like quality, shadows waving across it as he spoke.

'We have to get away from here,' he went on. 'Follow me – and be as quiet as you can.'

'But my parents …' said Dez, looking back at the road.

'All I can tell you is that it was very quick,' said the man, indicating that Dez should follow him through the bushes and away from the road.

'Who were those men? What happened?'

'I can't go into details now.' The man held a thorny branch back to let Dez through a small gap, and, too confused to do anything else, he followed.

When they reached the trees and were able to stand up, Dez was about to speak when he heard a soft sucking noise in the distance. The man stopped and looked at a small box in his hand. He smiled slightly.

'They've gone,' he muttered and began walking away from the road again, deeper into the forest.

'Who?' asked Dez, running to keep up with him and stumbling in the dark. 'Who's gone? Where are you taking me? Shouldn't we call the police … are *you* the police?'

'I will explain everything – as far as I can – when we get to where we're going,' came the reply. 'For the moment you just have to trust me.'

Trust. Small word, big responsibility. But for Dez there was no choice. Even though he'd been warned, ever since he could remember, not to go off with strangers, what choice did he have? Either stay where he was, stranded by the side of a French road in the gathering dark, or go with this man. Dez mentally flipped a coin, stood looking at the man looking at him, and then nodded.

'OK,' he said, wondering if he'd done the right thing.

Their journey was a short one. There wasn't exactly a path through the trees, and there was no light to see where they were going, but the man led the way without once bumping into anything and Dez followed his black-against-black shape like a puppy.

As he walked, his mind was in a turmoil. His parents were dead. Well, not his *real* parents – he was an adopted child – but they were the only parents he had. For all he knew his real parents could be dead as well, and it occurred to him that for this sort of thing to happen to a person twice in eleven years was totally unfair.

He'd been in foster homes until he was five and counted himself lucky to have been adopted at all. People only seemed to want babies they could pretend were their own, and when Ted and Mary Danby had come into his life it was like ten Christmases arriving at once. And now they were gone. In a way Dez was used to it; people had been going from his life all of his life, though usually it was in a far less dramatic way.

He was alone again, and he was going to have to get used to the idea.

A few minutes after leaving the roadside the man stopped in a clearing and Dez almost bumped into him.

'What's happened?' he asked, peering round the man. There was nothing to see.

'We're here.'

'Where?' said Dez, walking past the man and into the clearing.

'Careful.'

'Why? There's nothing he – *oof!*' It felt as if he'd walked straight into a tree, but when he stumbled back and looked there was nothing there.

'I told you to be careful,' said the man. He pointed his fist in Dez's direction and Dez heard the crackle of static as the air in front of him flickered. One moment there was nothing and the next he was staring at a sleek, ultra-modern van.

'How ... ?' Dez put his hand out and touched the vehicle with the tips of his fingers. It was real, it was solid, it was there.

'Intra-molecule expansion,' the man said, smiling as he walked forward and a door hissed opened in the side of the van.

'What?'

'That's how we do it,' the man said, waving at Dez to follow him inside. 'It's called "cloaking".'

Dez stood stock still and looked at the man, half of him lit by the yellow interior light of the van, his shadow cast on the leafy ground. Feelings crowded in on him like spectators at an accident, all wanting to be in front – amazement, fear and loss, all covered in the cold blanket of shock.

What was he doing here in this chilly French wood, alone with a stranger? Shouldn't he have waited by the car for the police to come? Why did he believe a word this man said? He could be anyone. What on earth, thought Dez, had made him think he'd be safer going here? From inside the van he heard what sounded like a soft chirruping. *Budgies?*

All this time the man had watched him, saying nothing, staying still. Then, just like his dad used to do, he put his hand on Dez's shoulder and patted it. The simple gesture made Dez feel a lot calmer, more at ease, and he knew, just somehow *knew*, that everything would be all right if he got in the van. He walked slowly to the door, hesitated, and then got in, the man following him. There was another sighing hiss of air as the door swung shut.

More whispers. More questions.

'Success?' they asked.

'As far as we can tell,' they answered.

'What?'

'There was an explosion.'

'Why?'

'The machine they were in was far cruder than we imagined, little more than a travelling bomb. But, as far as we can tell, we succeeded.'

'I hope so. Stay for another circuit or so, just to check. We will be in touch.'

Chapter 3

While the outside of the van looked … well, like a van, the inside was something else entirely. There was no way, Dez knew, that these four wheels could have rolled off a production line *anywhere* on Earth. But if they hadn't, where had they come from? A Hollywood special effects studio? His eyes almost out on stalks, he sank into a chair, totally confused.

Then he felt the seat mould itself to his body. It was the oddest sensation, like he was suspended in mid-air, being gently massaged – which was just what he needed after being flung out of a speeding car and across a road. The place had an odd smell (sort of mothbally, but nicer) and the more he looked the more he became aware he was surrounded by the most mind-boggling technology.

The van was divided into two compartments, the bit he and the man were sitting in and, through a small gap, the actual driving bit. Dez stared, mouth open, at large, flat screens. Some danced with weird hieroglyphics, others projected three-dimensional pictures – aerial views of wooded countryside, what looked like the solar system and other things he couldn't make out – and yet others gave the distinct impression that they were, in some odd way, *thinking*.

And all the time, in the background, he could hear strange bird-like squawking, cheeping noises. Was someone talking?

The more he looked, the more convinced he became that there was nothing twenty-first-century about the van, nothing at all. But (and this was what he was still finding hardest to grasp) if it wasn't twenty-first-century technology, what was it? Dez turned to look at the man, whose skin had now lost its waxy appearance, but he couldn't think of what to say.

'Maybe I should try and explain a few things, Jack,' said the man. Dez looked at him and frowned. 'Are you feeling all right?'

'Yeah, kind of … but how did you know my name was Jack?' Nobody called Dez "Jack" any more, not since primary school, not even his parents. His surname was Danby, and someone, he couldn't remember who, had nicknamed him "Desperate". He'd been Desperate Danby for a term or two, and simply Dez from then on. It was strange to be called Jack after so long, but then everything was strange at the moment.

'I know rather more than just your name, Jack.' The man reached over to a console, tapped it and said something Dez couldn't understand. A screen cleared and then threw up yet more of the dancing hieroglyphics that twisted and squirmed like coloured worms.

'Well, you don't know that no one calls me Jack.' Dez sat forward, and the back of the chair moved with him. 'And anyway, what's *your* name?'

'How rude of me,' replied the man, looking slightly surprised. 'My name is Yakob. So, if you aren't called Jack, what *are* you called?'

'Dez,' said Dez, watching as the man called Yakob tapped the console again. The worms tangoed. 'Everyone calls me Dez.'

'I shall as well.'

'You were going to explain things to me.' Dez rubbed his bruised shoulder as he spoke. 'What happened out there?' He took a deep breath, swallowed the lump that had suddenly appeared in his throat and pointed back to the road, 'Why are my, um ... why are my *parents* dead? And what were *you* doing there?'

'I was sent to rescue you, Jack – sorry, Dez.' Yakob leaned back in his chair. 'I came a long way to make sure you would be safe, and, to be honest, I arrived almost too late.'

'But I *am* safe, aren't I?'

'More by luck than anything to do with me,' said Yakob.

'What do you mean?'

'Somehow or other you were thrown out of your car.' Yakob fiddled with the small matchbox-sized thing in his hand. 'The Väd-Raatch meant you to die in that crash, and it was pure chance that you didn't. None of this,' his hand swept round the weird clutter of humming, seemingly alive stuff that surrounded them both, 'could have stopped it from happening.'

'Why would anyone want to kill *me*? What have *I* ever done? And anyway, who are they? What did you call them? The Vadwotsits?' Dez could feel things welling up inside him once more – things he couldn't control, like tears and stuff. He wanted to cry, but he couldn't quite remember how. Actually, what he *really* wanted to do was kick something very hard.

He was alive, but his parents weren't. He was alone in the world. No brothers, no sisters, no grandparents – just some sister of his father's, somewhere in Australia, who no one had heard from for years. And he was in the middle of the French countryside, a long way from home. Then he remembered they were moving house soon, and didn't really have a home at the moment. *Total* bummer.

Yakob looked at Dez in the kind of way people do when they don't quite know what to say, and took a deep breath. 'You'll have to listen to what my Wing Leader, Tor Kobal, has to tell you for the full story,' he said at last, reaching behind him and picking up a small silver oblong. 'But before I play you this, I have to tell you something you may find very hard to believe.'

'Harder to believe than some people I've never heard of trying to kill me?' interrupted Dez.

'Quite possibly.'

'Tell me, then.'

But before Yakob could say anything something in the van screeched and all the lights dimmed.

'What's happening?' gasped Dez.

'Scoutship overflight … low and slow,' Yakob said, then turned and muttered something his own language. Seconds later every screen in the van blanked and there was complete silence. Dez froze. In the yellow half-light he sat rigid in his chair, wondering what the heck was going on. He didn't dare say or do anything and as the seconds ticked by all he could do was try to stop his teeth from chattering. He wasn't cold, so he knew he must be frightened.

Then one of the holo-screens lit up next to Yakob, information of some sort streaming across it at a rate of knots.

'Can we, um … can we talk?' whispered Dez.

'We can.'

'What's a scoutship overflight?'

'The Väd-Raatch were checking the area,' explained Yakob. 'Being typically thorough.'

'Can they see us? Will they be able to find us?'

'They're not looking for us, and they don't know we're here,' said Yakob, studying the screen. 'And if you don't know what you're looking for, you very rarely find it.'

'So why all the precautions?' asked Dez.

'Because if they *did* happen to pick us up we'd be in real trouble.'

'I thought I was in real trouble already,' sighed Dez.

'This would be real trouble and then some more,' said Yakob, sitting back. 'Good, they're out of range … for the moment.'

'For the moment?'

Yakob turned and said something over his shoulder to whoever or whatever it was in the van he spoke to, and the lights brightened. 'They may come back,' he said, 'or they may not. What were we doing before all that?'

'You were going to tell me something you said I'd find hard to believe,' said Dez.

'Right, so I was. All right. I've already told you my name is Yakob, Yakob Pell. What I didn't say was that I am a Tylurian from Priam, a planet somewhere behind what I'm told you call the Cygnus Rift – that's in the Orion Arm of the Milky Way, 300,000 light years from here – give or take a light year.' Yakob pointed to himself. 'I am – how would you put it? – an alien.'

'You don't *look* like one,' Dez said, peering at Yakob, staring in a way he'd been told he never should. 'You look just like one of us.'

'Appearances can be deceptive.'

'Huh?' frowned Dez.

'Don't judge people by what they look like – they aren't always what they seem,' explained Yakob, reaching over and placing the silver thing on the console. There was the sound like a bottle of fizzy water opening as it changed colour and somehow became part of the surface. 'I'm going to play the holo now, so listen carefully.'

He waited for a second or two and then a cylinder

of light, about a metre high, shot up and Dez was gawping at the figure of a woman dressed in some kind of uniform. She looked like a very expensive plastic kit he'd seen in a comic shop once, and then she moved, waving her arm.

'That's my Wing Leader, Tor Kobal,' said Yakob.

'Hello, Jack,' said the small figure.

'She also doesn't know you're called Dez,' whispered Yakob, leaning forward.

'You are now safely in the hands of one of our best agents,' Tor Kobal continued. 'And it is time for me to tell you why ...'

The next half-hour was the most extraordinary of Dez's life.

Priam's star system, Tor Kobal told him, was dominated by two cultures, the Tylurians and the Väd-Raatch. These two had been sworn enemies for longer than anyone cared to remember, and the Tylurians, according to Tor Kobal a peace-loving race, had managed to keep the Väd-Raatch at bay and their home planet safe until very recently. The arrival on the scene of a bloodthirsty new leader had changed the Väd's tactics. They were now at war, with the single aim of totally destroying Tylurians.

To guard against this ever happening a weapon had been developed, but never actually made – a complex, oxygen-hungry bacteria that could wipe out the Väd-Raatch in a matter of weeks once released on their planet. The plans, said Tor, had been hidden in a safe place – in fact, split up into three parts and put somewhere the Väds would never find them. The threat of the weapon's existence had, for some time, been enough to ensure peace.

So far, so good, except that the Tylurians had discovered there was a Väd spy in their midst. They didn't know who it was, or how much he, or she, had found out, until an information download from the Tylurian High Command's central intelligence unit had been intercepted and halted.

The spy – obviously someone very high up in the Tylurian government able to gain access to the intelligence unit – had been stopped before they could get the information they were after. But, before the security forces could find out where they were operating from, the spy had shut down their own terminal – but not before they'd infected the Tylurian computer with a deadly bio-metric virus – a disease that had damaged, beyond repair, almost all the other files about the secret plans. The data they contained had been lost for ever.

The tiny holographic figure of Tor Kobal paused for breath. Dez looked at Yakob.

'What's all this got to do with me?' he asked.

'Wait, there's more,' Yakob said.

'You are probably wondering what all this has to do with you, Jack.' Tor started talking again and Dez found himself nodding at the hologram, even though it couldn't see him. 'And the reason is that we hid the information about our weapon – including the antidote – on your planet. To be exact, some eleven years ago we placed it in the genetic coding of three inhabitants of Earth. You are one of them.' The figure pointed in his general direction and then froze. Dez noticed that Yakob was tapping the console.

'Are you all right?' he asked. 'Shall I start the holo again?' Dez nodded. He wasn't all right! He was, to put it mildly, stunned. Eleven years ago? He'd only had his eleventh birthday three months before. He'd been messed around with by aliens when he was only three months old? Did this have anything to do with him being an orphan? A million questions raised their hands and demanded to be asked, but you couldn't talk to a hologram, only listen. He watched Yakob touch the surface of the console again.

'Hidden in the double helix, the twin spirals of your DNA, is one-third of the information required to make the secret weapon we need to stop the Väd-Raatch,' Tor continued. 'You may not believe this is possible, you may not believe that we could have done this – but you are sitting in a vehicle that has travelled well over a quarter of a million light years to find you, so please believe that *every* word I say is the truth.

'We thought we had chosen a hiding place the Väds would never find, but we hadn't reckoned on the traitor. We were lucky the spy was uncovered before they found out everything, although what they got was bad enough.

They had managed to get one name and location – yours – that was all. When we searched through the mess our central intelligence unit's memory was in, we found that all we now had was the same information the spy got, plus something they hadn't: the other two names and where they lived. They will be difficult to find, but not impossible.

'The race was then on to get to you before the Väds. They wanted you dead, and if you died we would not be able to build our weapon. You three are like pieces of a jigsaw puzzle – the picture is incomplete, and the information useless, without all of you being alive. I must end now. I am glad Captain Pell has succeeded, and I look forward to meeting you in person in the very near future.'

The hologram saluted, and then disappeared. Dez stared at where it had been, finding it hard to blink, let alone think. Tylurians? Väd-Raatch death squads? People from a planet three hundred *thousand* light years away? He ought to be hallucinating, but he knew he wasn't. This was real, this was happening. And what was more, it was happening to him, Dez Danby, 14 Avenscroft Road (until he moved), London, England, Northern Hemisphere, Earth, the Solar System.

He breathed out and realized that he'd been holding his breath for ages. He looked at Yakob. Yakob raised his eyebrows, as if to say 'Well?' and Dez rubbed his face with his hands before speaking.

'So, I'm a filing cabinet.'

'Excuse me?'

'Your lot thought I'd make a neat place to store stuff . . .' Dez frowned. 'How'd they come to choose *me*?'

'I've no idea, Dez. I was still in the Academy eleven years ago.' Yakob pressed the silver holo-chip and there was another *T-ssst!* as it disengaged from the surface of the console. 'All I know is, now I've found you, I have to tell Tor Kobal so she can send one of *Tyson's Grip's* cruisers here to pick you up.'

'Tyson's grip? What's that?'

'The T-class StarJumper we came here in – it's hidden far out beyond your system at the moment.' Yakob swivelled his chair and turned to face the console. 'Excuse me for a minute, would you?'

Dez watched as Yakob's fingers danced across the surfaces in front of him. As he watched he could hardly believe what he saw – things moved, other things disappeared and the whole area in front of Yakob seemed to reform into a new configuration. Then Yakob started speaking; it still sounded like total gibberish, but then it was a foreign language. About as foreign as you could get, thought Dez, realizing that what he really wanted was a drink.

'Done!' said Yakob, sitting back.

'What is?'

'I've just informed *Tyson's Grip* that I have you in safe keeping.'

'What happens now?'

'I will tell you . . .'

Chapter 4

Sitting holding a cup of something hot and wet that Yakob had given him, Dez listened to Yakob tell him that they were going to drive from the Dordogne to a pre-arranged site in the Alps, where a cruiser from *Tyson's Grip* would come and pick Dez up. Yakob would then go and find the other two people who had the code inside them.

'Why do we have to drive?' asked Dez, putting his empty cup down.

Whatever he'd been drinking had actually tasted quite nice. 'If you're so advanced, why can't you just teleport us there?' He snapped his fingers.

'I *could* fly,' said Yakob, 'but the cloaking device isn't working properly. As far as the diagnostics can tell one of its logic buffers has malfunctioned. It *thinks* it's working when it isn't.'

'It was working all right when I walked into the van!' interrupted Dez.

'That's because it only works properly when we aren't

moving. And I don't want to alert anyone to the fact that we're here by flying – your people or the Väds.'

'Why would the Väds still be here? They think I'm dead.'

Yakob fiddled with one of the controls and something, somewhere in the van, started to hum quietly. 'Remember the spy?' he asked. Dez nodded. 'They're still there in Central Command; they weren't caught. If they find out you're still alive we'll be in the firing line again.'

'So,' said Dez, getting up and walking over to look at the driving compartment, 'we can't fly, and the Väds might still be out there looking for me.' He turned. 'Have you got a gun, just in case?'

'I carry a needle laser; I also have side-mounted, melt-tipped rockets, front and rear Cold Pulse cannon and three-ply molecular shielding, just in case.'

'And a broken cloaking device.'

'Yes, and a broken cloaking device that will be fixed as soon as the cruiser arrives. Look,' Yakob got up and walked past Dez and sat in the driving seat, 'you're safer here than anywhere else on this planet.'

'I'd be even safer if you hadn't mucked around with me and made me into a target for a bunch of space gangsters who ended up killing my parents!' Dez did what he'd been wanting to do since getting into the van. He kicked something. Whatever it was simply absorbed the shock by letting his foot sink into it slightly, making him feel a bit foolish.

'I can only apologize for what has happened to you,'

said Yakob, ignoring Dez's outburst. 'I'm sure that when Tor finds out how badly things have gone wrong she'll be horrified. It was never meant to be like this – never.'

'Well, it *is* like this, and this is *supposed* to be my holiday! Some rotten holiday …' Dez plonked himself down in the seat next to Yakob. 'What's going to happen to me? I mean after this is all over?'

'I don't know. That is in the future. For now all I can say is that we must get to our destination within the next two days. When you meet Tor, you must ask her.'

'Well, let's go,' said Dez. 'I've never seen an Alp, so I suppose that's something to look forward to.'

'You are a brave kid, Dez,' Yakob touched something on the dashboard as he spoke. The lights in the van went out and the headlights switched on, illuminating the trees in front of them. He reached over with his right hand, taking Dez's hand and shaking it. 'I am very pleased to have met you, and only sorry that it is in such bad circumstances.'

'Me, too,' replied Dez, smiling despite how he felt. There was something about this man that made him unable to stay angry with him for long. Then a thought struck him. 'Has this thing got number plates and everything, in case we get stopped by the cops?'

Yakob muttered something in his own language and started turning the very unalien-looking steering wheel. 'Yes it has,' he grinned, looking at part of the windscreen, which now showed the view out of the back window as the van reversed, 'but thanks for the reminder!'

Once Yakob had driven the van out of the clearing and on to a rough track, he spoke again in his own language and a map appeared, low down on the windscreen. A red dot blinked in the bottom left-hand corner and a green one to the right. He pointed at the green one. 'That's where we have to go.'

'How far is it?'

'550-600 kilometres – about a day's drive.'

'But we don't have to be there for two days,' said Dez. 'What're we going to do for the rest of the time?'

'If we get there early, we rest. It's always good to have some spare time.'

Dez nodded, thinking that Yakob sounded just like his father – far better to be early and have to wait for hours than be even five minutes late for anything. He watched as the van moved quickly along the deeply rutted forest track, its suspension making it feel as if they were driving over the smoothest of motorways.

'You will drive carefully,' Dez said nervously.

'Very carefully,' replied Yakob. 'You are …'

'I know, "*safer here than anywhere else on this planet*" … but all the same, watch out for big trucks.'

An hour later they were still travelling along the same type of road, not fast, not slow. Poodling.

'Why don't you get on to a motorway? You know – an autoroute. Wouldn't that be quicker?' asked Dez.

'Could be, probably, but I prefer to stick to the less well-travelled routes.'

'Just in case?'

'Yes,' smiled Yakob, 'just in case.'

Dez fell silent, looking out of his side window. The van was a left-hand drive, like a proper continental car, and for some reason this made him feel safer. Looking at the small rear-view image on the windscreen Dez could see a police car – at least he *hoped* it was a police car. 'Yakob,' he said nervously, 'we're being followed.'

'I know, I've just done a scan. It's an ordinary car; I can't pick up anything unusual.'

'Could it be the Väds?' asked Dez.

'It could, but they'd have to be unarmed.'

'Why?'

'Because the arms they'd be carrying give off high resonance feedback when scanned,' replied Yakob, his eyes flitting to and from the rear-view screen.

'Oh …' Dez nodded, none the wiser.

'The plasmetal that laser weapons are made of has a particular sound signature.' Yakob accelerated, and the car behind also speeded up. 'And that car has no shielding. I'd know if they were carrying any.'

'What will we do if they stop us?'

'Act dumb.'

'One of my many talents,' said Dez.

'Happily,' said Yakob, pointing to one of the dashboard screens, 'I don't think we're going to have to put it to the test – they've just received a radio message calling them away.'

From just behind them a loud siren began to wail and

Dez jumped as he saw the police car's blue light begin to flash. Seconds later the white saloon car sped past the van and away into the night. As the red tail lights disappeared Dez realized his hands were tightly balled and slowly he unclenched them.

'Try and relax,' said Yakob. 'We've a long way to go and you're going to be a nervous wreck if you do that every time there's a car behind us. Why don't you tell me about yourself?'

Dez looked at Yakob. 'What do you want to know?'

'Oh, you know, everything – what it's like being you, here on Earth.' Yakob checked the rear-view image again and overtook the battered Renault bumbling along ahead of them. 'Loud, noisy, dirty, inefficient – why do they make things like that, let alone buy them? Sorry, talking to myself. You were going to say?'

'I don't know what to tell you,' frowned Dez. 'I'm just a kid. I don't do anything except fool around and go to school ... fool around *at* school as well.' He sat back and let the seat hug him like a big, fat auntie at a christening. 'Well, I'm eleven – but you know that. I like football, computer games – football computer games – and watching TV. I've got a dog called Rufus, two best friends – Tim and Cy – and I'm moving schools in September. Which is all right, 'cos I didn't really like the one I was at, but not all right 'cos I'm even less sure about the new one. And I'm moving house, which is definitely *not* all right, 'cos Tim and Cy won't be there.' He paused. 'Well, I *was* moving house and schools, but now ... who knows?'

'But what's it like living here?'

'I don't live *here*,' Dez explained. 'I live in England. This is France, and I've no idea what it's like to live here.'

'OK, what's it like living in England?'

'S'all right ... we've got a crap football team and my dad says – my dad *said* – it was better when he was a kid,' Dez turned in his seat. 'Now you tell me what it's like on Priam – you can see what it's like here.'

Yakob laughed, slapping the steering wheel as he did so. 'Well said, Dez! Good point!' He sat back in his seat and, flicking a switch, took his hands off the steering wheel and turned to look at his passenger.

'What are you *doing*? The road – look at the road!'

'It's all right, I've put everything on auto,' grinned Yakob. 'It's a better driver than me anyway, and now I can concentrate on talking to you.'

'Machines go wrong, like cloaking devices, remember?'

'Trust me,' said Yakob.

'I was always told never to trust strangers.'

'And what could be stranger than a man who says he comes from behind the Cygnus Rift?'

Dez nodded.

'OK, I'll drive,' sighed Yakob, turning back to the wheel. 'Well, Priam's bigger than your planet, has four moons and is in a system with twin suns, and our plants are all red, rather than green.'

'And where are the Väds?'

'Many thousands of your years ago we shared the planet with them, But after one particularly vicious war they left Priam. It took them some years to do, but they went and colonized another planet in our system – Anavrin – and made it their own.'

'But what's Priam like? Is it a nice place?'

'It's not perfect, nothing ever is; but some parts of it are beautiful, truly beautiful – even some of the cities, and it's hard to make a city attractive. Priam is very advanced, in comparison to Earth, as you've probably guessed.' Yakob indicated the van they were travelling in, and Dez nodded, even though he thought calling the thing he was sitting in 'advanced' was like calling a Ferrari 'quite fast'. Super-amazingly futuristic *might* come closer.

'Do you want to hear more?' Yakob inquired.

'You bet! What about school? Do you have schools up there?'

'Do we have *schools*!'

And as the darkened countryside sped past, the van eating up the distance between them and the Alps, Dez sat and listened, spellbound, to this strange man from beyond the stars spin tales of life on an alien planet.

Chapter 5

When Dez woke up he found the sun shining through the van's tinted windows and his seat tipped back, almost like a bed. He felt completely rested and ravenously hungry.

He yawned. 'When did I fall asleep?'

'Just before dawn. I'll never get used to just one sun – very odd!'

Outside Dez could see that they were still travelling on a smallish country road, fields on either side, some with crops, some with animals. It all looked very – what was that phrase he'd heard? – very chocolate-box.

'Where are we?'

'Outside somewhere called Lyon.'

'What time is it?'

Yakob looked at his wrist. 'Nearly 11.30, Earth time.'

'What? Almost lunch and I haven't even had breakfast yet! Can we stop for some food?'

'We don't have to,' Yakob pointed behind him. 'I've got food here.'

'But have you got a croissant – or better still, a glass of milk, eggs and bacon and a slice of hot buttered toast? That's the question.'

'The short answer to that is "no", but I do have a cup of mezz, some plakk and frew or a slice of tasmang. How about that?'

'I could eat a horse, so I suppose a plate of plakk and frew won't hurt me.' Dez sat up and his seat sat up with him. 'Can I eat your food?'

'There's only one way to find out,' Yakob smiled. 'Are you going to let me put *Stark Revenge* on auto so I can get you some food, or am I going to have to stop?'

'Stark revenge? What's that?'

'It's this craft's title; they all have titles.'

'What does it mean?' Dez looked puzzled. 'It doesn't make sense.'

'It doesn't *mean* anything. What does "Jack Danby" mean? Names are simply labels, something you give to a person or an object that makes it different from another one. They don't have to make sense; they just avoid confusion.'

'S'pose so … look, I think you'd better stop. I mean, the sight of this thing driving itself is going to look, you know, *odd*. We might have got away with it in the dark, but …'

'You're right,' said Yakob, pulling the van over to the side of the road and stopping. 'So, plakk and frew and a cup of mezz?'

'If that's what's on the menu.'

Yakob walked into the rear of the van. 'When you're hungry, anything tastes good. I'm sure that's as true here as it is on Priam.'

'We'll see,' replied Dez

Not long after Dez had finished his "meal" – even though it had tasted OK, he was still having trouble thinking of something blue as proper food – he noticed that there seemed to be rather more traffic in front of them than before. The road was quite twisty, and had hedges on either side, so they couldn't see very far ahead.

'Can you get the van to look round corners and find out why we've slowed down?' he asked.

'I could fly over everyone, but that might cause a bit of a stir,' said Yakob, peering ahead. 'We'll find out soon enough. Don't worry – we're doing fine for time.'

As they rounded the next bend the road straightened out and they could see some kind of road-block a few hundred metres in front.

'Now I can do something,' Yakob said, issuing what sounded like an order. In response a flat screen popped up and showed an image of what was happening in front of them. Yakob adjusted the controls and the picture became a close-up, with sound, of what was happening.

'*Excusez-moi, Monsieur; ça ne va pas vous prendre très longtemps, mais nous sommes à la recherche d'un évadé. C'est un criminel.*'

'Can you understand what he's saying?' Yakob pointed to a policeman who was wearing sunglasses and bending down to speak to the driver of the car at the head of the queue.

'I got "could do a lot better if he tried" in my French report last term.'

'No matter; we'll know soon enough – the queue's moving quite fast.'

'Must be something quite big,' mused Dez. 'I can see four or five unmarked cars as well as the police one.'

'The translator circuits have kicked in,' said Yakob, as subtitles in a weird script began appearing at the bottom of the little screen. 'It's something to do with an escaped criminal … armed and dangerous. He's saying – the policeman – that no one should approach him if they see him, and don't pick up any hitchhikers. What's a hitchhiker?'

'Someone standing by the road, asking for a lift. Look, they're making the driver open the boot so they can check inside!'

'People travel in such small places here?'

'No, Yakob, they …'

'Only joking!'

'An alien with a sense of humour!' Dez made a face. 'Don't joke with the policeman. My dad always said they thought you were up to something if you were too jokey – oh, no!'

'What's the matter?'

'What if they ask to see our passports and stuff? Mine's burnt to a crisp and you don't have one at all!'

'Not quite true. They gave me papers on the *Grip*

before I left. I haven't even looked at them yet, to be honest.' Yakob scratched his head. 'Do you think they'd believe us if we said yours had been stolen?'

'Can't you kind of *make* one?' asked Dez, a worried look on his face. 'I mean, if this mega-machine of yours can do breakfast, can't it magic up a passport?'

Yakob moved *Stark* forward a few metres as a car was let through the road block. It would be their turn in four cars' time. 'If we had a little more time I'm sure it could, but not right now, I'm afraid.'

'And you look nothing like my dad – they might think I've been kidnapped or something!'

'You worry too much.'

'I've got lots to worry about.'

Three cars to go.

'Must be a bad man, this escaped criminal,' said Yakob.

'Why?'

'Ten, maybe twelve men; lots of cars.'

'Just like on TV.'

'If you say so.'

Two cars to go.

'Have you ever seen any space monsters?' Dez was getting bored with all the waiting.

'My Astro-Nav tutor at the Academy was one of the ugliest people I've ever met – bad-tempered too.'

'No, I mean – you know, like real monsters, with a hundred eyes and loads of tentacles, blasting ray guns and stuff. That kind of thing.'

'Is that what you think it's like up there?' Yakob pointed and looked up at the roof of the van.

'That's what it's like in the movies.'

'The movies, whatever they are, sound more interesting.'

One car to go.

Dez glanced at the rear view screen and saw there were no cars behind them, and only one in front. They were almost alone, in the middle of the French countryside and surrounded by heavily armed policemen. The car in front moved off.

Suddenly the hollow feeling in the pit of Dez's stomach made him think something wasn't right. Maybe he *was* worrying too much, but maybe, just maybe, his survival instincts were turned full up. Was this a road block? Were these really policemen? The car in front disappeared from sight round a bend in the road.

'Scan them, Yakob – *scan them!*' A split second later he saw the policeman with sunglasses turn and nod to the men behind him. 'It's a trap!' he yelled. Everything was going in slow-motion once more, just like in the accident. He saw some of the policemen duck down into their cars, as if to pick something up, and as they stood he saw they were holding large, black things that could only be guns that looked as if they could burn a hole through a tank.

'Väds ...' he heard Yakob mutter. 'You were right ...'

'They're going to kill me!'

'Not if I have anything to do with it.'

'But you're not *doing* anything!'

'Hold on,' said Yakob. His arms straight out, his hands gripping the steering wheel, he yelled something at the top of his voice.

From being in a world where time had slowed down to a trickle, as if someone had hit his own personal pause button, Dez was suddenly thrown forcibly down into his seat; it absorbed most of the shock, but he still felt as if his stomach had been nailed to the road while the rest of him reached for the sky.

Out of the window everything had disappeared and all he could see was blue, and for a very long moment he had no idea what had happened. Then his brain caught up with reality. *Stark Revenge* had taken off. Vertically. It felt like 0-200 metres in next to no time.

'Don't *ever* ...' he said through gritted teeth, as Yakob yelled something in the general direction of the dashboard and he was pushed hard, back into his seat, ' ... try this at home ...'

Chapter 6

Stark Revenge was flying. How far off the ground, Dez had no idea, but everything looked incredibly tiny and a long way down. He'd flown before, but never in anything this small and never in a van. All around him those strange trilling noises babbled away, the windscreen was covered in flashing, blinking displays, and lights – red, green, yellow, blue – winked on the dashboard while screens showed ever-changing exterior views.

Dez noticed one screen in particular. It gave a view along the side of *Stark* and he could hardly believe his eyes. The van was no longer van-shaped! As he watched, it was changing, morphing into an aircraft.

'The van!' he exclaimed, turning to look at Yakob. 'It's changed!'

'Well, *you* try flying something the shape of a box. It's possible but no fun, I can tell you!'

Dez looked out of the window again. The sides of the van had curved out to make short, stubby wings, and a rear-view monitor showed that they'd 'grown' a small tailplane. As far as he could see, the skies were clear. They'd got away.

'Phew! That was close!'

'It still is,' muttered Yakob, his eyes flicking all over the dash as he spoke, his hands whipping out to make a small adjustment here and turn something on (or off, Dez couldn't tell) there.

'What d'you mean?' Dez looked around frantically. Nothing to be seen. Not even a bird. 'Where?'

Yakob indicated a pattern of pulsating lights on the dash. 'We've got company,' he said, turning up the zoom on the rear-view screen when the van bucked sideways. 'Pulse beam … there they are.'

Dez saw a couple of evil-looking black helicopter-type craft on the screen. He couldn't tell if they were gaining on them or whether the camera was still zooming in. Whichever it was, the things were far too close. 'How come we can see them? Can't they cloak their stuff?'

'They can, but they obviously don't care if they're seen …' he said.

'Are we going to die?'

'You want the truth?' The van shook again. 'Or …'

'The truth.'

'I don't know,' Yakob gripped the juddering steering wheel. 'But we'll soon find out.'

Dez kept his eyes firmly on Yakob, aware that his seat was holding him so tightly that he couldn't have got out of it even if he'd wanted to. The thought passed through his head that he wanted to go to the loo. Badly. Then, before he had a chance to think anything else, the van, or what it had turned into, flipped sideways and then looped the loop.

It felt as if the van was being flung about at random, like a squash ball in a grudge match, and the taste of plakk and frew rose in Dez's throat. The last thing he wanted to do was be sick. Correction, the *second*-to-last thing he wanted to do was be sick. Mostly, he didn't want to die.

'Why don't you shoot at them with those melt-tipped thingies of yours?'

'I'm too busy trying not to be shot *at*, is why.' Yakob whistled softly as a group of lights on Dez's side of the dash flared up. 'That was close!'

'What was?' Dez whirled round, and somewhere in front of them a shimmering, glassy sphere of air exploded silently.

'PhotoSonic cluster. Would've made quite a dent in the shielding.'

'How come they keep missing?'

'I was top of my Evasive Action class,' smiled Yakob grimly.

'No one could catch you?'

'Ninety-nine out of a hundred times.'

Stark dipped and skewed, almost skidding in the air as another glassy ball shattered to Dez's right, much closer than the last time.

'They're good,' Yakob grunted, powering *Stark* forward again. 'But I've got a feeling I'm better.'

'I hope it's more than a feeling,' Dez muttered to himself, grabbing the sides of his seat. There was a sudden jolt, all the lights dimmed and the sky went a deep, deep blue and then back to normal.

'Fooled them!' yelled Yakob, as *Stark* appeared to start flying backwards.

'Are we, you know, going back the way we came now?'

'In a manner of speaking.' Yakob was hunched forward over the steering wheel, staring intently at the map on the windscreen. 'We just warped slightly.'

'Warped? As in "Warp factor 5, Mr Sulu"? Like on *Star Trek*?'

'I wouldn't know about that. More like it being two o'clock, and then it being a couple of seconds to two.'

'*Time* travel? We went back in *time*?'

'Only a second or two, just enough to confuse the the Väds.'

'Me too,' said Dez. 'Where – *woo-o-o-ow!* Where are we going now?' The van was falling, nose first, in what seemed to him like a kamikaze dive straight for a large expanse of forest.

'Somewhere safe, safer than being up here anyway,' replied Yakob, as the trees rushed towards them. Just before it seemed inevitable that they would crash, Yakob pulled *Stark* up and they dropped slowly through the tangle of leafy branches, finding a space to go through where, from way up in the air, it had seemed impossible.

The next thing Dez knew, the van was settling in a tiny clearing deep in the forest. Yakob lowered *Stark*'s side windows, letting in the sounds and smells of the quiet, peaceful woodland, and then punched in the command for it to morph back into its van shape. Dez leaned out of his window and watched as the metallic wings disappeared soundlessly, flowing back into the main body of the vehicle in the same way as he'd seen mercury move on a dish in the science lab.

'How does it do that?'

'Intelligent metal. It can memorize shapes,' explained Yakob. '*Stark* has a dozen or so configurations – things it can become. Quite useful, really.'

'I think my dad would have called that an understatement.'

'I think your dad would have been right. Get back in, Dez – I'm going to cloak.'

Dez sat back down and they both sat in silence, waiting. 'Can I get out and have a look at us being invisible?'

'No point. Nothing to see,' grinned Yakob.

'How long are we going to have to wait?'

'As long as it takes.' Yakob yawned, stretched and got up. 'Until it's dark, probably.'

Dez stayed, watching life going on outside the cloaked van. Whatever panic their arrival had created amongst the animals in this part of the forest, they seemed to have forgotten about it now. He'd seen squirrels, a fox and a host of birds all going about their own particular business by the time Yakob came back, holding two cups of steaming liquid; he gave one to Dez.

'What did you say this was called?' he asked as he took a sip.

'Mezz.'

As Yakob was sitting down the dashboard lit up like a Christmas tree, and Dez got the distinct impression that *Stark* was actually tensing itself, getting ready for something to happen.

'Overflight,' said Yakob, bending over to look up out of the van's sloping windscreen.

'The Väds? But … but I thought we'd lost them?'

'We did, but they know we're still here somewhere.' Yakob examined various readouts on the dash. 'And they don't give up that easily.'

'What's *Stark* doing?' asked Dez, who could hear things happening all around him.

'It's dissipating heat from everything, including us – bringing the temperature down so it's the same as our surroundings. That way it doesn't look like we're here.'

'I thought we were cloaked and no one could see us.'

'We are, and no one can see us, but we still have what's called a heat autograph, and that can be picked up quite easily.'

Dez shivered slightly. He didn't know if it was simply panic or the van cooling down. 'Where are they?'

'Very low and right above us.'

In Dez's mind's eye he could see the crouched black shapes of the Väd craft hovering in the sky like evil mosquitoes, waiting to strike. If they found them they would do more than bite – he knew that. He tried to swallow and found he couldn't. Glancing at Yakob Dez thought the man looked as if he was made out of stone, while he felt as if *he* was constructed entirely out of jelly – pale, very frightened jelly.

Some lights on the dash flickered and Yakob let out a small, low sigh. 'They've gone,' he said.

'Are you sure?'

'Without going up there and taking a peek, which I'm not going to do, I'm prepared to believe the tried and tested instrumentation installed in *Stark* which, I am told, has an insignificant fail factor. Yes, I am sure.'

'What about the cloaking device?' muttered Dez.

'Give me a break, will you?' exclaimed Yakob. 'Nothing's perfect!'

Whispers again. Shouted whispers. Angry whispers.

'Report!' they said.

'We lost them.'

'Explain.'

'We think they warped.'

'Think?'

'They warped, and by the time we realized what had happened, they'd hidden.'

'Find them.'

'We've tried.'

'Try harder. Try much harder. Failure is not an option.'

Chapter 7

'What now?' said Dez. 'Are we safe?'

'Safe is a relative term.'

'Don't understand.'

'Well, we're safe enough where we are,' said Yakob, 'but we could be a lot safer elsewhere.'

'Let's go then!' Dez clapped his hands together. 'What are we waiting for? Step on the gas and accelerate *Stark* out of here!'

'Nothing's ever that easy, Dez.'

'How did I know you were going to say that? All grown ups say things like "nothing's ever that easy" and "whoever said it was supposed to be fair" ... even ones from Priam,' Dez ran his fingers through his hair. 'I thought at least you might be different.'

'It's not me. I can't change the circumstances; I can only work with them.'

'And what's that supposed to mean?'

'It means that we'll have to do some walking.'

'*Walking?* But it's *miles*! Why can't we drive there? If

the Väds have gone we'll be all right, won't we?'

'I told you, the Väds don't give up easily. They'll be on the lookout for us everywhere. Even if *Stark* changed its shape they might pick us up. I daren't drive out of here.'

'Won't walking be just as dangerous?' said Dez.

'No, because the last thing they'll be expecting us to do is leave our transport behind.'

'You're going to abandon it?'

Yakob shook his head. 'I'm going to leave it here and come back for it once I've delivered you.'

'You make me sound like a package.'

'No offence intended, but that's my job – delivering you to the scout ship from *Tyson's Grip* that'll be meeting us in around twenty-four hours from now.'

'Twenty-four hours and at the top of an Alp from now!' Dez looked as if he'd chewed on a lemon. 'How're we going to get there? You can't be serious about walking.'

'Part of the way, yes. To the next big town. It's not that far, only twenty or so kilometres.'

Twenty kilometres. Dez paused. For all that he'd been a metricated kid all his school life (and wouldn't know an ounce from a pint), when it came to kilometres he was lost. 'How long will it take us?'

'Oh, I don't know.' Yakob looked at the map displayed on the windscreen. 'Let's see ... about, say, five or six hours if you're really slow.'

'Five or six *hours*!' moaned Dez.

'Not all in one go, we'll stop about half-way and have a rest and some food.'

'Oh, great! A midnight feast round some old camp fire! I've never fancied camping much – are you *positive* we can't drive?'

'Positive,' replied Yakob firmly. 'It won't be so bad, although we can't have a fire as it might attract attention.'

'Might keep us warm as well.'

'I've got travelling packs; we'll be OK.'

'The only travelling pack I'm interested in has four wheels and an engine.'

'Are all boys like you?' Yakob looked him up and down.

'Like me how?'

'Lazy.'

'I'm not lazy!'

'You just don't like walking, right?' grinned Yakob.

'Not for six hours in the dark.' Dez sat round, facing the windscreen. He was in no mood to start getting ready for a twenty-kilometre walk either, but, from the short time he'd known Yakob, he could tell when the man was being serious and when he was joking. They were going for a walk.

Chapter 8

Dusk had just started to fall when Yakob said that it was time to go. They left *Stark Revenge*, cloaked and in maximum security mode, in the tiny clearing. Before leaving Yakob had squirted a coded message to *Tyson's Grip*, saying the meet was still on, and reminding Tor Kobal that he needed a new cloaking device.

Yakob had changed into more appropriate clothes and each of them was carrying a small dark green backpack. Dez felt a bit cold as they set off, but once they'd got into their stride he realized he was quite warm, and even thought he might have to take his sweatshirt off.

They kept mostly to small forest tracks, crossing main roads when they had to, and then only when there were no cars coming. Occasionally Yakob consulted a small electronic map, whose coloured screen glowed in the dark. As they walked, they talked about everything and anything to do with life on Earth and on Priam. Only after they'd been walking for an hour or so, and a sickle moon had risen in the night sky, did Dez realize that

Yakob had got him round to talking about the accident and his parents – two subjects that had been hovering in the back of his mind but he hadn't been allowing himself to think about.

'What were they like, your parents?' It was a simple enough question, but it made Dez stop walking when Yakob asked it.

'I've never really thought about them like that,' he replied. 'They were just, you know, *there*. It's hard to imagine that they aren't now. Too many things have been happening for it to sink in properly.'

'It will take some time.'

'But not being there is for ever, Yakob.' Dez started to walk again. 'I mean, you can't get *Stark* to warp again – to when they were alive – and stop the accident, can you?'

'No, I can't. I wish I could, but anything more than the couple of seconds' jump we did back there would be a serious time-effect warp. Even if it were possible, it could be dangerous and wouldn't solve anything, anyway.'

'Why not?'

'Someone once worked it out – some really clever scientist developed a theory – the Whole Story Theory, it's called.'

'How does that go then?' Dez jumped over a fallen tree.

'It says that everything that is going to happen *will* happen, no matter what you do.'

'Why bother then?' asked Dez, looking back as Yakob stepped over the tree.

'A good question.'

'I mean, if that was true, and I was going to pass all my exams, then why should I do any work at all?'

'Ah!' Yakob smiled. 'But you *don't* know. None of us knows anything until it happens, and then it's too late. That's why you *have* to bother – that's why no one's ever managed to disprove the Whole Story Theory.'

'Sounds like a cop-out to me. And anyway, if you can warp a little, what's so dangerous about warping a lot?'

'Warping one or two IOT's-'

'Eye-owetees?'

'Increments of Time – seconds to you ... anyway, warping one or two IOT's doesn't allow anything but the most infinitesimal changes to the Time Line. And changing the Time Line isn't like simply changing your clothes – it affects everything for everybody and it's permanent. Apart from that it would take the most stupendous amounts of energy to do it, which even we don't have.'

'Oh ...'

'Do you understand?'

'I don't understand anything at the moment.' Dez put both hands in his jeans pockets and hunched his shoulders. 'I don't understand why I was chosen to have my DN-rotten-A messed around with; I don't understand why you Tylurians and the Väds can't do your fighting elsewhere, and I don't understand why I'm trudging through this manky forest at the dead of night!'

'I think it's probably time to take a rest.'

'Probably,' humphed Dez. 'Are we nearly there?'

'About half-way. We'll have some food, you sleep for a bit and then we'll get to the town around nine o'clock tomorrow morning.'

Yakob moved off the path and into the brush, clearing a space where they could sit down. He shrugged off his backpack and took Dez's from him. The food he prepared wasn't like anything Dez had had before, but he was too tired to ask its name. He ate what he was given and just as he was about to lie down Yakob threw him a roll of something very light.

'Unwrap that and get inside,' he said. 'It'll keep you warm.'

'What is it?'

'It keeps all your body heat in.'

'Like a sleeping bag?'

'That would be a very good name for it.' Yakob sounded as if he was smiling. 'Sleep well.'

Sleep is a strange thing. One moment you're wide awake, aware of everything around you, all the small noises sounding so much louder, and the next minute you're awake again. You don't know, if you can't see a clock, how long you've been sleeping. It could be minutes, it could be hours, and dreams that seem to last a lifetime can happen in the blinking of an eye.

When Dez woke up he had no idea what time it was, how long he'd been asleep, or what had woken him. As he fumbled to check his back-lit digital watch (4.30!) he wished he wasn't awake because he knew what would happen – what always happened to him when he woke in the middle of the night – he'd lie there thinking of loads of things he didn't want to think about and freaking himself out.

'Yakob?'

There was a moment's silence, then: 'What?'

'You awake?'

'I am now … are you all right?'

'Yeah … suppose so …'

'I know a bit of how you must feel … I am alone here too, a long way from home, and with the fate of my whole planet resting on my shoulders. You never asked to be a part of this and neither did I.'

'They *made* you come here? You didn't volunteer?'

'It was my duty.' Yakob put a hand on Dez's shoulder. 'They told me I was the person best qualified. I had no choice.'

'I thought only kids never got any choice – you know, got told what they'd got to do.' Dez looked up at Yakob and saw that he was staring up into the star-spattered sky. Out in the country, away from civilization, there were so many flickering pin-points of light it made him feel dizzy to look at it. 'Where's Priam?'

'I've no idea,' sighed Yakob. 'It all looks so different from down here.'

'How did you learn to speak English so well?'

'Are you trying to take my mind off things, or do you

always make such sudden changes of subject?'

'All my teachers say I've got a butterfly mind, always flitting around.' Dez handed the torch back. 'Well?'

'I learnt it on the way here. I'm still learning it.'

'Adults always say that.'

'Say what?'

'You never stop learning.' Dez shivered, wrapping the thin material tighter round him.

'Adults are right, then.'

'What a horrible thought! I'm fed up with learning *now* – I don't want to be doing it in twenty years' time!'

They waited and watched as the dawn came up, the skyline turning a delicate pale blue, seeping colour into the blackness. Around them things began to take shape, and what had been mysteries turned into boringly ordinary bushes and trees.

With the rising sun warming them up by the minute, they sat and ate some food. Yakob did something to two foil packets and whatever was in it heated them up. The plastic bottles they carried held a clear fluid that tasted quite fruity, but Dez had no idea what sort of fruit.

'What wouldn't I give for a Coke right now!' he said as he finished off his drink.

'When we get to the town you can get one. What is it?'

'Fizzy-pop.'

'Oh …' Yakob looked confused. 'Good.'

'So, what would happen if this weapon of yours was

actually used? Would the Väds roll around gagging? Would they turn purple – even better, turn inside out?'

'I don't know *how* it's supposed to work – only the High Command knows the details.'

'And the spy and the Väds.'

'True.'

'Some secret!'

'True also.'

They walked in silence for a time, and then came to a point where the track met a road. It was long and straight and shaded on one side by trees. Close to where they were standing Dez could see what looked like a bus stop, and in the distance, to his left, a single-decker bus was trundling towards them.

'Yakob?' he said, as the Tylurian was about to cross the road.

'Yes?'

Dez pointed to his right. 'Is that the way to town?'

Yakob looked. 'Uh-huh. Why?'

'Can we catch the bus, pl-e-e-e-ease?'

'We haven't got any money.'

'*You* might not, but,' Dez patted his bumbag, '*I* have.'

'You have?'

'Yes. Well, enough for the bus fare.'

'All right,' smiled Yakob. 'I've never been on a bus.'

Chapter 9

The bus was quite crowded, but they managed to get a seat each, one behind the other. It was going to a town called Chambéry, a few kilometres further than the town they'd planned to walk to, and luckily nearer their final destination – and Dez had enough money for the tickets.

Up ahead they could see the road start its climb towards the snow-covered peaks. It looked cold up there, even though the sun was shining and it was getting hotter by the minute in the bus. The road they were on was following the course of a river, and the river was in full flow, fed by the melting snow from high up in the mountains.

Surrounded by the chatter and buzz of a motley collection of French people – grandmas, children, farmers and others – Dez and Yakob passed the time observing their fellow passengers and taking in the scenery. At some point the person next to Yakob got off and he moved over to the window and let Dez come and sit next to him.

Just after they'd driven past the sign telling them they were entering Chambéry, Dez noticed a car pulled off to the side of the road with its bonnet up. A man was sitting on the grille, not looking at the engine.

'Nice place to break down,' Dez said. There was no reply from Yakob and Dez looked up at him. His face was serious. 'What's the matter?'

'I want you to go and sit at the back of the bus by yourself.'

'Why? We're nearly there. What would I want to do that for?'

'Because I think that man back there was a Väd – *don't* turn round!' Yakob began to talk very fast, bending down and whispering in Dez's ear. 'Stay on the bus when I get off in the town centre – they'll be looking for two people, one of them a child. Get off at the next stop and find somewhere to stay out of sight. I'll come and get you.'

'How? How will you find me?' Dez suddenly felt the happiness of the last few hours wash away, to be replaced by a creeping fear.

Yakob pressed what looked like a coin into his hand. 'Don't lose this. I'll find you. Now go to the back and keep your head down!'

Again, like the first time they'd met, Dez felt an odd calmness, as if everything would be OK if he did exactly what Yakob said. As he walked to the back of the bus he glanced over his shoulder. Yakob was looking left and right out of the bus, watching the road like a hawk. As far as Dez could see, there were no other "broken-down" cars parked on the sides of the road.

He sat, hunched, on the back bench seat next to an old man who smelt of garlic and cigarette smoke. He looked as if he wanted to talk, and Dez tried to ignore him. Dez looked at his watch. 11.30. They'd been on the go since just after dawn and ordinarily he'd have been starving. Now, though his stomach felt empty, it was a different kind of emptiness, and one not requiring any sort of food at all.

The bus stopped.

Dez sat up slightly and watched a clutch of passengers get off, Yakob among them. He didn't look back or wave or anything. It was as if they'd never met and Dez hadn't ever felt so lonely in all his life. On top of everything else that had happened, now his only friend in the whole world (the entire *universe*) was walking off the bus.

The doors closed and the driver moved off.

'*Parlez-vous français?*'

Dez turned to the old man. 'Me? No, I mean *non*.' He chewed his lower lip as he thought. '*Je*, um ... *je ne parle pas français, monsieur* ... sorry, *pardonnez moi*.'

'I speak little Henglish,' said the old man. 'You very young to travel halone?'

'I'm meeting someone. They're, um, picking me up at the next stop.' Dez's eyes darted sideways to look out of the bus window. There was no sign of Yakob. 'I'm all right, really.'

'*En vacance* ... on 'oliday?'

'Er, yes, holiday … with my, um, family.' To Dez's horror, as the bus accelerated out of the town he saw another car by the side of the road, this time with its boot open, and a man standing by it with some tools in his hands. He sank down in his seat so that only his baseball cap would be visible.

'Are you feeling all right?' the old man rolled his R's as if he had a handful of gravel in his throat.

'Fine – a bit tired.'

'You get out at ze next stop, you say?'

'The next stop, yes. I'm, um, meeting someone there.'

'Zere is *un café*. It belong my son – you can sit zere, have, maybe, a sandwich?' The way the old man spoke it sounded more like *zaandweeech*, but Dez knew what he meant.

'Thank you, but—'

'Bien!' the old man smiled, showing an almost complete set of rather brown teeth.

There was a loud hiss of air brakes, the engine roaring loudly as the bus slowed to go round a bend. Up ahead Dez could see a stop sign, right next to a small café, and beside him he was aware of the old man picking up a bag from the floor and getting ready to stand.

He had no choice – he had to get off with him. If he didn't Yakob might never find him, even with the tiny gizmo he had in his pocket. He stood and let the old man go up the gangway to the door, following in his shuffling footsteps.

Outside on the road he watched the twin doors shut

and the bus drive off. He looked back the way they'd come. Who would be the first to arrive? Yakob, to pick him up, or a Väd death squad to make a toasted *zaandweeech* out of him? There were some things, he felt sure, that an eleven-year-old boy (on holiday) shouldn't have to think about. And this was definitely one of them.

Dez was sitting at a table near the window. He had demolished the most delicious ham sandwich he'd ever tasted, was on his second bottle of Orangina and had now spent almost all his Euros. Looking out of the window he saw a dark blue saloon coming from the direction of the town, one of its indicators starting to flash as it slowed down. Maybe this was Yakob.

Dez looked at the man getting out of the car. He was wearing a white floppy sun hat, dark glasses, khaki trousers and what looked like fairly serious walking shoes. Dez's heart sank. It wasn't Yakob. Then it sank even further as the ghastly thought occurred to him that it could well be a Väd.

He looked round the small café, his mouth suddenly dry as a sandpit. Was there a back entrance? Could he get to it in time? Would there be someone waiting for him if he did? Questions, questions … Dez was rooted to his chair, unable to move. He heard the hinges squeak as the café door opened. He didn't dare look round.

'Dez?' said a voice behind him.

It *was* Yakob! He could have leapt for joy as he turned

to look. Dez jumped up and ran over to him. 'Thought you'd never get here!'

'Got caught in some traffic. Sorry I'm a bit late.' Yakob took off his sunglasses and smiled a tight smile. 'We should go.'

* * *

'How did you manage to get this?' Dez asked as he got into the passenger seat of the brand new Citroën and reached for the seatbelt.

'I hired it.'

'What with? You don't have any money!'

'I persuaded a machine outside a bank to give me some.'

'Persuaded?' Dez gave the dashboard the once-over. After the one in *Stark Revenge* it looked like something off a Fisher Price toy, only not as colourful.

'The machine wasn't very intelligent.' Yakob started the car. 'There are smarter *plants* on Priam – it was easy.'

'Why the new clothes? And where did you learn to speak French since you got off the bus?'

'I can learn very quickly by listening; it's something we are taught. By the time I left the bus I'd got most of it figured out.' Yakob pulled out on to the road and accelerated. The automatic gearbox did the rest. 'And I got the clothes to confuse anyone who might have been watching the bus. Did you see the car waiting this side of the town?'

'Yeah,' said Dez, frowning. 'How did you know they were Väds?'

'I had a feeling – I think you call it intuition – and even if I was wrong, which I don't think I was, being cautious never hurt anyone.'

Dez fiddled around with the levers down the side of his seat and found the one that made it recline. He leant back and when Yakob next looked over at him he found that the boy was fast asleep, slumped in his seat with his mouth slightly open.

The sun was beginning to set when Dez woke up. He stretched and yawned and then sat up with a jerk.

'How long have I been asleep?'

'Four hours. Nearer five, actually.' Yakob pointed out of the window. 'Have a look at where we are.'

Dez brought the back of his seat up and saw they were high up in the mountains, travelling on one of those roads carved out of solid rock with a sheer drop to certain death on one side. His side.

He looked in awe at the black and white stripes flashing by on the low concrete wall that was the only thing between him and a final sky-dive, and was lost for words. High above the valley birds were flying parallel – *parallel!* – with the car.

'Amazing view, eh?'

'I think I preferred it when I was asleep. Do you have to drive so close to the edge?'

'You scared of heights?' asked Yakob as the road swung round in a tight curve and started to climb even higher.

'Don't think so, but I've never been this high before.'

Yakob indicated and overtook the car in front. 'If you like, we can stop at the next restaurant – would you like some food?'

Dez dragged his eyes away from the view. 'You bet!' he replied.

No more than five minutes later they were standing in the restaurant's car park, shivering from the cold.

'Let's get inside quick – I'm desperate for a pee!' said Dez, hopping about and rubbing his arms.

'After you, Desperate!' grinned Yakob, bowing Dez towards the front door.

When Dez emerged from the toilet he found Yakob already seated at a window table, reading a newspaper; he pushed a menu over towards Dez. 'Take your pick, I'm paying!'

'The bank in Chambéry's paying,' said Dez, opening the thick, leather-bound book. 'It's all in French!'

'*Quelle surprise!*'

'Oh, very funny!' Dez closed the menu. 'You order, *mon-sewer*. Anything as long as it hasn't got mushrooms, broccoli or cauliflower in it.'

Yakob raised his eyebrows.

'And it must have chips.'

'Your wish is my command.' Yakob looked around and waved at a waiter, who came straight to the table. '*Deux steaks, frites, un café et un Coca – pas de champignons, s'il vous plaît.*'

'Steak and chips! My favourite!' said Dez, sitting back and rubbing his stomach.

'So you *do* speak French.'

'Yeah, I'm fluent in food.' He pointed at the paper. 'What's in the news?'

'We are.'

'We are? What d'you mean?' Dez leaned forward as Yakob folded the paper and turned the front page towards him. He saw a large, very fuzzy picture of something hovering in the air over some trees. A large headline below it screamed: *LES OVNI ARRIVENT!*

'Our little meeting with the Väd-Raatch didn't go totally unnoticed.' Yakob took the paper back. 'And the radio has been full of it all afternoon – I was listening while you were asleep. Apparently our flight paths took us up high enough for this country's defence forces to pick up on their … what's it called?'

'Radar.'

'That's it, radar.' Yakob put the paper down.

'Who took the photograph?'

The waiter came over with their drinks, putting them on the table. 'One very scared farmer, apparently,' said Yakob when he'd gone.

'Doesn't look much like *Stark*.'

'So-called military "experts" are calling the picture a fake, and looking at it I don't blame them.'

'Everything's all right then.' Dez could see their waiter coming back with two plates loaded with food, chips piled high.

'Except that it seems, according to the radio, that

everybody who owns a pair of binoculars is going to be out tonight watching the sky.'

'So?' queried Dez as the plates were set in front of them.

'So we'll have to be even more careful.'

'Mushrooms! You ask for *no* mushrooms, I heard you!'

'It's not a problem … give yours to me.'

Dez forked his mushrooms off his plate and on to Yakob's. 'Why will we have to be more careful? No one's going to be looking way up here, are they?'

'Who knows? Maybe.'

'Better safe than sorry?' asked Dez, cutting off a piece of steak, so soft it was like butter, and watching the juice spread across his plate.

'Much better,' agreed Yakob. 'It's the only way to make sure you live a long and happy life.' He put his knife and fork down. 'By the way, there was a small piece about your "accident" as well; the police are mystified as to how it happened, but have listed all three of you as dead. I thought I should tell you.'

The meat never got to Dez's mouth. 'They think *I'm* dead as well?'

'Yes. The explosion left very little of anything, apparently.'

Dez blinked and took a deep breath. He was past the point where crying about what had happened to his parents would help. He missed them, missed them badly, but nothing would ever bring them back and all he could do now was look forward. Surviving whatever came next was all he was able to think about.

'I'm dead.' He looked down at his plate and sniffed.

'Do you feel all right?'

'I feel kind of empty,' said Dez. 'But I can't tell if that's because of what's happened or because I'm so hungry.' He picked up his fork again. 'I suppose there's only one way to find out …'

CHAPTER 10

It was pitch dark. The moon was hiding behind clouds and only the occasional star was visible through the gaps. Dez, who could still taste the ice-cream (with chocolate sauce) that he'd had for dessert, had given up trying to read the map by the light of the dashboard. The clock said it was 23.15.

Yakob drove very slowly with his headlights dipped. He was looking, he'd explained, for a small unmade track that would take them nearer to their rendezvous point with the scout ship.

'Are we on time?'

'We have forty-five minutes to get there.' He slowed down almost to a stop and swung the car hard right, off the smooth tarmac. 'Here it is …'

All Dez could see was a space between the brush just wide enough to take the Citroën. The car bounced and heaved over the large rocks and stones that littered the rutted track. 'You should've got an off-roader,' he told Yakob.

'I *should* be driving *Stark*, but I can't,' replied Yakob, coaxing the vehicle carefully up the track. There was a muffled *CLUNK* behind them.

'Whoops!'

'Whoops indeed. I hope that wasn't anything vital,' Yakob stopped the car and listened.

'Maybe we should have a look. If something's wrong you'll never get back to *Stark* after you've dropped me off.'

'Come on then.' Yakob opened his door and got out. Dez did the same and found Yakob at the rear of the Citroën, shining his torch at one of the tyres. It was flat.

'Why did it do that?' Yakob asked.

'Must've hit a sharp stone or something.'

'Isn't it self-inflating?'

'This is Earth, Yakob, not Priam,' said Dez. 'We'll have to change it.'

'What for?'

'The spare, what else? Come on, it's in the boot.' Dez popped the tailgate open.

'Have you done this before?'

'No, but I've watched my dad a few times.' Dez took the torch off Yakob and began poking around in the well. 'And if he could do it, it can't be *that* difficult – my mum always said he was useless at mending things.'

'Will it take long?'

'Shouldn't. Why?' Dez found the jack and took it out.

'We still have to get to the meeting point.'

'Well, don't just stand there – help me get the wheel out!' grinned Dez.

* * *

Because of the uneven track it had actually taken a lot longer than Dez thought it would to change the wheel, the whole process not helped one bit by Yakob's huffy complaining about archaic, ancient, antiquated and *awful* Earth technology.

It was now 23.40; only twenty minutes to go.

'Do you think we should park this thing here and hike the rest of the way?' Dez suggested.

'I thought you didn't like walking,' said Yakob, steering the car gingerly round a bend.

'I don't, but I'm thinking of you.'

'Very kind, and it's appreciated.' Yakob fell silent, and for the next few minutes he concentrated on driving while Dez sat on the edge of his seat, watching their slow progress. 'As soon as I find somewhere, that's exactly what I'll do.'

The road suddenly flattened out and Dez could see a place up ahead of them where the track widened slightly. Yakob pulled over and parked the car, turning the engine off, dousing the lights and sitting back with a sigh. In the silence Dez could hear the radiator fan whirring. When that stopped all that was left was the ticking of the engine as it cooled down. It sounded like an insect.

'Now we walk,' said Yakob, reaching over into the back of the car and getting his rucksack. 'Ready?'

'Ready.' Dez picked his bag up from between his feet and opened his door. The interior light came on and he saw Yakob smile.

'These machines aren't so stupid after all!'

'They've got computers in them,' Dez said, locking his door and closing it.

'Why give a tin box a brain?'

'*Stark*'s got a brain.'

'It's a polymorphous hybrid transport unit; it needs one.' Yakob looked at his wrist. 'Come on, we haven't got far to go.'

Fifteen minutes left.

* * *

Using the torch to guide them, they walked quickly in the cold night air, their breath blossoming out in front of them. They followed the track for some way and then Yakob pointed to a rocky slope and they scrambled up it, their hands and feet searching for holds, stones skittering down behind them as they climbed.

By the time they reached the top the track was some twenty or so metres below and Dez was out of breath and sweating from the effort. In front of him, in the beam of the torch, he could see they were on the edge of a wide, flat outcrop of rock, a wall of mountain rising up to their right.

'This it?' he wheezed.

'This is it.'

'It's like a natural helicopter landing pad.'

'It *is* a natural scout ship landing pad.' Yakob swung

the torch over to where the mountainside met the level rock. The beam found something that looked like a cave entrance. 'Let's wait over there, out of sight.'

'Just in case?' grinned Dez.

'As always.'

It wasn't really a cave, merely a hollow in the rock. Huddled in it and wrapped in the heat-retaining sleeping bag, Dez felt safe and warm if not comfortable, but he'd lately come to realize that you couldn't have everything. He looked at his watch, pressing the button to see the time.

'Five minutes to twelve,' he said.

'Five minutes to go, then. We made it.'

'Just.' Dez took a deep breath.

'They'll be here soon.'

'Midnight on the dot?'

'That's the plan.'

'That's what we call the Witching Hour, when the ghoulies and ghosties come out to play.'

'You like monsters?'

'I like the *idea* of monsters ... I wouldn't want to actually meet one.'

'With any luck you never will.'

'What do you mean?' Dez frowned. 'Monsters don't exist!'

'The Väd-Raatch do, and they're enough to make anyone's flesh crawl ...' There was a high-pitched but soft beeping noise, like a phone ringing very far away. Yakob gave Dez the torch and reached into one of his pockets, bringing out a tiny box. A small red light on it was flickering. 'Any moment now.'

Dez looked out at the flat expanse of rock, grey against the black velvet curtain of sky. It was empty. Then the beeping stopped and became a single tone. Dez noticed that the red light had turned green, and as it did so it seemed as if all the air around them had been sucked away – he could almost hear a *FFFFF-WHPPP!* – and blown back again, like a giant had taken a deep breath and exhaled.

There was still nothing out on the small plateau.

'What was that?' Dez asked.

'That's called being on time.'

'But there's nothing there!'

'Either you are very forgetful or you have an extremely short memory.' Yakob pressed the box in his hand and an orange light joined the green one.

'What have I forgotten?'

'Cloaking.'

'You mean the cruiser's arrived?' Dez squeezed the torch, sending a beam of light out on to the rock, and started to get up. Yakob reached out and pulled him back down again.

'Turn that off and don't move! You *must* stay here until I tell you to come out.'

As he spoke there was a hiss of escaping air. Out in the middle of the landing spot a thin line of light, like three sides of a round-edged square, appeared in the night sky a metre and a half off the ground. It looked totally weird, so odd that at first Dez's brain couldn't make any sense of the information it was receiving from his eyes. Then the thin line of light got thicker and thicker and Dez could hear the whine of a motor.

'It's a door!' he whispered to himself.

'They've forgotten to turn the lights off!' muttered Yakob.

'Do they come on when you open the door of a scout ship as well?' said Dez, nudging Yakob, with his elbow. The light suddenly went out, but Dez could still hear the motor as it carried on opening.

'They must be nervous,' commented Yakob, as the pitch of the motor changed.

'Not half as nervous as I am – what's happening now?'

'They're putting down the steps.'

'Can you see anything?' said Dez, peering hard into the gloom.

'Not too much.'

Then, as Dez's eyes got used to the dark, he could make out a patch of the night sky that wasn't quite so black. In it he thought he could see a figure moving and when the shadowy figure had reached the ground (was that a gun he could see in his hand?) he heard a voice calling Yakob's name.

'Stay here.'

'I'm not going anywhere, me,' said Dez, watching Yakob get up and run low across the flat rock to meet the waiting figure.

Dez strained to hear what they were saying, then remembered that even if he could he wouldn't be able to understand a word of it. He could see that Yakob was asking for something – something, from the way the other man was moving his hands, that he didn't have with him.

The next thing he knew, both men were walking back up the steps and into the scout ship. He was left completely alone, and even the sleeping bag wrapped round him couldn't stop the shivering. He huddled as far back against the rock as he could, scrunching himself up like a hedgehog.

Dez felt abandoned, exposed, at the mercy of whoever or whatever might choose to have a go at him. He peeked at his watch. The figures 00.05.45 peeked back and it took him a moment to work out what they meant. He looked at the watch again. 00.06.05 … six minutes and five seconds past twelve. If he kept using the back-light at this rate, he thought, the battery would run out and he'd have no idea what the time was. Then he saw two figures appear in the grey square of the door and his fear took a hike to the back of his mind once more.

He was so glad to see Yakob he wanted to wave, to get up and shout and run over and clap him on the back. But he knew he mustn't. He'd been told to stay still, stay quiet and stay alive. So he waited and he watched until, *finally*, he heard his name being called.

'Coming!' he said, starting to unwrap the sleeping bag. But it was all tangled up with his feet and all he succeeded in doing was rolling over like a sack of potatoes. When he looked up he was facing away from Yakob, across to the right of the rocky plateau. There, hanging in the air, were the blacker than black shapes of the Väd craft that had attacked them the previous day.

He opened his mouth to shout a warning, but nothing came out.

Chapter 11

Things began to happen, and they began to happen very fast.

Dez found his voice and yelled at Yakob to get down. The Tylurian standing by the steps to the scout ship crouched down and fired a stuttering pulse of bright white laser fire at the Väds, yelling something at Yakob as he disappeared inside his ship.

Then Yakob started to run towards him, and Dez saw the ground between them erupt. A hail of explosive blasts sent shock waves through the rock and sharp *C-RAACKS!* echoed off the mountainside. It was like being in a shoot'em-up vid game, except this was more real than real, and so fast-moving that there wasn't time to be scared.

As the air around him sucked and blew, like it had a few moments before, Dez saw Yakob dive for cover, there was a blast so loud he thought his eardrums had surely burst.

'Where's my bag?' Yakob yelled above the noise as he pushed Dez back into the tiny cave. 'My bag!'

Dez fumbled and found it. 'Here,' he said, ducking as splinters of rock ricocheted around him. He watched as the flashing lights exploding in the air lit the scene, making every action jerky and puppet-like. He saw Yakob put something in the rucksack and take a gun out. It looked small – too small to be of any use against what was being thrown at them. Still, better than nothing, he thought.

'We've got to move!' Yakob pushed Dez behind him, reaching round the lip of the cave and firing the lightweight hand-held laser in the direction of the Väds.

'Where?' Dez yelled back.

'Anywhere but here! Next time I fire, run, get over the edge and just slide!' Yakob took a deep breath, '*Go!*'

Dez went. Something told him that stopping to think might be the last thing he ever did – no matter that he was about to throw himself over a twenty-metre drop while alien craft used him for target practice.

He went into a slide, as if about to make a really ace football tackle, and felt himself start to roll down the rock face. Something whistled past him as he disappeared over the edge, exploding some metres away, and he joined the cascade of rocks and stones in the stampede to be first to hit the track below.

Above him he could hear the *ZAP! ZAP! ZAP!* of Yakob's laser gun, then, as he reached the ground, a cry of pain. Turning round he looked up and saw the silhouette of a figure come tumbling over the edge.

He began scrambling back up as Yakob, feet and arms splayed out to slow himself, slid towards him.

'Yakob!' he yelled hoarsely. 'Are you OK?' If Yakob was dead then his own chances of survival were going to be worse than nil.

The Tylurian came to a halt next to him. 'Yes … and no,' he whispered, breathing heavily. 'I'm alive, but they hit me.'

'Where?'

'We don't have time for that; we've got to get further away.' Yakob let himself slide the rest of the way to the track. Instead of making off left towards the car, he ran across the track and dived into the bushes on the other side.

'It's *that* way!' hissed Dez, pointing even though Yakob's back was to him.

'Can't use it,' grunted Yakob, forcing his way through the thick brush. 'They'd pick us off in no time.'

Dez didn't wait to argue. He scuttled across the track, feeling as if there was a great big luminous bull's-eye on his back. Pushing his way into the brush he followed Yakob down the steep slope, thrusting branches out of his way with one hand and grabbing others to stop himself from falling.

The vegetation seemed to be attacking him from every side, thorns digging into him and tearing at his clothes. He didn't care because at least he was still alive, still hurting, gasping for air and still getting away. In front of him he could see and hear Yakob steam-rollering his way down the slope, and then stopping. Dez skidded to a halt, a branch thwacking him in the face.

'Ow!' He batted it away. 'Why have we stopped?'

'I think something's about to happen.' Yakob was taking deep, quick breaths and Dez could see him wince with pain as he dug his left hand into his trouser pocket and took out the little black box. The green light was still on.

'What?'

'Listen …' Yakob stood still, like a cat waiting to pounce on a mouse.

KA-WHUUUMP!

The air was split by a series of furious explosions and a fist of hot air punched them both in the face, making them reel and stagger backwards.

'We got them!' grinned Yakob. He held the box out so that Dez could see it properly. The green light blinked three times and then went out.

'That mean something?'

'It was the scout ship signing off.' Yakob put the communicator away. 'I wasn't sure they were still here, for all I knew the Väds could have got them – it was such chaos out there *anything* was possible.'

'So the scout ship blew up the baddies … does that mean your lot will be back to get me?'

'I'm afraid not,' sighed Yakob. 'Not right now, anyway.'

'Why?'

'There's a good chance they weren't the only Väd ships

in the area. If they come back it could start all over again, and we can't risk that.'

'I'm still stuck here then?'

'Yes, stuck here and stuck with me.' Yakob picked up a branch and began to hack at the bushes. 'We must get back to *Stark* immediately.'

'Can't we get our breath back? I mean the Väds are gone, we should be OK now, shouldn't we?'

'We may be, but that performance back there should have this place crawling with your people any moment now, wouldn't you say?'

As if in answer to Yakob's question a lone siren wail whooped from somewhere in the distance, setting off an eerie echoing reply.

'Police,' said Dez.

'And that's just the start of it,' Yakob slashed his way through the bushes with the branch. 'This will be a busy place by dawn.'

'They'll have plenty to look at.' Dez ducked as a branch Yakob had pushed aside came whipping back at him.

'How do you mean "plenty to look at"?'

'Well, they weren't playing games up there, were they? I mean, that was a *serious* firework display.'

'Very serious,' Yakob muttered. 'Come on, let's get into the trees; we don't want to be spotted.'

'And the Väd gunships, they blew up, didn't they? There'll be loads of bits lying around – souvenirs.' Dez followed Yakob, jogging down the slope.

'No, no souvenirs,' replied Yakob, slowing down once

they were under cover of the trees. 'The explosions were the result of vaporizer salvos. They'll be lucky to find dust.'

'Could the Väds have done that to *Stark* when they were chasing us?'

'Could have and would have, if they'd got the chance.'

'Blimey!' Dez trotted after Yakob in silence for a few minutes, his mind buzzing as he replayed the screamingly insane few minutes when his life had hung by a thread – for the second time in two days, he reminded himself. What on Earth would Tim and Cy think, if he ever got to tell them the story? He decided they'd think he was a few players short of a football team, so nothing new there.

It occurred to him, as he jogged along – breathing fine, head clear, not even sweating – that, oddly enough, he hadn't felt so good in ages. Maybe there was something to this exercise lark, or maybe, more likely, he was simply glad to be in one piece. Whichever it was he realized he was ridiculously happy to be jogging down an Alp at – he checked his watch – a quarter to one in the morning.

His dad would have been amazed – his son, sole heir to the Danby millions (ha-ha!) and dedicated couch potato, actually enjoying a run.

They stopped when they came to the river and both of them got down and scooped up handfuls of achingly cold, but delicious water.

'Never tastes like this out of a tap,' Dez said, wiping his hands on his jeans.

'It's good; just like on Priam.' Yakob sat back on his

heels, shaking drops of water off his fingers. 'It always tastes better closest to the source.'

'Is your arm still hurting?'

'My arm? No, not really.' Yakob turned it to him to have a look and Dez could see a neat hole on either side of the sleeve. 'A high-boost flux shot.'

'What's that when it's at home?'

'A type of laser. Lucky really – if they'd hit me with a deep resonator I'd probably have lost the arm.'

'Why?' Dez moved round to have a closer look.

'Deep resonators make a tiny hole when they hit and then spread out in an arc. Very messy.'

'No kidding!' Dez stood up. 'Hasn't it left a hole in your arm?'

In reply Yakob rolled his sleeve up and showed Dez the two tiny scars, black against his pale skin. There was hardly anything to look at.

'Don't you bleed?' queried Dez, reaching out and touching Yakob's arm. 'You're not a, like, *robot*, are you?' The skin felt quite normal for a person (a *creature*?) from a planet 300,000 light years away who drove an invisible van.

'No,' replied Yakob, rolling his sleeve down. 'I'm not a robot, but then I'm not human either.'

Dez stood and looked at Yakob. The clouds had cleared a little and although it was still dark there was a pale light from the sky which made him look as if he'd been sculpted. He'd known, almost from the moment they'd met, that Yakob was an alien, but he hadn't really had the time to think about what that meant. Too much had happened; there'd been too many close shaves and far too much excitement.

He was about to ask more questions when they heard the sound of a helicopter in the distance, the deep, rhythmic throbbing of its rotor blades becoming louder by the second.

'That's not the ...'

'No, it's not the Väds,' Yakob answered the unfinished question. 'But we should move on, and keep out of sight. If we can put a bit more distance between us and this area, we can sleep till dawn and then make the nearest town for breakfast.'

'Triff!' Dez grinned at the thought of food. And then he remembered something, something he'd been meaning to ask Yakob. 'Why did you go into the scout ship, back up there on the plateau? Looked like you were having an argument with that other person.'

'I was.'

'What about?' asked Dez, as they started to follow the river.

'He hadn't brought the new cloaking device out with him; we went back into the ship to get it,' Yakob shrugged as he walked. 'He was nervous, I suppose.'

'Not half as nervous as I was. I thought I'd never see you again – I thought I was going to die when the Väds appeared!'

'It was bad up there. We nearly lost everything. That spy is making life very difficult.'

'Why can't they catch whoever it is?'

'They're too good, or too highly placed or, what's more likely, both.'

'Why would a Tylurian want to help the Väds if the Väds want to kill Tylurians?' Dez's stomach rumbled. 'Have we got any food left?'

'Money and yes,' replied Yakob, stopping for a moment.

'What?'

'Back where I come from we have a saying which translates something like *Money has no enemies*.' Yakob took off his rucksack, opened a pouch pocket and dug around inside it.

'My gran, who was a bit odd, had this embroidered picture that said *Money is the Root of All Evil*.' Dez accepted the silver-wrapped bar that Yakob gave him. 'I dunno. I thought money was just money – stuff to buy stuff with.'

'That's because you've never had large amounts of it.'

Dez opened the foil package. 'I've got £280 in my building society!' He bit into the bar. 'Mmmm!' he said. 'Crunchy, chewy and sweet – what are they called, Space Bars?'

Yakob watched Dez demolish his food while slowly opening his own bar. 'No, it's called OPR, actually.' He saw Dez frown, unable to talk because his mouth was crammed full. 'Off-Planet Rations.'

'Not very catchy.'

'Filling though.'

'Did you get the new cloaking device after all that?'

Yakob patted his backpack. 'Safe and sound.'

'Not a complete disaster then?'

'Not as long as we can get back to *Stark* in one piece.'

As they made their way down river it became obvious that there was an increasing amount of activity in the area. More and more sirens wailed eerily in the night, the sky occasionally lighting up with flashes. The quiet alpine night was quiet no more.

But it was all happening further and further away as they jogged down the valley. Not for one moment did it occur to Dez that their escape had been too easy, and when the helicopter roared overhead he was so stunned that he stopped running and stood stock still, like an animal caught in a car's headlights, looking up to see where the noise was coming from.

Yakob ran back to get him, dragging him towards the trees as a spotlight lanced through the dark and started to sweep the ground around them, its incredibly bright white beam looking almost solid, almost touchable.

The combination of the noise, the buffeting wind and the probing light threw Dez's mind into a whirl. He couldn't think straight. Part of him knew that it wasn't the Väds, that it was just a helicopter, but part of him expected to be vaporized at any moment.

He flung himself on to the ground and scrambled behind a tree trunk. 'What are they doing?' he yelled, in an effort to make himself heard above the din.

'Probably trying to find out what happened,' Yakob

yelled back, taking off his backpack and reaching inside it.

Dez watched, open-mouthed, as Yakob took out his laser pistol. 'Are you going to *shoot* them?'

'Not them, their light.' He leant against the tree trunk for support and took aim, steadying his right wrist with his left hand and following the helicopter as it hovered in the air, swaying.

The spotlight swung around lazily, stopping here and there and making the shadows of what it found dance madly on the ground.

'Stay still, stay still!' muttered Yakob as he sighted down the barrel, one eye closed. The beam turned and began to trace a path towards their hiding place. Yakob took a deep breath and held it. The beam crept nearer, wavering slightly as the person controlling it aimed it up the slope.

Dez, now also holding his breath, watched as Yakob pulled the trigger. The moment the spotlight was about to hit them the end of the laser pistol glowed and then the world went black. Still noisy, but black.

'Yes!' Dez punched the air and clapped Yakob on the shoulder. 'What a star!'

Yakob grinned and moved back behind the tree. 'My aim is true.'

A thought struck Dez. 'Won't they know someone's here now you've done that?'

'They'll think their equipment's failed and go back to base. I didn't blow the thing up, I simply burnt it out.'

As if it had heard what Yakob had said, the helicopter rose up, banked and roared away, its tail-light flashing angrily.

'D'you know,' said Dez, leaning back against the tree and scratching his scalp with both hands, 'if nothing exciting *ever* happens to me *ever* again in my *whole* life I won't care. Honest.' He looked up at Yakob, who was standing, listening. 'Can we go somewhere and have a little kip? I'm trashed.'

'Translate.'

Dez yawned. 'I'm tired.'

'Me too, but we should go a little further maybe.'

'OK, you're the boss.' Dez got up and yawned again. 'Let's hit the road, Yakob.'

About an hour later, and nearly a kilometre farther on, Yakob called a halt for the night. It was nearly 2.30 in the morning and a cold wind had sprung up. Way back in the distance they could still hear and see evidence of the frantic searching that must have been going on around the site of the battle between the Tylurian scout ship and the Väd craft.

They found somewhere out of the wind, unfolded their sleeping bags and got in, using their backpacks as pillows. It wasn't a bed, thought Dez, as he curled up in a ball, and it wasn't home, but he didn't care. At least he'd survived another day.

'Sleep well, Dez,' said Yakob, patting him on the back.

'I will …'

The airwaves almost hiss with poisonous conversation. In the world of the Väd-Raatch failure is a disease.

'What happened?'

'We don't know. Communication has ceased with the hunter units.'

'Nothing?'

'Nothing.'

'Have you sent reinforcements?'

'Too risky. There's an extremely high level of activity down there.'

'Action is never *too risky when the survival of our race is at stake.'*

'We will try.'

'Trying is not good enough. Our target is just one small creature, after all.'

Chapter 12

When Dez woke up the sun was shining. He rolled on to his back, stretched and sat up, holding the sleeping bag up to his neck so as not to let any warm air out. 'What's the time?'

'Time you got up.'

'Ha-ha!' Still holding the sleeping bag tight with his right hand, Dez pushed his left hand out and squinted down at his watch. '6.30! I'm going back to sleep!'

'We still have a way to go. The nearest place we can rent another car from is about eight or nine not very easy kilometres away. If we go fairly soon we might just get there by lunchtime.'

Dez groaned, slumped in a heap on the ground and then started to crawl out of his bag on all fours. 'This is worse than term-time.'

He slouched over to the river and splashed some water in his face, the shock of the icy cold making him gasp. He stood and looked down at himself. His clothes were a mess, torn, dirty and crumpled, and his hands were filthy and covered in small cuts.

He glanced at Yakob. He looked no better. 'How are we going to walk into some French town and rent a car looking like this? We'll get arrested!'

'We do look a bit like a couple of what we would call, um, roamers!' Yakob smiled as he stood up and looked down at himself.

'We call them tramps, and we look a *lot* like a couple of them!'

After a half-hearted attempt at dusting themselves off and wiping themselves down, the two of them looked like a pair of slightly cleaner tramps. It would, Dez thought, have to do.

It was close to 7.30 when they set off in the direction of somewhere called St Jean. As before, they kept off the roads, staying with the river as much as possible and trying to keep out of sight of any cars. As they got closer to St Jean this became impossible and they decided that it would be all right – and much quicker – to join the road and finish their journey as if they were hikers.

They noticed that traffic was becoming quite heavy in the direction of the peak where they'd been the previous night. At the first shop they came to Yakob bought a couple of bars of chocolate and a newspaper and they sat by the side of the road and took a break.

'What does the paper say?' asked Dez, between mouthfuls.

'The headline says "*LA GUERRE DES ÉTOILES!*" and there's a lot of utter nonsense about fleets of spaceships and nuclear explosions – these are stories for children!' Yakob put a piece of chocolate in his mouth and read on. 'Oh!' he said, looking up and nodding his head. '*This* is good!'

'What is?'

'We have apparently been kidnapped by aliens from – some "expert" says – the Andromeda system. Ha!'

'Well, we were nearly killed by some aliens, so he wasn't so far off.'

'True, but the *Andromeda* system! It's ridiculous!'

'Why?'

'Everyone knows there isn't a civilization in the Andromeda system that can split the atom, let alone master interstellar travel.'

'Everyone on Priam might, but what do we know down here? Any pictures?'

Yakob flicked through the paper. 'There are pictures of people trying to get up there.' He held the paper open so Dez could see the photo of a traffic jam.

'Why do they think we've been captured by aliens then?'

'They found our car. Someone at that restaurant we stopped at spotted us driving off up the mountain.' Yakob turned back a page. 'It says, let me see ... "*The mystery couple – thought to be father and son – were last seen leaving* Le Bon Goût *at about 10 o'clock, and their car, hired that day in Chambéry, was found abandoned near the site of last night's extraordinary incident. A white sun hat and a baseball cap were left in the car, but otherwise no sign has been found of them."'*

'I've disappeared twice in two days – I think that must be something of a record.' Dez popped the last piece of chocolate in his mouth. 'I liked that cap as well. D'you think it'll be three days in a row when they find this next car dumped?'

'*If* we get another car.' Yakob folded the newspaper and put it down. 'I hope they haven't all been hired by idiots trying to get up the mountains.'

'Let's go and find out, shall we?' Dez reached out and pulled Yakob up and they walked off towards the town.

As they came closer to the centre, more shops began to appear on the streets. Dez stopped outside one and looked at his reflection, and that of Yakob standing next to him.

'Do you have enough money to buy some new clothes?' he asked.

'Sure.'

'*And* hire the car?'

'Yes.'

'There's a sports shop two doors down.' Dez pointed to a sign sticking out into the street. 'I'm fed up with looking like a scarecrow.'

Ten minutes later saw them both back out on the pavement dressed as if they were about to go to the sports track. And after a visit to a restaurant with a reasonable toilet, Dez for one felt a hundred times better than he had when he'd woken up that morning.

It was nearly lunchtime and the streets were almost deserted. They were walking up a steep hill, following the directions of the restaurant owner, when Yakob suddenly stopped and pulled Dez into a nearby doorway.

'Why'd you do that?'

'I think I just saw a Väd.'

'What, *here*?'

'Shhh!' Yakob leaned forward slightly to look back up the street. 'He's walking this way.'

'What are you going to do?' whispered Dez. 'Shoot him?'

'Can't. I may be wrong.'

'Great.' Dez turned to look at the door behind them. He reached out and turned the handle. Locked. Even greater. He turned to see what Yakob was doing and found he wasn't there. His mind froze; he couldn't think and for a moment he couldn't move. Where could he have gone?

Making an extraordinary effort he forced himself into action and peered out into the street. A few metres up the pavement he saw Yakob walking towards a man in a grey suit. He saw him stop and ask the man something. He saw the man look down at his wrist, and as he did so he saw Yakob's shoulders relax as he turned away, nodding to the man.

'What were you *doing*?' he asked when Yakob came back.

'Checking,' replied Yakob. 'Let's get on …'

'So he wasn't a Väd?'

'No, he just looked like one of the men I saw outside Chambéry.'

'But ...' Dez watched Yakob walk off down the street, bemused.

Yakob looked round. 'What?'

'How could you tell?'

'Tell what?'

'If he's a Väd of course, what else?'

'There would be signs,' said Yakob mysteriously, carrying on walking.

'OK,' Dez nodded to himself, kicking at a stone, '*don't* tell me then.'

Dez hung back, keeping himself to himself until, some two hundred metres away, he saw the sign for the car hire firm.

'What are we going to get this time?' Dez asked, catching Yakob as he opened the door to the office.

'Anything they've got.'

To Dez's delight the owner told them he'd just had a four-wheel drive Suzuki returned that morning. It was checked and ready to go. Dez took off his backpack and sat on a chair by the counter. As they waited for the man to fill in some papers in the back office a policeman walked in and approached the counter. He looked at them both and Dez, who wore guilt like a neon sign, immediately got up and went over to examine the car tyre pressure chart as closely as he could.

He didn't know why he felt guilty. Neither he nor Yakob had done anything wrong – except "borrow" some money from a bank's cash machine. And they were supposed to have been kidnapped by aliens, of course. As he looked at the blur of type in front of him he supposed he could be feeling guilty because it seemed as if he was on the run, not just from the Väds, but from the whole world. The policeman started talking to Yakob.

Dez strained to understand what was being said, but his French simply wasn't good enough to make out anything but the occasional word. He cursed himself for not paying more attention in class, and vowed that, should he live to ever do French again, he would be all ears all the time.

The policeman sounded as if he was giving orders, but policemen everywhere always seemed to sound like that. Dez didn't dare say anything; he didn't even dare turn round in case the policeman noticed him and started asking him questions. He was going cross-eyed staring at the chart, so he moved along a bit and found himself looking at a large map of Europe.

He stood back a pace and looked up and over to the left hand side. There was England (or was it Britain? he could never remember), all green and tiny and floating off the coast of France. Would he ever get to see it again, or would this rotten secret code they'd stuck in his rotten DNA put the kybosh on that? Lost in thought he jumped a mile when a hand tapped him on the shoulder. He turned, half expecting to see Yakob in handcuffs and the policeman pointing a gun at him.

It was Yakob, without handcuffs. 'The car's waiting for us round the back,' he said.

'Great!' Dez turned and made for the door. Yakob joined him outside and they went looking for the entrance to the garage where the Suzuki was parked. 'What did that *gendarme* want?'

'Nothing really.'

'He sounded as if he was telling you off or something.'

'He was telling me that it would be inadvisable to take a certain route up the mountains today because there are roadblocks everywhere. I told him we were going in quite the opposite direction.'

Dez was about to reply when he heard a shout.

'Attendez!'

He looked back and saw the policeman holding something in one hand and beckoning them back with the other. 'What does he want?' All his panic, guilt and fear came flooding back and he felt like haring off as fast as he could.

'It's your backpack,' said Yakob, putting a hand on Dez's shoulder as if he knew what he was thinking. 'You left it in the office.'

They drove out of St Jean and followed the signs for Lyon, making sure they didn't go through Chambéry. It wasn't just the thought of the spooky Väd lookouts that made the longer trip worthwhile; Yakob didn't want to risk being recognized, especially by the man he'd rented the car from. As far as either of them could tell, they weren't spotted or followed by anyone.

'Have we been visited by aliens for a long time?' asked Dez, chewing on some gum to help his popping ears.

'As far as I know *we* came here first around the time you were born. I don't recall ever reading anything about this system, but someone must've known about your planet to have picked it.'

'There's always stories about UFOs and flying saucers, but no one's ever seen a real one and all the photos are like that one in the paper, all blurry.'

'You've seen a couple – you've even flown in one.'

'Me?' Dez looked up from fiddling with his mp3 player. It was the one major casualty from the Battle of the Plateau.

'UFO stands for Unidentified Flying Object, doesn't it? I think *Stark* fits into that category very well, wouldn't you say?'

'Yeah. Trouble is, who'd ever believe me? I saw a programme once, on TV, where they interviewed people who said they'd been in flying saucers and they all looked like complete nutters.' Dez fell silent for a moment. 'I haven't gone mad, have I? I mean, this *is* all real, isn't it?'

'Afraid so, Dez.'

'So I'm not going to wake up in my bed and find it's all been a terrible dream, like in the movies?'

'This is about as real as it gets.'

'I had a feeling it was.' Dez did what his mum would

never let him do and put his feet up on the dashboard. 'I've got a good imagination, but even *I* couldn't have dreamed up the Väd-Raatch.'

They drove on for what seemed like ages and then Yakob turned the car off the main road and on to a small track.

'Where are we?'

'Not far from where we left *Stark,* about half an hour's walk.'

'Only half an hour?' Dez undid his seat-belt as Yakob parked the Suzuki out of sight. 'That's hardly a walk at all!'

'Well, *there's* a change of attitude,' grinned Yakob, switching off the engine and reaching for his backpack. 'When I first met you the thought of half an hour's walk caused something of an uproar.'

'I've changed,' said Dez getting out and closing the door. 'Being a dead person does that to you.'

'It's true, you have changed.' Yakob joined Dez and they started walking. 'You are an amazing person, Dez.'

'I'm not amazing; why should *I* be amazing? You're the amazing one, with your laser guns and cloaking devices and not bleeding when you're shot.'

'That's just who I am and the job I do, I can't help it.' Yakob stopped walking. 'You have had to deal with some terrible things in the last few days and you've come through it all with your sense of humour intact; you've been scared, and you don't mind admitting it, and you have the wisdom to know that the only thing you can do now is look to what the future holds. I hope I could be like you if I was in your position.'

Dez gave an embarrassed shrug and carried on walking; he'd never been called wise before and had no idea how to react.

When they were reached the edge a clearing that looked to Dez exactly like the last few he'd seen, Yakob stopped, took out the small communicator Dez had last seen up on the plateau and pressed it. It beeped and Dez could hear an answer from the invisible *Stark*. He scanned the clearing and was amazed to see a bird walking about, suspended in mid-air.

'Look,' he nudged Yakob. 'Magic!'

'Look,' replied Yakob, pressing the box again and uncloaking the van. 'More magic.'

The bird, frightened either by their arrival or by the sudden appearance of something very solid underneath it, flew off. They walked over, and Yakob was just about to unlock the van when the air above them was split by an almighty roar.

'What was that?' shouted Dez as the sound reached a peak and then began to die away.

Yakob quickly opened *Stark*'s door and got in. Dez followed and watched as he sat down in front of a console.

'Well?'

'*Stark*'s checking,' said Yakob, his fingers racing over the bumpy surfaces in front of him as screens lit up and holo-displays threw pictures out at him. 'Low-level jet overflight. Must be the military still searching for flying saucers.'

The ringing in Dez's ears had begun to fade when he heard another sound: the sucking *WHUPP-WHUPP-WHUPP!* of a helicopter. 'Is that one of theirs?'

'Theirs?'

'The Väds.'

'No, no it's not,' said Yakob. 'And it's going off in the opposite direction as well.'

'We're safe?'

'We're safe.'

'Thank goodness!' Dez sat down. He couldn't believe the relief, the sheer pleasure of sinking into *Stark*'s soft, friendly, welcoming seats. He revelled in the comfort, tilting his chair and lying back as Yakob disappeared into the front of the van. The jets and the helicopter had almost been one scare too many.

'How are we going to get out of here without being seen?' Dez called out.

Yakob came back up, holding something small and gold-coloured in his hand. 'We are now fully operational. We can fly and no one can see us!'

'What's that?' Dez sat up and pointed at the thing in Yakob's hand.

'The old cloaking circuit.'

'*That* tiny thing?'

'That indeed.'

'What are we going to do now? I mean now that you haven't been able to deliver me to the scout ship.'

Yakob sat down. 'The plan was, remember, for me to go off and find the other two parts of the jigsaw puzzle. Get the second and third people with the altered DNA off-planet as fast as possible and up to *Tyson's Grip*.'

'And now?'

'Still the same, except I'll have an extra passenger.'

'Is that going to be a problem?'

'It will be for you,' said Yakob, putting the broken cloaking device down. 'Every time unit you spend here you're in danger. We're going to have to be extra careful.'

Dez tilted his seat back up. 'I feel as if I've got a deadly disease inside me, like I could die any moment from it, and there isn't any cure.'

'There *is* a cure.'

'What?'

'As soon as you reach Priam, and the code is read, you'll no longer be of any interest to the Väds. Instant cure.'

'So, Doctor, how long do you think it will be before I can have the treatment?'

Yakob sighed. 'That depends on how quickly I can find the other two.'

'Where are they?'

Yakob was suddenly getting very busy, muttering to himself, or to *Stark*. It was hard to tell, and Dez realized he'd taken for granted the fact that Yakob talked to the van, but what – or possibly who – was he talking to? He'd ask later; now he wanted the answer to another, rather more important question.

'I said, where are they?' repeated Dez.

'Who?'

'The other two.' Suddenly all the windows went dark, although the light inside the van remained the same, just like day. 'What's happening?'

'Nothing, nothing,' said Yakob. 'The others, yes ... well, one is in Africa, somewhere called Lagos, and the other is in America – New York, the place is called.'

'Where are we going first?'

Yakob looked at a map that had appeared on the darkened windscreen. 'Africa. It's nearest.'

'And who's there? What's their name?'

'I only have the first two initials, and the general area where they live.' Yakob consulted a small screen covered in Tylurian script. 'BK. Their initials are BK, and I have to find this person with no help at all.'

Dez looked round at *Stark*. Its lights flashed and pulsated, the displays were displaying like crazy and the whole place hummed with artificial intelligence. It occurred to him that it could hardly be called "no help at all".

'Can I get a drink?' he asked, getting up.

'Sure, I'll get you a cup,' said Yakob, joining Dez in the back of the van. 'What would you like?'

'Anything.'

'Mezz?'

'Some of that juice?' Dez looked at his watch. 'When are we leaving?'

'We left a few minutes ago.'

Dez grabbed the edge of the console, even though nothing had happened. 'We're *flying*?'
'We're nearly there,' grinned Yakob.

Somewhere in the unending vastness of space a transmission circuit opens.
'You have something to report?'
'We've picked up a trace. Someone's on the move.'
'Follow them.'
The circuit closes. For now.

Chapter 13

Dez sank back in his chair as *Stark Revenge* arrived in Africa. Somewhere in the Nigerian city of Lagos was another person with rather more information in their chromosomes than they knew about. The thought made him frown, and when he glanced up he found Yakob looking at him.

'Everything all right?'

'Everything's fine, for now,' said Dez. 'But it's all going to start again, isn't it?'

'Soon.'

'Too soon for me. I wish there was a "Stop" button.'

'What on?' asked Yakob.

'Life.'

'If it was made on this planet it probably wouldn't work.'

'Are we there yet?' asked Dez, who was bored and getting fidgety.

'Yes, we're there,' said Yakob, who was hunched over a control panel that was making squealing, babbling noises like a psychotic budgie. To his right a large, incredibly detailed 3D map hovered, like a mutated tray, in the air. Dez could see it was raining over one of the mountain ranges. Yakob kept glancing at the map and then talking to the control panel. It was, thought Dez, quite the weirdest conversation he'd ever heard.

'What are you doing?'

'Trying to work out where to land.'

'Where are we then?'

'About a klik above Lagos,' muttered Yakob over his shoulder. 'I'm scanning for any signs of watchers and overflights.'

'And?'

'And what?'

'And are there any?'

'They've got to be there *somewhere* – the Väds don't give up that easily – but I can't find a single trace of them.'

'Well just take *Stark* down and let's get on with it,' Dez shifted in his seat. 'The quicker we start, the quicker we'll finish. That's what my headmaster used to say, anyway.'

'Practical sort of man was he, your headmaster?'

'Not really,' said Dez, sitting back and remembering. 'We called him The Wol because he looked just like the owl in *Winnie-the-Pooh*.'

'Winnie the what?'

'It's a kid's book.'

'Oh … did you like him?' asked Yakob, turning round in his chair.

'Didn't like him, didn't hate him,' said Dez, stopping and frowning. 'Don't think I've ever *hated* anyone – until now.'

'Now?'

'Yeah, I hate the Väds for what they've done to me. Killing my parents and making me run for my life.'

'You don't hate the Tylurians, do you?'

'Why should I?' Dez frowned.

'For making you a target.'

'I wish they hadn't messed about with me, but at least you're trying to put things right and not atomize me.'

'No matter how well plans are made, it seems that something will always go wrong.' Yakob looked back at the console. 'Even with all our technology we still can't get things absolutely right.'

'My dad called it Murphy's Law.'

'Murphy's Law?'

'Yeah.' Dez thought for a moment. 'If it *can* go wrong, it *will* go wrong – that's what he always used to say.'

Yakob smiled and nodded. 'I think the last few days have proved him to be quite correct.'

Behind him the deranged budgie began squawking again and Yakob swung his chair back to look at the control panel and the levitating map. Lightning flashed from the miniature storm clouds, but there was no sound of thunder.

'We're going down,' said Yakob. '*Stark*'s chosen a landing site.'

'Attaboy!' grinned Dez.

'Actually,' replied Yakob, 'you mean, atta-girl.'

Dez felt a slight quiver in his stomach as the van (he still thought of it as that, even though they were one klik up in the deep blue sky) began its descent. 'What?'

'They have distinct personalities, these constructs,' explained Yakob, getting up and walking to the front seats as the map dissolved in the air. 'They're complex individuals that are, in many ways, superior to us – and each one is a unique individual, just like we are. Some are male and some female. *Stark*'s the latter.'

Dez looked at his surroundings with amazement as he followed Yakob. 'Do *all* your machines have personalities?' he asked, looking back at the toilet.

'Only the ones with intelligence,' Yakob sat down as the dashboard and the windscreen, which had been mirrored, cleared.

'Jeez!' Dez almost fell into his seat as he saw the ground coming up to meet them at an incredible rate. 'We're going to crash!'

'No, we're going to land very quietly and softly and no one will know that we're here,' said Yakob calmly, as the ground stopped approaching like a runaway train and *Stark* began to glide slowly like a feather, swaying slightly from side to side. 'You'll get used to this, soon enough.'

'Thanks,' Dez grunted.

In the silence that followed their landing Dez watched the exterior of the craft change shape, but not back into the van they'd travelled through France in. This time

Stark took on the appearance of a dun-coloured, no-nonsense off-roader. No matter how many times he saw that happen, he thought, it was always going to be one very strange experience. Metal just wasn't supposed to do that – but then everything that had happened to him since he'd met Yakob wasn't *supposed* to have happened.

But it had, there was no doubt about that.

Chapter 14

'So, how are we going to find this "B" person?'

'Look everywhere.'

'How can you do that?'

Yakob looked over at Dez and raised an eyebrow. 'You are here, sitting in *Stark Revenge*, and you ask a question like that?'

'We aren't really going to blend in with the surroundings dressed like this, are we? How's *Stark* going to get round that little problem?'

'You wait here and get to know each other,' said Yakob, standing up. 'I'll be back in a minute or two.'

Dez sat looking at *Stark*'s dashboard. How did you start to get to know a machine, even one that you now knew was intelligent? And female. He'd never been very good with girls. And, as he couldn't speak Tylurian, what was he supposed to do?

'Hello, Dez.' *Stark*'s voice even sounded female, friendly too, and nothing like anything Dez had heard in the van before. 'How are you?'

'You speak English?'

'I do.'

'Oh … right,' he replied, wondering if, now, he really was going mad. 'So, um … how are you?'

'I'm enjoying myself, especially now that Yakob has replaced my cloaking unit – it wasn't much fun when that was broken. I felt somehow naked.'

Dez was at a loss for how to reply to that. The bizarre image of a naked, embarrassed van, its wheels covering its engine and rear axle, sprang to mind.

'Have you always been a van?' enquired Dez, and immediately wished he hadn't. Stupid question!

'Interesting,' said *Stark*'s voice. 'I've never thought of myself as anything but me. *Stark Revenge* is my first assignment, so in that way I suppose I have always been what you call a van.'

'Why didn't you talk to me before?'

'To be perfectly honest,' said the voice, 'I was busy and it never occurred to me. I'm sorry for being so rude.'

'It's OK; been a bit weird for everyone, I suppose. By the way, what's your name?' asked Dez. He was getting used to this. It was a bit like having an invisible friend. 'What does Yakob call you?'

'He calls me all sorts of things!' *Stark*'s voice laughed. 'Often quite unrepeatable things when there's a problem. But, to answer your question, I am what is best translated as a Bio-syntonic Intelligence.'

'Where did you come from?' asked Dez.

'I was grown,' the voice replied.

'Grown?'

'Yes, in a laboratory.'

'Like test-tube babies?' asked Dez.

'Possibly, although I'm not entirely sure what you mean by that.'

'Oh ...' Dez wasn't exactly sure what he meant either.

'Bio-syntonic means that I am, like you, a combination of many different elements working together in complete harmony. But *you* are the result of a complex biological accident; the difference with me is simply one of design and production – someone made me.'

'Yeah, really?' Dez wasn't quite sure how to take being called a biological accident. 'Can't call you bio-syntonic, can I – bit of a mouthful. Could I call you Bess for short?'

'That would be nice, Dez. I like that name.'

Nobody said anything for a moment or two, as if the two of them were getting used to the new circumstances. Then Dez broke the silence.

'Bess? Could you show me where we are – you know, with your long-range cameras?'

'I can do that, certainly.'

In front of him three of the dashboard screens lit up, each showing a different picture. On one he could see dry, scrubby fields with not much growing in them; in another was a street with mostly single-storey houses; the picture on the third screen kept jumping nearer and nearer to some children playing.

'It's getting close to midday here, not many people about,' said Bess.

'How far away can you see?'

'On a clear day, for ever.'

'Yeah, really,' smiled Dez.

'OK, on a clear day – or night – I can "see" to the horizon,' Bess explained. 'But the atmosphere on your planet, especially round the towns and cities, can make that impossible.'

'Pollution,' said Dez. 'It's the pits. Everybody knows it's happening, but no one'll do anything about it. We're all going to end up breathing canned air, if you ask me.'

'You could be right,' said Yakob. Dez hadn't heard him come back to the front of the van and he whirled round in his seat.

'Yakob?'

'Yes, what do you think? Will I fit in now?'

Dez's mouth hung open, the perfect fly trap. In front of him stood a man with skin the colour of mahogany. Oiled mahogany. Warm and dark. He was still dressed in the same jeans and T-shirt that Yakob had been wearing, but everything else had changed, except for the voice.

'H-how?'

'Know-how!' grinned Yakob.

Chapter 15

Dez was beginning to find things a little hard to take. First, the van, *Stark Revenge*, had turned out to be a girl – or a woman, or at least *female* – and then Yakob changed completely *everything* about himself!

There seemed to be no certainties any more. He came from a life where everything mostly stayed the same – the way it *should* be – the kind of life where you knew where you stood, you knew what the rules were, and just about everything had its place. And your parents, even if they were your *step*-parents, were there to see fair play. You had somewhere you belonged.

Not any more …

'What's going on, Yakob?' he asked. 'Why have you done that?'

'You were right about fitting in, Dez,' said Yakob, his teeth so white against his skin they almost seemed to glow. 'I can move about much more easily like this.'

'But your face! It's so – so *different*.' Dez stared at Yakob. The man's features shimmered ever so slightly as he looked at them. 'How did you *do* that?'

'Asked nicely,' smiled Yakob, turning and saying something in Tylurian.

'If Bess speaks English, why don't you talk to her in that, so's I can understand what's going on?'

'Bess?'

'She told me she was a bio-syntonic intelligence and Bess seemed like a friendlier name,' explained Dez. 'She likes it, don't you, Bess?'

'Yes, I do.'

'Glad to see you two are getting along so well,' smiled Yakob. 'OK, why not turn this into an English-speaking zone. All right with you, er, Bess?'

'Fine by me. What was it you wanted me to do?'

'A search,' said Yakob, closing his eyes as he thought. 'Look for all the people, aged eleven, with the initial "B", who live in the Ikoye district, please.'

'OK,' said Bess.

'What happens now?' asked Dez. 'How will she do that, from here?'

'She'll lock on to the nearest ultra-high frequency broadcast and seed some worms into it. Then we wait; it shouldn't take long.'

'"Seed some worms?"' frowned Dez.

'It's like a spy program,' explained Bess. 'They can look for anything I want by searching for any dense clusters of information activity and then "burrow" into all the available databases until they find the information we need. Then they bring it back.'

'What do they look like?'

'This,' said Bess, and one of the screens, the one showing the empty fields, blanked and then threw up a mass of weird notation. 'Beautiful, aren't they?'

'Only if you understand what you're looking at,' laughed Yakob.

Dez pointed at the screen where the children were playing. 'It could be anyone, even one of them.'

'We'll find him or her.'

'They could be on holiday, or visiting an aunt,' said Dez. 'So even if you find them in the computer they may not actually *be* here. What happens then?'

'We carry on looking.'

'Triff.' Waiting wasn't one of the things Dez was very good at.

'List coming in,' said Bess.

'What have we got?' asked Yakob, leaning forward in his seat.

'Twenty-seven possibles in the frame – nineteen girls and eight boys,' said Bess as a stream of hieroglyphs replaced the worm program.

'Can you translate them for me?' asked Dez.

'Want, want, want,' said Bess, with what sounded like a smile in her voice. Then the hieroglyphs melted into English script.

'Thanks.'

'My pleasure.'

'What happens now, Yakob?'

'I go out and have a look.'

'But how will you know which of those kids is the right one? You can't just wander up and *ask*, can you? I mean, we don't even know we've got this stuff inside us, do we?' Dez sat back with a pleased expression on his face, as if he'd scored a point.

'You keep forgetting where you are, Dez.' Yakob dug into his jeans pocket and pulled out the tiny black communicator.

'What's that going to do?'

'Sniff.'

'*Sniff?*'

'Each of you three special people had a unique pheromone micro-grafted into your cell structure, along with the code,' Yakob held up the device. 'This can detect it.'

'I didn't understand a word of that.'

'You *smell* different,' said Bess.

'Exactly,' smiled Yakob, pointing the communicator towards Dez. It beeped and a green light flashed on and off. 'You could be a quarter klik away and in the middle of a sweaty crowd of thousands, and it would find you.'

Dez made a face. 'Even if I used deodorant?'

'Even if you took a bath in it.'

Yakob spent almost an hour pottering about the van before he left. He prepared some food for the two of them, ate it, tidied up, checked things and then started searching around for something.

'What have you lost?' asked Dez, who had discovered

that Bess knew how to play draughts and had got her to create a 3D holo-board. They were on their third game and she had won them all.

'For something to be lost it must be impossible to find.' Yakob opened a storage area he'd already looked in twice and began taking things out. 'What *I'm* looking for is simply mislaid.'

'Where I come from something's lost until you find it,' said Dez, taking one of Bess's pieces and then watching as Bess proceeded to swipe three of his.

'It's the same where he comes from,' commented Bess. 'Only he won't admit it.'

'There they are!' Yakob drew his arm out of the storage space to reveal he was holding a pair of black-framed sun-glasses.

'You could've saved yourself a lot of time and just bought a pair from a shop.'

'Not like these.' Yakob put them on. 'Show him, Bess.'

A screen next to him turned on and Dez found himself looking at the back of his own head.

'They've got microcam transmitters in them.' Yakob turned his head, changing the picture on the screen. 'You can follow me wherever I go!'

And as he left the van, they did just that.

Chapter 16

Fifteen defeats later Dez was fed up with losing at draughts, and half an hour after that bored with looking at the pictures Yakob was broadcasting back to *Stark*. He had been told to stay in the cloaked van; stay put and stay quiet were his instructions. But he was itching for something to do and, almost before he knew what was happening, he found himself walking away from *Stark*, off in the direction he'd seen Yakob go.

The van's doors hadn't been locked and Dez's decision to go had been so illogical that Bess hadn't had a chance to stop him. This was a *military* exercise; orders were supposed to *obeyed* and people were *not* expected to act on impulse. Dez was outside and closing the van's door before Bess could react.

Behind him he thought he could hear her calling his name, and he did think of going back. But only for a moment. Instead he strode on with the sun beating down, so hot he thought he should have steam coming out of his ears. Summer in Nigeria was like being in an oven and the air shimmered and waved.

All Dez could see in the heat haze were a few small buildings dotted about, and in the distance the buildings he'd looked at on *Stark*'s screens. It took him ten minutes to reach them and what little shade they offered, and, although it wasn't Disneyland, it was more exciting than sitting around in the van.

The trip to the Dordogne was the first time Dez had ever been out of England. France was certainly abroad – they drove on the wrong side of the road – but it wasn't really *foreign*. Not like this place.

Lagos, at least the bit he was wandering around, smelled, sounded and looked different – unlike anything he'd ever imagined. Dez liked watching documentaries on TV, but as he walked through the streets he realized that what you saw and heard on the box wasn't even a fraction of what it was like actually to *be* there. Being in this place made his skin tingle.

Keeping an eye on the way he'd come, Dez found a wide, palm-lined street crowded with shops, stalls, cafés and hawking, hollering traders. Women walked by with babies strapped to their backs and what looked like their own body weight in merchandise perched precariously on their heads. Here you could buy food, fabrics, pots and pans, live animals (soon to be more food? he wondered) jewellery and furniture. And everywhere music played, hard, bright rhythms spilling out of tinny loudspeakers. The noise was incredible.

Dez sat on the ground in the shade of a tree. He'd stay for a while and just soak up the atmosphere. If Yakob found "B", whoever they were, as easily as he said he could then they might well be on their way very soon. And he had an idea that a return trip to Nigeria might not be an easy thing to organize.

No one seemed to be taking much notice of him as he watched the insanely vibrant world go by, and soon Dez lost himself in the lawless tango of events that seemed to be happening for the sheer joy of it.

Out of the ceaselessly shifting crowd an old man, his black skin almost grey from the dust, shuffled over and stood in front of him. He said something, rubbing his thumb against two fingers. Money, thought Dez; he wants some money and all I've got is a couple of Euros.

Unzipping the pouch he took out some change and put it in the beggar's hand. The old man's face broke into a huge toothless grin and he patted Dez on the shoulder before hobbling away into the crowd.

Then Dez felt another hand grip his shoulder from behind. Hard.

Through his mind raced the ghastly thought that it was Väds. They'd found him! He'd been stupid enough to disobey Yakob's orders and expose himself to danger and his worst nightmare had come true. He was going to be hauled off this lively, happy street and taken somewhere to be vaporized.

He didn't dare look but kept his eyes fixed on the ground. Ants rushed to and fro, unaware of the tragedy taking place above them, and Dez took his lead from them. Leaping to his feet he wrenched his shoulder away and ran, his feet pounding on the dusty road, eyes searching for gaps in the shifting crowd, ears filled with the thumping of his heart.

He was aware that people were looking at him. Puzzled faces stared, hands reached out and violently patterned cloth swept over him as he barged his way through. It didn't for one minute occur to him that he had no idea where he was going; all he wanted to do was escape. Every second he stayed out of the grip of that hand was a bonus.

And then he tripped, falling in a tangle of arms and legs.

'What are you doing here?' said a voice.

Dez looked up. Staring down at him was a tall man wearing sun-glasses, dressed in a swathe of colourful local clothes and with a matching pill-box hat tipped forward on his head. He was panting and frowning, his forehead beaded with sweat.

'I thought I told you to stay with *Stark.*'

'Yakob?' queried Dez, finally finding his voice. He got up and stared at the impressive figure looming over him, ignoring the looks of the slightly perplexed market traders. 'Where did you get the clothes?'

'Never mind that.' Yakob put one hand on his hip and wagged an angry finger at him. 'You're very silly to do this – you could have got lost, anything! And why did you run away?'

'I thought you were the Väds.'

'Exactly! I *could* have been one of them.'

'I'm sorry, I won't do it again, I promise.' Dez suddenly became aware that where they were standing had become a little pool of quiet. He glanced sideways and saw that people had stopped what they were doing and were looking at them. 'We're being watched,' he said.

'I can see that,' muttered Yakob. '*I* fit in but you don't, and we're making a bit of a scene.'

Someone in the crowd said something to Yakob and he replied in what sounded to Dez like perfectly fluent dialect. If only he could learn to speak maths that easily ...

'They want to know why you were running away, why I'm shouting at you,' said Yakob, speaking with a huge, false grin on his face.

'What did you tell them?'

'That you were the son of a friend from England, that you'd wandered off and I was worried.'

'Good story,' said Dez.

'And not one I want to have to tell again,' said Yakob, looking back down the market. 'I can see a policeman coming. Let's get going.'

As Dez turned to go he heard a metallic clatter behind him, and when he looked round he saw a thunder-shower of coins spinning and bouncing on the pavement. As Yakob took his arm and guided him away, the space they left was filled by a mass of people frantically trying to sweep up as much money as they could. The babble level rose to an even higher volume.

'Why did you do that?' Dez yelled over his shoulder.

'Didn't want to be followed,' came the reply as Yakob gently prodded Dez to go left and make for a side street.

Dez was pushing through the crowds when a pair of khaki-clad legs strode in front of him and stopped. He had been concentrating on weaving his way through the people, and took a moment to look up at the man standing in his way. The ugly automatic rifle he was holding gleamed dully in the sunlight, its black paintwork chipped and scratched, making it look like some old toy.

The soldier jabbed the rifle at Dez as he spoke to Yakob, the barrel's spiralled rifling clearly visible as the muzzle waved only centimetres from his face. He could smell the grease that covered it.

'Is he arresting us?'

'Not yet,' muttered Yakob, and said something to the soldier.

Dez didn't know what to do next. He listened to the sing-song conversation going on between Yakob, extraordinary in his colourful disguise, and the soldier, immovable in his dusty uniform. He couldn't tell what was happening; Yakob sounded polite and reasonable, the soldier somehow uninterested.

Yakob suddenly put his right arm out, as if to shake hands, and the soldier let go of the rifle grip and did the same. Dez thought he heard the rustle of paper as the two men nodded at each other and the soldier stood to one side to let them pass. Without waiting to be told Dez scooted off down the side street. He heard Yakob call to him to slow down.

'Don't get lost now!'

'I was just getting away.' Dez turned to wait for Yakob to catch up. 'What happened back there?'

'He wanted to know why we were so eager to leave.'

'What did you say? It must've looked dead suspicious, chucking that money around like that.'

'I told him it was an accident, a hole in my pocket,' said Yakob. 'Just small change I couldn't be bothered to pick up.'

'And he believed you?'

'After I made it worth his while.' Yakob smiled.

'I *thought* I heard something! You passed him money when you shook hands – bribed him!'

'We say "smoothed the path",' said Yakob, hurrying Dez forward. 'It appears some things are the same no matter which sun is shining down on you.'

'Or suns,' said Dez, weaving his way through the crowds. 'Must be really weird having two of them in the sky at once.'

'I miss the sight.'

'Are you homesick?'

'Homesick?' Yakob was silent for a long moment. 'I suppose I am.'

'Me too,' sighed Dez. 'And I haven't really got a home to go back to any more.'

Chapter 17

On the way back to *Stark Revenge* they stopped at a stall that looked as if it might collapse under the strain if just one more item was put on it. Yakob bought some bananas and oranges, and then got a couple of cans of drink from a nearby shop.

'I suppose you've been at the money machines again,' said Dez, as they began the long, dusty walk through the streets.

'Might've been.'

'You'd be a bit stumped if we pitched up somewhere they didn't have any.' Dez kicked a stone out of his way. 'People aren't as easy to fool as machines.'

'Don't be so sure – and don't look round!' Yakob's voice suddenly sounded oddly clipped and strained.

'Why?'

'Just do as I say …'

'It's the Väds …' Dez stopped in mid-stride.

'Maybe.'

'What are we going to do?'

'Get away from here – quick, before they see you.' Yakob came close to Dez and put his arm round his shoulders, turning him and walking back the way they'd come.

'How d'you know they haven't already seen me?'

'You're still breathing.'

'Great!' Dez felt like being sick, the acid taste of half-digested fruit rising in his throat. 'But what if there are more of them back this way?'

'I'm getting you off the street so I can do something about the way you look.'

Before Dez had a chance to ask what that might be, he found himself being hustled inside what looked like a cross between a party and a general store. The shop – what you could see of it from all the stuff hanging from its porch as well as the ceiling inside – was crowded with people.

Yakob and Dez joined the throng, losing themselves amongst the shoppers picking and poking at the crammed shelves. For a few minutes they walked up and down, Yakob squinting at the displays as if searching for something.

Then Dez found himself being pulled down an aisle, Yakob muttering 'This will do ...' as he reached up for a colourful mask that came complete with green raffia hair.

'And?' said Dez, none the wiser.

'You wear this and a long-sleeved T-shirt,' said Yakob, picking one up from a nearby basket, 'and no one will know *where* you come from – you could be bald with yellow spots wearing these.'

Back out on the street, his hands stuffed in his pockets, Dez felt hot, sweaty and ridiculous – though he realized it was definitely preferable to be a live idiot than a dead sensible person. They were keeping to the emptier side streets and he felt jittery and nervous as he couldn't see very well, the two holes in the mask giving him almost no view at all. And the raffia hair was making his neck itch.

'Triff idea this, Yakob. Not.'

'Better than walking about in full view.'

'Can you see anyone we want to avoid?'

Silence.

'Yakob?' Dez swung round, the twin holes, bright spots in the dark of the mask, giving him a weird binocular image of the dusty street. He heard a door slam and then …

Nothing.

'Yakob …' Dez tore the mask off and stared about. The street was empty. Where could he have gone – was Yakob playing some kind of trick? He didn't think so.

And then he heard it … a grunting, scuffling noise. But where was it coming from? He was beginning to feel sick with fear again, looking left, right, up at shuttered windows, but where to search first?

'Yakob!' he yelled. An answering throttled gurgle came from behind a rickety wooden door set into a mud brick wall a few metres back down the street. Mask still in hand, Dez ran towards the door and pushed it open.

Writhing in the dirt yard were two figures. The one on the ground was definitely Yakob, and the one with his hands at Yakob's throat was some person in a suit; they were locked in almost silent combat, but for all the lack of noise it was obviously a battle to the death. And Yakob was losing.

Without even thinking Dez dropped the mask and leapt, screaming, on to the back of the man attacking Yakob. He tore into him; he pummelled, he kicked, he punched and he scratched and then he felt a bone-shaking punch in his side and he was flung like a rag doll into the dirt.

All the breath in his body had gone and tiny bright lights whirled in front of his eyes. Gasping for breath, Dez pulled his head up in time to see Yakob land a sledgehammer punch. His attacker's neck snapped back with a sharp cracking sound and he slumped sideways, Yakob pushing him away as he got up.

It was then that Dez saw the small, grizzle-haired old lady, broom held in her wizened hands like an axe, standing in the doorway of the house the yard belonged to. She was staring at them, her mouth open.

Yakob, brushing dust off his clothes, said something to her in local dialect as he limped over to Dez and pulled him up. She shook the broom as she replied.

'She's saying that if she had a telephone, she'd call the police,' panted Yakob, wincing as he spoke. 'So we'd better move before she decides to go and find one and do it anyway.'

Dez nodded. He couldn't speak yet to save his life, and the two of them shuffled quickly out of the yard. On the ground behind them the man in the suit lay face down in the dirt.

'Was it … a Väd?' asked Dez. His breath was still coming in fits and starts and his side hurt; Yakob nodded. 'Is he dead?'

'Probably.'

'How did he find us?'

'Don't really know; luck, maybe. He came out of nowhere,' said Yakob. 'I didn't have a chance to warn you, it all happened so fast – one moment we were on the street, the next I was dying in that little old lady's back yard.'

'You nearly *died*?'

'I did.'

'And I'd've been next,' said Dez. 'I suppose I'd better put the mask back on.'

'I suppose you better had.'

Turning a corner they heard the sound of someone screaming; the old lady, it seemed, was going to get her policemen. They started to walk faster.

Neither Dez nor Yakob spoke for some time. What had happened was both a warning and an example of the dangers they faced; the Väds were everywhere and could strike at any time. Out in the open the risks seemed to be getting bigger all the time.

Finally, away in the distance, Dez could see the stand

of trees where *Stark* was waiting for them, and wondered what Bess would have to say about his running off and what had happened to them since. It was a bit much, really, having two people on his case.

'Oh, yeah!' he said, suddenly remembering what he'd been meaning to ask Yakob. 'Did you find "B"?'

'I have located her,' said Yakob, his limp now almost gone.

'You did? Why didn't you tell me before?' Dez stopped suddenly. '*Her?*'

'Beatrice Okonkwo, eleven years old like you, and I really haven't had a chance to tell you before,' said Yakob, shooing Dez on. 'She's at a school not so far from here.'

'What are you going to do – walk up to her and say "Beatrice, you don't know me, but I'm an alien from Priam and I need to get hold of some stuff that was bunged into your body when you were little?" She'll think you're completely barking.'

'I'm not going to walk up to her and say anything – you are.'

'Me?' Dez's feet forgot where they were and he stumbled, just catching himself before he fell. 'What do you mean?'

'It's too hot to go into details out here. I'll tell you when we get back to *Stark*.' Yakob started walking faster. 'And don't be surprised if – what do you call her, Bess?' Dez nodded. 'If Bess has a few words to say to you about walking out on her like that. She's annoyed.'

'I had a feeling she might be.' Dez raised his eyebrows. 'Bit like having an auntie, or an older sister.'

'I wouldn't know.'

'Neither would I, but I've got a good imagination.'

Beatrice Okonkwo's school wasn't very far from where *Stark* was hidden, but it was too late to do anything because it had already closed for the day. They spent the rest of the afternoon recuperating from the trauma of the Väd's attack.

Yakob put some cooling ointment on Dez's bruised side and then, to pass the time, showed him how *Stark* worked; Dez was amazed to find that although Bess controlled everything, she had a team of drone intelligences that did all the boring, repetitive work. They were the ones that sounded like budgies that'd drunk too much coffee, twittering at Yakob when they wanted to tell him something or other.

At some point Yakob sent a tiny remote camera, no bigger than a large bumble bee, high up above *Stark* to do an aerial scan. It wasn't cloaked but was so small and stayed up such a short time that Yakob thought it a risk worth taking. The remote's electronic images of the surrounding area, and its almost instant check on all possible frequencies, showed telltale signs of Väd activity, but they were being very careful. As Yakob said, it would have been a major surprise if the remote hadn't spotted something, after what had happened.

It was midday, scorching hot with hardly a breeze in the air, and the light was so bright it hurt. Dez, who now had a stupendous tan (courtesy of some tiny pills Yakob had given him to colour his skin), was looking at the world through a pair of mirrored dark glasses. Part of him still felt like he was on holiday.

He was with Yakob and they were sitting outside a café just down the street from Beatrice's school. Dez looked at his watch.

'She'll be out soon,' he said.

'Nervous?'

'No, not really.' Dez looked at his watch again. 'Not about meeting her – it's the Väds.'

'They won't recognize you now; you look like you've been living here all your life.' Yakob looked out of the café window. 'You remember what to do, don't you?'

'Yeah, you'll be waiting in that alleyway over there,' Dez pointed across the street, 'and all I've got to do is ask for help … convince her to come with me.'

'Simple.'

'If only!'

'Here they are,' said Yakob.

Dez looked towards the school and saw a stream of kids running towards the gates. 'They look a bit young.'

'They're the small one's who get let out first.' Yakob finished off his cup of black coffee. 'Beatrice will be one of the last; she's top year.'

'You know a lot about the place.'

'Did my research.'

'You mean Bess did.' Dez drained his can of a local cola drink, so sweet it made his tongue dance.

'Same difference.'

The two of them sat and watched as the children running by them got bigger and older. Then Yakob nudged Dez.

'There she is – the one with the red and blue satchel.'

Dez's eyes flitted over the straggle of children and found the satchel. He looked at its owner. She was on her own, her hair pulled back into a bun and with small gold hoop earrings in each ear. It occurred to him that she looked quite pretty.

Yakob nudged Dez again. 'Time to go,' he said.

Dez got up and took off his new sun-glasses. His palms felt damp and he wiped them on his shorts. They still felt damp as he stepped out of the café and began to make his way towards the girl who, like him, carried secret information so valuable it could be the death of her.

Dodging through the chattering kids, Dez suddenly realized the flaws in Yakob's plan. Why was he picking on this particular girl? Why hadn't he asked someone else – an adult – to help him? He felt like turning tail, but he was now only a few metres from her and he knew Yakob would be watching. He stopped and waited for the girl to come nearer to him.

'Er, excuse me?' he pointed falteringly at her. 'Do you, you know, speak English?'

She ignored him and carried on walking.

'Beatrice?' said Dez, desperate to make her stop. A frown clouded the girl's face as she did exactly that.

'Yes … do I know you?'

'No, but …'

'Well, go away then,' she said.

'I need your help, and … and *you* need my help as well – there's something I have to tell you that's *really* important!' This wasn't going the way it was supposed to at all, thought Dez. He looked around desperately and saw some other kids coming towards them, pointing. 'I've *got* to talk to you – somewhere private!'

'What's going on, Treece?' said a tall, skinny boy. 'Who's this?'

'I think he's crazy,' said Treece. 'He keeps saying I need his help and he wants to go somewhere private.'

'Who are you, strange boy?' The skinny boy poked Dez in the chest, hard. 'What d'you want?'

'I must've made a mistake,' said Dez, watching as Treece's friends circled him. 'I'm lost, that's all … lost. I don't know where I am.' Someone behind him gave him a shove, and the circle got smaller.

'Why'd you pick on Treece?' said another boy.

'She looked, you know, friendly.' Dez tried to smile. What were these kids going to do? Beat him up right there on the street? Where the heck was Yakob? He looked for a gap in the ring of scowling faces, a way out, and as he did so he caught sight of the Tylurian's bright pill-box hat at the corner of the alley.

Taking a deep breath he picked the smallest kid and

barged straight at him, pushing him out of the way and running for it. Behind him he could hear cat-calls and jeering, but as far as he could tell, no one was following. Skidding to a halt in the alley he glanced over his shoulder and saw Treece and her friends wandering off, as if nothing had happened.

'Great plan, Yakob!' he said. 'So simple it went like clockwork.'

'It was worth a try.'

'Thanks a lot – I nearly got trashed by that bunch!' Dez said angrily. 'Next time you have a triffic little idea *you* see if it's worth a try.'

'I'm sorry; I didn't know she'd be like that.' Yakob looked a bit sheepish. 'Some things are obviously *not* the same wherever you are. Are you OK?'

'Yeah, but I screwed up, didn't I,' Dez sighed. 'I knew I'd be no good at this sort of thing – what are we going to do now?'

'Kidnap her,' said Yakob, turning and walking off down the alley.

Dez, too stunned to answer, had to run to catch him up.

'Are they there?' came the query on the cryo-plasma screen.

'Yes.'

'Pinpointed?'

'Not exactly. We picked up a faint trace of scanning activity, but it was over before we had time to triangulate. We have people on the street, though. They reported an incident in a market, but it was impossible to get through the crowds – this city is out of control. And ...'

'And what? Are you holding something back?'

'We had them both and, ah – they got away.'

'Put the person responsible on a charge!'

'I'm afraid that's impossible.'

'Why?'

'He's dead. We just managed to retrieve the body before the local authorities got to it ... his neck was broken.'

'They're making fools of us! They must be found, and quickly!'

Chapter 18

They were going to kidnap someone. The thought lay there, over Dez's head, like a sleeping threat. He was sitting in the passenger seat, watching Yakob drive *Stark*, in its new disguise, nearer to Treece's house. He just hoped the Tylurian knew more about doing this kind of thing than he did of the rather simpler job of talking to someone in the street. And hope was all Dez could do.

As they drove through the darkened streets to the Ikoye district every system *Stark* possessed was on high alert, watching, waiting, seeking, searching, sensitive to the merest twitch of a moth's wing. Dez could feel the tension as if he was wearing it next to his skin.

Infra-red cameras made the pitch-dark appear almost like day and Dez felt a bit odd knowing that he could see so much without being seen himself.

'Which is her house?' he asked.

'The one with the white fence round it.'

'They've *all* got white fences, Yakob.'

'Right in front.' Yakob pointed. He'd taken off his

flowing robes and was back in jeans and a sweatshirt, though still dark-skinned. 'With the flowering bushes at the gates. Show him, Bess.'

The screen in front of him zoomed into a close-up of a decorated ironwork arch spanning a pair of metal gates.

'Thanks,' said Dez.

'No problem,' replied Bess.

'It's half past three.' Dez showed Yakob his watch. 'Are you going in?'

'No point in waiting; it'll be dawn soon.' Yakob reached over to the dashboard, picked up the microcam glasses and twisted one of the arms. The lenses cleared and he put them on.

'Do they have sound *and* vision?'

'They do,' Yakob opened the van door and got out. 'See you later.'

Dez watched him sprint over towards the fence, stop, look round and then swiftly climb up and over. A screen in front of him showed the sweep of garden as Yakob looked around. From one of the speakers came the sound of a low, rasping growl. Yakob had obviously heard it too as he looked in the direction it was coming from.

'Guard animal,' they heard him say.

'Guard *dog*,' muttered Dez as he saw a large, smooth-haired Doberman come into view. Its nose was wrinkled, its teeth bared and he could see the hackles on the back of its neck bristling. 'Vicious.'

For a long moment Dez was lost in his thoughts about

his dog, all alone in the kennels, waiting for the family to return and take him home. A feeling of absolute sadness came over him; for both of them life was never going to be the same. He missed Rufus and had an awful feeling that he'd never see the old boy again. Another low growl brought Dez back down to earth and he saw the Doberman's face large on one of the screens, jowls quivering, saliva dripping off them.

He watched as the animal came slowly towards Yakob, each step cool and deliberate, its eyes fixed on his face. It was, Dez felt as he watched the screen, almost as if it was looking straight at *him*. He found himself sitting still and tense in his seat. Then he heard the strangest thing. From the speakers came a different growl, this one slightly lower, with an almost questioning tone to it.

'What's that?' he asked, watching with amazement as the Doberman stopped, its ears cocking as it turned its head to one side, quizzically.

'It's Yakob,' said Bess.

'Yakob? He speaks *dog* as well?'

'A bit,' replied Bess.

'Obviously the bit that matters,' said Dez, as he watched the dog wag its tail. Its hackles went down and the dog looked away, then sat down. 'Crisis over?'

'This one.'

'He's off!' Dez pointed to the screen showing Yakob was approaching the house. 'How's he going to get in, Bess?'

'You'll see.'

Dez was glued to the screen. Yakob walked slowly round the house, a long, low, single-storey building, obviously inspecting each window and door he came to. He did a complete circuit, meeting the Doberman on his way and giving the animal a friendly pat on the head. That was one guard dog, thought Dez, who'd be down the Job Centre when its owners found their daughter missing in the morning.

Mumbling something about the back door being the easiest and safest route in, Yakob jogged off again and was soon kneeling down and peering at the lock. Into the picture came his hands, one of them holding what looked like a black screwdriver, and Dez watched as Yakob pushed it into the lock. The blade moulded itself to the pattern of the keyslot as it went in, and then Yakob pressed something on the handle. As the blade began to glow Dez heard a soft *CLICK* and saw the door swing open.

'He's in,' he whispered, even though he didn't have to.

'And all he has to do is get out again,' said Bess.

Yakob was in the kitchen, its work surfaces gleaming and everything neat and tidy; from there he went along a wood-floored corridor and into a large hallway. Off this ran two more corridors, and there were three doors, including the big double front door, as well. Yakob's head turned left then right as he inspected the lie of the land.

The hall had what looked like a thick patterned carpet on the floor and there were pictures and a mirror on the walls. At one point Yakob strayed in front of the mirror and there he was, looking at them in the van. He grinned and waved. Then the sound seemed to be turned up, the speakers in the van whistling very softly.

'What happened?' asked Dez.

'He's turned the mic volume up,' said Bess, 'so he can hear if anyone's awake in a room.'

It was weird to watch someone invade a strange house and drift around it like a phantom, silent and all-seeing. There was a feeling of power about it, and Dez wondered if that was what cat-burglars felt when they sneaked about as people slept. You were there, but you left no trace of coming or going, except, if you were a burglar, empty spaces where you'd taken things.

Yakob started walking again, and the picture showed Yakob going up to the door opposite the entrance and Dez could hear the low rumble of someone snoring. Unlikely to be Treece, he thought. Yakob thought so too and went down the corridor to his right until he came to another door. He listened and then slowly turned the handle, opening the door bit by bit. The noise sounded deafening in the van, and Dez began to worry that whoever was inside would be woken, until he realized the mics were still on "high".

Asleep on the bed, sprawled across it sideways, was a boy. Treece must have an older brother. Yakob closed the door and went back up to the hall and turned left, stopping when a floorboard creaked, waiting for a moment and then carrying on, past more pictures, until he came to a door. It was covered in stickers and hand-drawn notices with things like KEEP OUT, GO AWAY and NO ENTRY written on them. From the little Dez knew of her, he thought it sounded just like Treece.

Yakob opened the door and slipped in.

The room was a riot of frills and lacy bits, and Dez could just tell that everything had to be pink – curtains, bedcover, sheets, the lot. Dolls littered every flat surface and clothes were scattered everywhere. The place was a mess. Yakob seemed as amazed by the state of the room as Dez was, looking here and there for some moments before focusing his attention on the sleeping figure of Treece.

She was lying on her back, with one arm cradling her head and her mouth slightly open. She still had her earrings in, but her hair was no longer tied back and was strewn over her pillow.

'Pretty girl,' said Bess.

Dez looked up from the screen and sat back in his seat. 'Yeah, she is,' he said. 'But about as friendly as her rotten dog – at least she was to me.'

'Girls, eh?'

'Yeah ...' Dez heard Bess laugh quietly, and then fall silent. 'What's the matter?'

'She's waking up.'

'How do you know?' Dez leant forward to look at the screen. 'She looks fast asleep to me.'

'Her levels have changed. She's surfacing – fast!'

'Levels?'

'Functions that show the state the brain is in,' explained Bess. 'I must warn Yakob.'

But it was too late. Unable to do anything but watch, Dez saw Treece's eyes on the screen blink open and shut and then open again. Open so wide there was white showing all round the irises.

And then she screamed.

Chapter 19

The scream echoed around the van, shrill and piercing like glass being scratched by a diamond. Dez jammed his fingers in his ears.

'Yow!' he yelled. 'Turn it *down*, Bess – she'll wake the whole neighbourhood!'

'We're sound-proofed.'

'Well, *I'm* not!'

The sound in the van lowered and Dez looked back at the screen. Yakob's hand had come into view and he was holding something out towards Treece. The scream died away on her lips and she lay in the bed, staring up at him. Slowly her mouth closed and her eyes shut.

'How did he *do* that?'

'Simple hypno-pulse,' explained Bess. 'Short-acting, but effective.' She turned the sound up again and Dez could hear voices.

'Her parents have woken up!' he said.

'Afraid so.'

'What's he going to do?'

'If I were him I'd hide,' said Bess.

'If I were him I'd hurry up; I can hear footsteps coming down the hall.' Dez watched as Yakob scanned the bedroom again and moved quickly over to a pair of cupboard doors. He saw them open and felt himself bend with Yakob as the Tylurian ducked into the closet and pulled the door to behind him.

The screen darkened and then grew lighter bit by bit as the microcams adjusted to the almost complete lack of light. In the gloom Dez could just about make out the clutter Yakob had pushed himself behind.

Dez heard the bedroom door open and a voice call Treece's name. He could also hear Yakob's breathing, shallow and regular, but amplified in the van so that it seemed he was right behind him.

From the sound of it, both Treece's parents were now in the bedroom. Dez couldn't understand what either of them were saying, but it was clear the mother was worried, her voice at a higher pitch, and the father was calming her down. They were walking round the room and Dez heard windows being checked. Would they do the same to the cupboards? He held his breath in anticipation and realized that Yakob was doing the same thing.

Then he heard a whisper, a soft kiss, and the bedroom door closing. He sighed with relief, a sound echoed by the speakers in the van.

'Close,' said Bess.

'No kidding,' Dez nodded. 'And they're awake now

– how's he going to get her out?' He saw the doors of the closet open slowly on the screen, revealing Treece still fast asleep on her bed.

Yakob moved quietly towards her and the picture showed a close-up of her face.

'Still under the influence,' said Bess.

'How much longer?' Dez peered at the screen.

'Hard to say.'

Yakob moved away from the bed and Dez could see he was collecting some clothes and a pair of shoes and putting them in a plastic bag he'd found.

'I'm coming out the front door,' he whispered. 'Be ready to go.'

Wrapping the bed cover round the girl, Yakob lifted her up as if she weighed nothing and went to the door. He opened it, listened and, hearing nothing, moved out and along the corridor. He came into the hall and stopped once more. The house was full of small, inconsequential little noises that could mean anything or nothing.

'I'll be glad when this is over,' said Dez.

'Not looking forward to a life of crime, then?' asked Bess.

'No way! I'm a nervous wreck now and I'm not even *in* the house.'

Something odd started to happen to the screen linked to Yakob's microcams, the picture and sound momentarily breaking up.

'Eh?' Dez leant forward. 'What's going on?' he asked as the picture cleared.

'Unattributable malfunction,' replied Bess.

'What?'

'I don't know.' Bess sounded worried.

'Dez?' Yakob's voice boomed over the speakers.

'Yeah?'

'I need your help. She's waking up and I haven't time to do anything.'

'What can I do?' Dez shifted in his seat and looked out of the van at the house. There was no sign of any activity.

'Come and meet me in case she wakes up.'

'This is *not* a good idea,' said Bess. 'What's he thinking of?'

'Let me out, Bess!' said Dez as he tried to open his door.

'I don't like it.'

'Why?' Dez pressed the lock again. 'Come on Bess – I've got to go and help him!'

'This goes against all procedures.'

'I'm coming out,' said Yakob's voice.

'Bess!'

'All right, but take a communicator.'

A panel in the dashboard flipped open and Dez saw a small black box, just like the one Yakob carried. Picking it up and putting it in his pocket he heard the door lock click and he got out.

'Be careful,' warned Bess. 'Be *very* careful!'

'I will,' replied Dez, the butterflies starting to swarm in his stomach.

The air was cool and there was a slight breeze fanning him as he ran out of the trees and across the dry, scrubby grass towards Treece's house. He was half-way there when he saw the front door open and Yakob, carrying his sheet-wrapped bundle, appear on the porch.

Dez waved.

Then, for some reason he couldn't fathom, everything locked up. His legs and arms wouldn't work and he crumpled to the ground as if someone had taken the ignition key out and his motor had stopped.

In the distance he could hear Yakob's voice and then he felt rough hands pick him up. He was facing down and all he could see was the ground rushing by underneath him, a blur of booted feet – not his – stamping the dust as they ran. He could hear voices, gruff, guttural voices – and the sound of laboured breathing.

His mind raced. What was happening? Nothing made any kind of sense and he felt like a piece of not very treasured luggage as he was carted unceremoniously off into the unknown. Somehow the Väds had found out where they were, but surely Yakob must have realized there was a danger of them doing that, so why had he asked him to come out of hiding? He'd walked straight into a well-laid trap.

Dez wanted to scream as the air around him went a blistering white and his ears felt as if someone had stuck a needle in them, but his voice was as useless as the rest of his body. Struggling was out of the question; everything he owned was as limp as yesterday's salad, but neither could he relax. As the seconds built inexorably into a minute he knew that the unthinkable had happened. He'd been captured by the Väd-Raatch and what was left of his life was running away like sand in an egg-timer. Dez's only thought was that he hoped it would be quick.

And then the hands holding him let go and he fell.

'What the hell happened?' demanded Yakob, as he laid Treece's sleeping form carefully on to one of the chairs. She shifted slightly under the bright pink bed cover and settled down again.

'You tell me,' said Bess. 'But do it *after* I get us out of here – I'm going into a low geo-stationary orbit until I can get a fix on everything.'

'Did you record it all?'

'Silly me, I forgot to switch the cameras on … of *course* I recorded it all!' Bess sealed *Stark Revenge* and hurled it a klik and a half into the dawn sky where it hung, invisible, above the quiet Lagos suburb.

Checking that Treece was still out for the count, Yakob went up front and watched as Bess re-ran the 30 seconds of imagery each of the four front cameras had caught.

Camera 1 had been trained on the front door of Treece's house. It showed Yakob coming out and catching sight of Dez. Urgently waving for him to go back he then fumbled behind him for precious seconds until he found his laser pistol. Yakob shook his head as he watched himself duck behind a large bush to keep Treece out of danger.

'My hands were tied,' he muttered to himself. The clip finished and Bess started to run Camera 2.

This view showed Dez appear from offscreen and start to run towards the house, waving as he saw Yakob. Then, like he'd fallen asleep mid-stride, he collapsed and two uniformed figures wearing visored helmets de-cloaked and picked him up. As they ran Yakob saw the tiny photon grenade Bess had fired explode in front of them, its brilliant light freezing the picture for a brief moment. There were going to be a lot of cats and dogs with sore heads the next day, thought Yakob, because the photon grenade also gave off a massive blast of ultra-sound, but the Väds must have been shielded as they just carried on running. Camera 2 followed them as they disappeared into the open hatch of their cloaked ship.

Camera 3 had followed Dez in close-up and gave readings of his heartbeat and breathing – both, Yakob was relieved to see, were normal. Camera 4 had worked out where the Väd soldiers were making for and had zoomed in on the open hatchway the moment it appeared. Its final shot was of Dez dropping to the floor.

'They knew we were here,' said Yakob.

'Something – or some*one* – obviously tipped them off.'

'They have to have cracked my broadcast frequency as well,' Yakob sighed. 'Tell me again what happened when I was in the house.'

'I'll show you,' said Bess, and up on screen came the moment when Yakob's transmission had blanked and returned with him asking Dez to come and help.

'They jacked in and over-rode the sound channel,' said Yakob. 'Must've synthed my voice. Very clever.'

'I should've done a match.'

'It's not your fault; it all happened so quickly.'

'Why did they take him? Why not just kill him then and there?'

'I don't know,' said Yakob, getting up and massaging his neck with one hand. 'I can't figure that one out at all. Something must have changed.'

'We have it.'

'Alive?'

'Everything in working order, as ordered.'

'What about the other one?'

'Circumstances didn't allow us to get them both – the counter-attack was very swift.'

'Get what information you can from the creature without harming it, and stay there until you find the second one. New orders from Anavrin now dictate we need all three.'

'Would it be impertinent to ask why?'

'It would, but I see no reason why you shouldn't know. Overlord Garel wants to punish the Tylurians for even thinking of devising such a horrific weapon to use against us, let alone actually designing it. He wants those plans intact so we can make the weapon … and use it.'

'It is no more than they deserve.'

'Quite. So make sure it happens. Any more losses and heads will roll.'

Chapter 20

It had all happened so fast. One minute he'd been running towards Treece's house and the next he was a heap on the ground, the only thing working being his mind. And that was on overdrive.

As he lay on the cold metal floor, his cheek pressed on the scuffed, dented paintwork, his thoughts were like pieces of paper in a hurricane. Trying to catch one and concentrate on it was impossible; they slipped through his mental fingers and were gone.

Slowly, as the pain in his ears subsided, Dez realized that he could blink and move his eyes. The effect of whatever they had done to him must be wearing off slightly – and if he could be sure of only one thing it was that "they" meant the Väds, who didn't, for some inexplicable reason, want him dead. Yet.

He knew he wasn't tied up; he could just make out one of his hands lying limply in front of him, and he gave up trying to move. There was no point. Instead he began attempting to see where exactly he was and who he was with.

From his position on the floor his view was restricted because he couldn't turn his head. All he could really see properly was what was in front of him, and that was a wall about a metre away. It was a dull green, like the floor, which it joined in a rough weld. Everything was all bolts and hard edges and the whole place had a sort of military air about it.

It reminded Dez of the time they'd gone on a school trip to the Imperial War Museum. No matter what age it came from, army stuff always had the same look to it – no frills and built to be battered. This place was completely different from *Stark*, with its soft lighting and gentle curves; the van wasn't designed to kill, although it was perfectly capable of protecting itself from attack, but the Väd ship was very obviously a battle craft and nothing else.

Forcing his eyes up as far as they would go – which in effect meant looking sideways, as if he was trying to see his own right ear – Dez saw a control panel set into the wall. It had buttons and a small screen and was covered in indecipherable squiggles. Väd-speak, thought Dez, as he felt, rather than heard, the thud of approaching footsteps. The floor vibrated as they got nearer and then hands roughly picked him up and turned him over. His head lolled back like a newborn baby's and for the first time he could see one of his captors.

He (Dez presumed it was a he) was dressed in a blue uniform with no markings on it, of the same dull shade as the floor and walls. The material, which looked like a tough nylon, was fastened with plastic tabs up to the neck and the Väd was wearing what looked very much like a skiing helmet, complete with a dark mirrored visor.

Somehow not knowing what the Väd looked like was worse, scarier even. Were they monsters? Did they have three eyes or something? Did they have big tongues and slaver a lot? Dez found himself trying to see under the visor for tell-tale signs of dribble – a ridiculous thing to be doing when there were bigger things to worry about.

And then he was being hauled through a doorway and into another room, his head bouncing around like one of those dogs in the back window of a car. A voice behind him said something and Dez found himself being hitched up and put on a chair, gloved hands on each shoulder to stop him from falling off. His head swung forward and he found himself staring at his feet. It occurred to him that he could really do with a new pair of trainers.

'You're designation is "Jack Danby",' said a slightly muffled voice.

Somebody's gloved hand took his chin, lifting it up, and Dez saw himself reflected in the visor in front of him. He looked moronic, all his facial muscles completely slack and lifeless. The Väd took his hand away and as Dez's head fell down again he felt a tingling in his neck and around his mouth; sensations were slowly returning and he found he could pull his head up.

'You can talk now,' said the Väd.

'Ghhhow, Ah khhan,' said Dez, his tongue feeling three sizes too big for his mouth.

'Try harder.'

'Kk-hay.' Dez felt spittle run down his chin. He was the one dribbling now.

'You're designation is "Jack Danby",' the Väd repeated.

'Yes … I am.'

'Do you know the tri-scan co-ordinates for the Tylurian scout ship?'

Dez shook his head slowly. 'No … no, I don't.' The Väd spoke perfect English, but the tone of his voice was much harder, less friendly than Yakob's, and he had a heavy accent. Staring at the big glass eye of the visor made it seem as if you were talking to a goldfish bowl.

'How many of them are there land-side?' the voice said.

'Don't know. What's "land-side"?'

'Did they get the other creature?'

'What "creature"?'

'What is the designation of the *third* creature?'

'What?'

Someone to Dez's left said something to the Väd interrogating him and he nodded, turning back to Dez. 'So, you're lying and you're not lying; you know how many they have land-side,' he ticked a finger. 'You know which creature I'm talking about, but not if they've got it,' another finger. 'And you don't know the name of the third creature we want.'

'How?' said Dez, inching his head to the left to see the other person who'd been talking. The back of a uniformed figure was hunched over some equipment.

'Mind probe,' said the Väd in front of him. 'You can't lie to us.'

'Why haven't you killed me?'

'Plans change. We have new orders – you are going back to Anavrin, along with the others when we get them. Which we will, have no doubt.'

'But you killed my parents!' yelled Dez, lurching forward and feeling the hands on his shoulders tighten their grip and pull him back.

'That was then. This is now,' said the Väd, turning and walking away, his hands clasped behind his back. 'We need you alive for the moment.'

'I *hate* you!' screamed Dez.

'Why?' the Väd turned to look at him. 'I'm simply doing my job.'

'I'm not *business*, I'm a *person*!' hissed Dez. 'Or don't you understand the difference?'

'I understand very little about you creatures, and, to be honest, I care less.' The Väd reached up with both hands and touched something on his helmet. There was a soft click as the visor swung forward like the top of a CD player, and he took the helmet off.

Dez's jaw dropped involuntarily. Blue skin! They had blue skin! He swallowed and stared wide-eyed at the

Väd; his head was covered with what looked like short spikes and he had small, hooded eyes with red irises and thin vertical pupils. His nose was long and narrow and ended in two flat nostrils, below which was a wide lipless mouth.

'All I care about is completing my task.'

Dez watched with amazement as the Väd spoke, his lips parting to show two rows of fine, pointed teeth and a darting tongue. A forked one. Dark red. Gross.

'I do not like trouble, and you have caused me no small amount of it,' said the Väd, tucking his helmet under one arm. 'This will all be over soon. Whatever your Tylurian friend has told you, he will fail.'

'You say!' said Dez, sounding a lot braver than he felt.

'I do.'

'What are you going to do to me? Are you going to leave me like this?' asked Dez, feeling his anger rise. 'I'm thirsty, I want a drink – and I'm hungry too; are you going to get one of *your* creatures to feed me?'

The Väd snorted, almost a sneeze, and his tongue slipped out between his lips. He turned to the person sitting at the vast bank of equipment and said something. Dez got the feeling of pins and needles all over his body.

'You'll be put under guard and supplied with something to eat and drink,' he said.

'And then?' Dez flexed his hands and stretched out a foot. He could move again, although he was still being firmly pressed into the chair by the two people behind him.

The Väd's spiny "hair" suddenly rose off his scalp and his mouth split to show his teeth. 'You are an arrogant creature, you show little respect in the presence of authority. Where *I* come from you would be punished severely for your attitude.'

'Well, we're not where *you* come from,' said Dez. 'We're where *I* come from, and here it's the people who mistreat kids that get punished!'

'Take him away,' said the Väd, turning on his heels and walking out of the room. 'I have things to attend to; I'll deal with him later.'

The two Väds grabbed Dez and pulled him to his feet. 'I don't need your help,' he said, shaking their hands off. His legs felt all wobbly and he had to sit down again quickly before he fell to the floor. 'I *don't* need your help,' he repeated, gritting his teeth and slowly getting up again.

The two Väd crewmen stood and watched him as he got his balance, willing himself to stand upright, on his own, no assistance required. He needed to do this, to show them he was more than just a scared kid. He *was* scared, but he was angry as well, and his anger cancelled out the fear of the unknown and gave him control. He looked round at the crewmen.

'Let's go,' he said.

Chapter 21

It was quiet inside *Stark Revenge*, even the machines seemed to be hushed, waiting for something to happen. Yakob sat bolt upright in his chair, watching Treece as she slept. He was turning a small coin over and over and over in his hand.

'You should wake her,' said Bess. 'She isn't going to bite.'

'I know that.'

'So do it.'

'I can't concentrate, I'm worried about Dez. I need time to think about what to do about *him* before I start dealing with her.' Yakob pointed at Treece.

'I'll think about Dez, you get to work on the girl. Division of labour, Yakob; that's one reason why I'm here.'

'OK, OK, OK,' sighed Yakob. 'I'll wake her, all right?'

'See you later. Have fun.'

'Very likely!' Yakob got up and walked over to stand by the chair Treece was lying on. She looked so peaceful it seemed a shame to disturb her and put her through what was bound to be a strange and probably frightening experience.

The last thing she would remember was going to sleep in her nice, if untidy, bedroom. She was going to wake up in another world. Yakob got out the small black box and held it over the girl's face, pressing a combination of buttons. In the subdued light of the van's interior he saw her eyelids flicker and he glanced over at one of the consoles.

Shimmering in the air were half a dozen or so different coloured lines weaving lazy patterns in the air, each one a visual record of heartbeat, breathing, pupil dilation and various brain activities. Yakob could see that Treece was slowly surfacing, climbing out of the warm depths of sleep, leaving dreams and random journeys through memory behind. It would, he thought, be a cold bath of an awakening.

'Papa?' said a small voice.

Yakob looked back at the reclined chair. 'No, not Papa,' he said.

'Where am I?' Treece sat up and rubbed her face with her hands. 'Who are you?'

'Treece,' said Yakob, sitting down in a chair, 'this is going to take some explaining ...'

'I'm dreaming!' interrupted Treece, lying down, curling her legs up and closing her eyes. 'Go away ...'

'I can't go away, and you're not dreaming,' said Yakob patiently. 'Do you remember a boy coming up to you yesterday, outside your school? He asked for your help … you told *him* to go away too.'

Treece visibly stiffened, her muscles tensing. She opened her eyes again and looked at Yakob. 'How did you know that?'

'I was there with him, watching.'

'Where is he now?' Treece sat up and looked around the van for the first time, her eyes widening. Above the console the heartbeat readout jolted and began a faster red rhythm in the air, and the four brain-activity patterns speeded up their multi-coloured dance.

'Let me explain a few things,' said Yakob, taking a deep breath and crossing his legs. 'That boy, Dez is his name, should have been here to help me, but he's … um … lost … for the moment.'

'Help you do what?' said Treece, half looking at Yakob and half staring at the pulsing readouts. 'What are they?' she asked, pointing at them.

'VSIs – Vital Signs Indicators.' Yakob said something to the control drone and the light show ended. 'I had to make sure you were all right.'

'But …'

'Look, this hasn't gone the way I'd planned it.' Yakob scratched his head. 'In fact nothing has since I arrived here.'

'In Lagos?' Confusion seemed to be stopping Treece from losing it completely. Her mind, unable to grasp what was happening, had gone into neutral and was waiting for the reality it understood to return.

'No, not Lagos,' said Yakob. 'Earth.'

Silence descended on *Stark Revenge* like a vulture to a kill.

'Earth?'

'Yes, I'm not from this planet.' Yakob started to fiddle with the coin again, making it roll across the tops of his fingers, left to right and back again. 'There's no easy way to tell you this, Treece, so I'll just jump in and start at the beginning.'

Yakob got up and began to talk. He told Treece about the secret information, and where it had been hidden; he explained she was one of the three most important people on the planet and how Dez had been captured. Fom the look on Treece's face he knew he wasn't doing a very good job so he sat down again.

'I'd like you to watch something,' he said, slotting a holo into a console. The 3D image of Tor Kobal appeared and waved, just as she had to Dez.

'Beatrice,' she said, 'by now Yakob Pell will have explained—'

'I don't want to hear any more!' screamed Treece, pushing a finger in each ear and turning away, sobbing. 'I'm dreaming, this is a nightmare! You're mad – it's all *lies*!'

Yakob didn't know what to do. Dez had been easy to deal with, all things considered; Treece, on the other hand, seemed on the verge of a complete breakdown. He stopped the holo. He'd replay it later, when – if – the time was right.

'Bess?'

'Yes?'

'Help.'

'She's frightened out of her wits,' said Bess. 'Tell her it's all going to be all right, calm her down.'

Yakob was about to say something when Treece spoke. 'This isn't a dream, is it,' she said. It wasn't a question. 'I'm awake and when I open my eyes I'll still be in this ... this place.'

'Yes.'

Treece turned round and sat up. 'If you're an alien, like you say, prove it. Prove it now!'

This was not a demand Yakob had anticipated and it stopped him in his tracks. What should he do? For a moment his mind went blank, and then he felt his skin heat up slightly and he had the strange sensation morphing always gave him – like his flesh was actually *crawling.*

He looked at Treece. She had a fixed grin on her face, the kind you have when you've no idea what else to do.

'Thanks, Bess,' said Yakob. He didn't need to look in a mirror to know that Treece had just watched him change from a typical dark-skinned West African into a typical fair, blue-eyed European.

'No problem,' said Bess. 'I think she believes you now.'

'It's all ... true ...' said Treece, her voice small and frightened.

'I'm afraid so.'

'Play her the Tor Kobal holo again,' said Bess.

'Who's that?' asked Treece, looking round to see where the other person was. 'Is there someone else here?'

'In a manner of speaking ... I'll introduce you properly later.' Yakob told a drone to start the holo and let his Wing Leader carry on telling her part of the story.

When she'd finished and signed off Yakob got up. 'Want a drink?'

'No,' replied Treece. 'No, thank you.'

'Are you OK?'

'Yeah ... how did, um, how did Dez take this? You know, when you told him about everything.' Treece looked around and waved a hand about.

'It was slightly different for him.' Yakob sat down again. 'He was really thrown in at the deep end, with the Väd attack and his foster-parents being killed. He didn't have time to think about things – and he could see from the start I was telling the truth.'

'I'm adopted,' said Treece, looking thoughtful.

'Did we know that, Bess?' enquired Yakob.

'No, nothing in the mem-banks. Must've been trashed by the virus.'

'Who *is* that?'

'I beg your pardon!' smiled Yakob. 'May I introduce this vehicle's Bio-syntonic Intelligence, christened "Bess" by Dez. Say hello, Bess.'

'Hello, Treece, welcome aboard *Stark Revenge*,' said Bess. 'I've had some thoughts about Dez,' she continued, changing the subject.

'Go on.'

'We have to assume they now want him alive, or they'd have killed him outside Treece's house, and I've been trying to work out why.'

'Any ideas?' enquired Yakob.

'A very nasty one.'

'What?'

'They want the information he holds. I can't see any other reason.'

Yakob frowned and nodded his head slowly. 'Makes a horrible kind of sense,' he said.

'But he has a chance,' Bess said.

'To do what?' asked Yakob, eyebrows raising in surprise.

'He has a communicator.'

'What?'

'You didn't think I'd let him out a second time without one, did you?'

'Let's hope the Väds don't find it,' said Yakob, standing up. 'Put the scanners on the ultra-high gain.'

'I already have.'

'What's happened to him? Where is he?' asked Treece, who had kept a confused silence throughout.

'Not exactly sure,' Yakob, frowned. 'And somehow or another, I've got to get him back.'

'How?' said Treece.

'Bess?'

'Don't look at me; you're the one in charge …'

Chapter 22

'Where's the guy in charge?' Dez yelled at the Väd soldier outside the cell – he now thought of them as soldiers, with their blue uniforms, helmets and guns. 'Come on, where is he?'

Dez was angry. He'd been poked and shoved along a rabbit warren of dimly-lit corridors and pushed into a room the size of a large cupboard. It had a metal grille for a door, a nasty smell, nothing to sit on except the floor and an armed guard outside. Prison. He was in prison!

Although he'd tried to see as much as he could on his way through the Väd ship, it had been impossible to gain much information. The two guards had herded him along at such a pace that he'd tripped a couple of times, stumbling on to all fours, only to be hauled back up and pushed forward again.

'Get me the man in charge!' yelled Dez, kicking the grille for good measure. But it was no good; the guard appeared to be completely unaware of his existence. He was standing sideways to the cell, his mirrored visor reflecting everything Dez did on its smooth, fish-eyed surface.

He flopped to the ground, an involuntary shiver running up his spine from the contact with the cold metal. How the heck was he going to get out of this mess? He felt like he imagined a dog on Death Row at the vet's must feel: unloved, dejected, depressed and totally off his food.

Dez looked at the metal plate and mug on the floor beside him. It had been pushed through a space at the bottom of the grille by his guard five minutes after the door had slammed shut. He doubted he'd ever be hungry enough to eat the slop on the plate, and the stuff in the mug looked like dirty dishwater – *was* dirty dishwater, for all he knew.

His eyes drifted across the graffiti. It was everywhere, scratched into the paint by previous occupants of the cell; stick-figure drawings and illegible scrawls covered the walls and floor, evidence of the many residents who had wiled away their captivity in this dark, tiny space. Dez peered out of the door past the guard. The cells he could see opposite him were empty and there wasn't another sound in the place. No other bad boys on board.

Dez racked his brain, trying to think what to do next. The Väd craft he was on had to be way bigger than *Stark Revenge*, and he could be anywhere. In the increasingly unlikely event that he escaped from his captors, he'd be lost. Knockout. But *how* to escape? The door appeared to be lockless, devoid of anything remotely resembling a handle, the spaces in the grille were so small his little finger got jammed in them, *and* there was a guard outside.

Looking around his cell, in the dirty light cast by a small panel in the ceiling, he noticed a pair of metal clamps bolted to the wall. He stood up and had a closer look at them. It took him a minute or two to work out, but then he realized they were for holding someone's wrists. The thought that he could have been fastened to the wall, unable to move, made him break out in a cold sweat.

Dez yawned. The air was stale and he was getting a headache. He also felt bruised from all the manhandling he'd had since leaving *Stark* and running towards Treece's house. He wondered what she was doing, what they all were doing; had he been abandoned, or would Yakob have some cunning plan to get him back? Sitting in this fetid box, deep in the bowels of an evil alien spacecraft, being rescued was at the very bottom of the short list of things that were likely to happen to him.

Dez stared at the guard. He hadn't moved since he went on duty, standing legs apart, arms resting on the stubby-barrelled weapon hanging round his neck. He was like some kind of vid-game robot and Dez wanted to do something to make the him react – make him do *anything*, even if it was simply to look his way, or walk over and tell him to shut it. Then the tiny match-light of a notion sputtered into life and Dez prayed it wouldn't go out, that it would burst into flame and be a really bright idea. His life, he knew, depended on it.

Hunched in the corner of the cell he worked on the thought, turning it over in his mind, trying to figure out how it might work and where it could possibly go wrong. He played the scene in his head what seemed like a hundred times, every different way it could happen. And then he thought some more. He knew he didn't have very much time – the big cheese could come back at any moment, get him dragged off and have his mind read, or whatever it was they were going to do to him.

It was now or never.

Dez took a deep breath and held it. At school he'd once been timed and had lasted about a minute and a half, a class record. He counted the seconds inside his head: *ten...fifteen...twenty*...the pressure was building up... *twenty-five...thirty...thirty-five*...he could feel a burning sensation in his lungs and there was a whistling in his ears...*forty...forty-five...fifty*...he was sweating and could feel his cheeks were red...*fifty-five...sixty...sixty-five*...his heartbeat sounded incredibly loud in his brain and his chest was as tight as a drumskin...*seventy...seventy-five... eighty*...he was reaching his limit and knew it, he was about to burst...*eighty-five...ninety...ninety-five*...he'd beaten his record!

He let go with a wild sigh and flung himself out flat, sending the mug and plate spinning and clattering against the door. Then he began to groan and twitch, his arms and legs doing a mad, epileptic thrash. For good measure he went completely cross-eyed.

If this didn't work, if there was no reaction at all from the guard, he was lost. The thought lent Dez even more energy and he began to grunt as he arched his back and flung his head from side to side. And then he stopped, lying stiff on the floor, fisting and unfisting his hands and staring at the ceiling.

One quick flick of his eyes showed him that his plan might be working. The guard was standing at the cell door, one hand up to the right-hand side, looking down at him. Was it working? It *had* to be working! Dez started to moan, a low banshee wail coming from deep in his throat, and rocked from to side to side. If the guard thought this was normal behaviour for Earth boys, that would be it.

Then he heard the cell door click as it was opened...

Chapter 23

Mentally crossing his fingers and toes (and re-crossing his eyes, in case that helped), Dez waited until the Väd was standing over him. He didn't consider himself a violent person and avoided fights unless absolutely necessary, but this was different. This guard represented everything he'd come to hate so totally over the last few days; these people had killed his parents – snuffed them out with as little thought as you'd give to turning off a light, the pigs. And they could just as easily kill him too, he knew that.

Dez braced himself, concentrating all his attention and energy on what he was about to do next. Letting out a sharp, karate-style scream he aimed an almighty kick between the guard's legs. The toe of his trainer powered into the Väd's crotch and Dez felt like yelling 'Goal!' as the guard let out an agonized gasp and fell to the floor, clutching himself and writhing in pain.

'Yes!' said Dez, scrambling upright. 'Gotcha!'

The guard's rifle strap was tangled in his arms,

impossible to unwrap, so Dez made do with taking the hand gun from the holster patched to his trouser leg. Moving swiftly out of the cell he closed the door behind him, smiling as he heard the satisfying *CLICK* of the lock engaging.

He spent precious seconds checking out the area he was in. The other cells, a dozen or so, might be empty, but was he being tracked by cameras? Not seeing any, Dez ran to the only door in the place. No handle. *No handle!* He swore loudly. Under the circumstances, he thought, he was allowed.

Next to the door was a control panel like the one he'd seen when he first arrived. The small vid screen was a flat grey blank, but Dez was sure that if he tried to punch the buttons – probably the only way to open the door – he'd alert someone to what he was doing. Stymied. A dead end. Trapped in a slightly bigger prison. His shoulders slumped and his arms hung down.

Then he realized he was holding the pistol.

He looked at it properly for the first time. It had an oval-shaped barrel about 20 centimetres long and was made out of some kind of dark green, almost plastic-like material. It was quite big in his hand and didn't have a trigger or sights and the end of the barrel appeared to have some kind of glass lens in it. A laser? Maybe he should do a test shot to see what it did.

Dez looked round the prison area and aimed the pistol at one of the empty cells. Pulling back what would be his trigger finger – if there'd been a trigger – he saw a pulse of pure white light leap towards it and there was a loud boiling hiss. His eyes took a moment to recover, and when they did he saw the grille was a blackened mess, wisps of smoke curling up to the ceiling. Result!

He turned back to the door and was wondering what to do next when noticed there was a square pad on the right hand side, about waist high. He reached out tentatively and pressed it. To his amazement he door swung open. For a second he didn't move, and then, with the smell of fried metal pricking his nose, he crept out into the corridor.

It was gloomily lit, like it'd been in the cell, and with his back to the wall, the gun held firmly in his hand, Dez crab-walked his way along the corridor until he came to some stairs. Standing at the bottom he waited, listening for any signs that there was someone about. As far as he could tell, everything was quiet.

Too quiet? Weren't you supposed to worry if things were too quiet?

Dez knew he'd be found cowering in a corner if he let thoughts like that influence him. Taking a deep breath he tiptoed up the stairs and ran down the next corridor he found himself in, stopping when he came to a large circular well that seemed to go up into the darkness for ever. Off it were three more openings.

He stood and looked down each corridor in turn. He felt a bit like the bloke in Greek mythology, wandering in the labyrinth – what horrors awaited him along those passages? The Väds, with their blue lizardy faces, red eyes and flicking tongues, were every bit as freakish and awful as any Minotaur.

For no reason, other than "why not?", he chose the right-hand corridor and started down it. Some way along he found a metre-square cube recessed into the wall, about a metre and a half up from the floor. He stopped by it and looked inside. He felt he needed some time to think about what he was doing, plan ahead a bit. If he carried on just blundering about he was bound to be caught, and this place looked like a good enough hiding place where he could sit for a moment and ponder. He slid into the shadowed recess and sat back.

As he leant against the side Dez realized he'd been tensed up, like the spring in a jack-in-a-box, ever since he'd whacked the Väd guard and run. Relaxing made his muscles hurt, but at least he was still alive and the lack of any sirens or alarm bells ringing made him fairly confident the Väds didn't know he'd got out. Yet.

He had no idea how long it had been since his escape; looking at his watch was the last thing on his mind at the time. He looked at it now though, pressing the button for the light. 5.05 a.m., just over an hour and a half since Yakob had landed *Stark* outside Treece's house. Amazing how much could happen to a person in such a short time.

Dez shifted his backside to get more comfortable and the open-sided cube he was hiding in moved slightly. In the distance he could hear a soft hum, but he wasn't quick enough in putting two and two together. Before he could jump out the cube began moving upwards and it now had four solid sides. He was trapped in some kind of lift!

He froze. He was going to be delivered right into the hands of the Väds, even before they knew he'd escaped. Dez put a hand out and felt the wall moving at some speed; he sat back and pointed the gun at where the opening would appear. He'd shoot whoever was waiting for him and be done with it. Go out in a blaze of glory.

Then he saw a thin strip of light at the top of the cube, quickly widening as the lift began passing another floor. This must be it. Dez levelled the pistol as the gap got bigger and then he realized he was looking at the uniformed backs of two Väds, deep in conversation.

The lift carried on moving, the gap widening. The Väds carried on talking, their harsh, guttural voices echoing in the lift cube. Dez was almost paralysed with shock – he'd wound himself up with the thought of someone being there and having to fire at them, and now, as he sailed up past the floor, he had to be as quiet as a mouse and not make a move and then he was out of danger. For now.

It seemed to take an age to reach the next floor and when the tell-tale chink of light appeared at the top of the cube once more it took a moment for Dez to see that the passage was empty – and then that the lift wasn't stopping!

Leaping forward, he somersaulted over the rising lip and fell with a sickening thud on the passageway floor.

Momentarily dazed, Dez took a good few seconds to collect himself; he got up, rubbing his bruised shoulder, and loped off down the corridor in search of another, safer, resting place. He found it round the next corner. A large pile of metal boxes had been stacked up where the corridor widened out, and Dez saw there was a small space left between them and the wall, just large enough for him to squeeze into. Once he'd sat down and pulled a couple of the boxes in front of him he was completely hidden.

This was even more cramped than the lift, but at least it wasn't about to move, he thought as he put the pistol down and rubbed his face, massaging the tiredness from his eyes. He could be anywhere on the Väd ship and he had no idea where the ship itself could be. Even if he found an exit door there was a good chance it would only lead to deep space. Holding his breath for a minute and a half wouldn't be much good there.

If the ship was still on Earth there was nothing to say that it'd be near Lagos or even in Nigeria. Still, thought Dez, anywhere would be better than Anavrin, which is where he'd end up if the Väds found him. Then he heard the footsteps.

They came from behind him and it sounded like two or three people approaching. He waited, curled in a ball, eyes closed tight, some ancient, primaeval safety mechanism in his brain kicking in – *If I can't see them they can't see me* – and bit his lip.

He could hear voices as the Väds got nearer and then

the footsteps stopped right beside the boxes. One of the voices gave what sounded like an order and Dez heard a crate above him being moved. He'd been crazy to think that he'd be able to hide aboard this ship, or move about unnoticed, *or* find an escape route. Completely crazy.

Even if he got out of this hole, all that would happen was that they'd get him eventually, and go ballistic because he'd caused so much trouble. The noise of the box being moved stopped. Another voice was calling from somewhere down the corridor; it had an urgent ring to it and Dez opened an eye and uncurled a bit. The box was being pushed back in place and then the footsteps began to move away, down the corridor.

In the silence Dez let out a heartfelt sigh. Had someone discovered the guard? Did they know he'd escaped? He was ageing years every minute in this place and he was sure he'd have white hair inside an hour if he didn't get out fast. He pushed aside the boxes in front of him and peered out. No one in sight either way, but to be on the safe side he'd go in the opposite direction to that the Väds had taken.

Shadow-dodging his way down the corridor, his throat as dry as his palms were wet, Dez stumbled out on to a walkway, up near the ceiling of a vast hangar. In the gloom he could make out a number of strange shapes down below him, and it was only as his eyes got used to the lack of light that he realized what he was looking at: a half-dozen or so black, insect-like craft of the type that had chased *Stark* over the French countryside.

Voices from far away behind him shook Dez into action. There was only one way to go – into the hangar. As he made his way down the metal staircase he felt as if he was entering some huge wasps' nest where the occupants slept, waiting to wake and get him. Once down at floor level he felt his way in the darkness, weaving through the cold black pursuit craft, trying not to touch anything. He was in between two of them when the lights came on.

Freezing where he stood, Dez frantically looked round for some cover. Two metres away an open hatch beckoned, and he had little choice but to accept the offer. Crouching low, he ran over to it and clambered into the cockpit.

A dozen armed men clattered down the stairs, following their squad leader into the silent hangar. He stopped when he reached the floor and his men gathered round him.

'You two, search this place thoroughly!' he barked, pointing at the first couple of soldiers. 'He can't have gone far. The rest of you, follow me.'

'If we don't find anything, should we buzz you on the headset to find out where to go to next?' asked one of the pair.

'Don't you people have brains?' snapped the squad leader. 'I've already *told* you – all broadcast activity is being kept to an absolute minimum because of the shielding malfunction. That's why the cameras weren't in operation and the creature hasn't been spotted already. When you've checked in here, follow us through the workshops and maintenance depots.'

'Sir!' Both the men saluted, standing rigidly to attention as the rest of the squad ran off.

'Typical!' said one of them, taking his helmet off and smoothing back the spines on his head.

'What is?'

'Leaving just two of us to do this whole place – and we don't even have camera back-up! I hate this stupid war …'

'Careful, you never know who's listening.'

The soldier put his helmet back on. 'Well, at least the infra-red's working on my visor display. How about yours?'

'On and off,' the other replied. 'I have to thump it sometimes.'

'I bet the Tylurians don't have to put up with junk equipment like ours.' The soldier clicked down his visor and turned the display on. 'I've heard they've got some amazing gear.'

'You ever met a Tylurian?'

'No.'

'Me neither.'

'Come on, we'd better start this search …'

Hunched down in the tiny space behind the pilot's seat, Dez heard the bulk of the Väds clumping out of the hangar, leaving two (three?) soldiers behind.

Their conversation, though he couldn't understand a word, sounded oddly casual for what he assumed were hardened space warriors.

It was fairly obvious his disappearance had been discovered, but would they look everywhere? It was too late to find somewhere else to hide, somewhere easier to get out of, so he just hoped they weren't going to be ultra-efficient. But in the back of his mind lurked the thought that he wasn't going to get off that easily. After all, they had come half-way across the Universe to find him.

Dez could hear voices calling to each other and then the sound of footsteps began to come closer; determined not to be found cowering like a mouse, he brought the laser up ready to fire. From the deep shadows he had a reasonable view between the seats and the open door. Into that gap came a Väd, helmet visor down, laser blaster held in both hands. He was turning his head slowly left and right and then he stopped and bent down to look under the helicopter.

Dez held his breath.

To his amazement, the Väd stood bolt upright and began banging the side of his helmet with one of his gloved hands. The visor then swung up and the Väd took the helmet off, spitting on the floor as he did so; as he poked around inside it he yelled something. An answering call echoed from the other side of the hangar and the Väd shoved his helmet back on, leaving the visor up, and stalked off, angrily slamming the helicopter's door shut as he went.

Dez waited for five minutes to be sure he was alone and then crept out from behind the seat and opened the door, which swung out with a soft click and a hiss.

A nerve-wracking quarter of an hour later found Dez, his eyes now used to the subdued Väd lighting, huddled in the doorway of what appeared to be a cargo bay. It looked as though no one was there and he darted inside, negotiating his way through the stacks of boxes to hide behind a tall crate. The air was cooler here and he found himself shivering, cold sweat running down his back.

He'd just made himself as comfortable as he could when he heard voices coming into the bay. He risked a quick peek and saw a pair of Väds wandering through the door. They were unarmed and seemed to be dressed in some kind of overalls. As he watched they walked over to the opposite wall and one of them held his wrist up close to his face, as if looking at a watch.

In the dull yellow light Dez could see they were standing by a larger version of the control panel he'd almost nuked to get out of the cells. The man who'd been looking at his wrist said something to his companion and then pressed a series of buttons.

The lights went out. In the almost tangible black Dez picked up the sound of motors whirring and something large moving; there was a sigh of air and the cargo bay suddenly seemed to feel much larger. He couldn't imagine what was going on and craned his neck around the crate in an effort to see something, anything, of what was happening.

Like a cinema screen opening the wrong way – downwards instead of sideways – a wide grey oblong was opening up in front of him, no more than three metres away. As it got bigger Dez could just make out a tree-lined horizon. He could hear vaguely familiar noises and smell real air. Fresh air. *Earth* air.

Chapter 24

'Why are you opening the cargo bay doors, sir? Didn't you get the Commander's message that the creature has escaped and a search was in progress?'

'Of course I did, but the schedule says we have to do regular system checks.' The Chief Tech pointed to a screen in front of him. 'And the schedule says we have to do them *now*.'

'But ...'

'Don't worry.'

'I still think we should have waited until he's been caught, sir. With the shielding problems ...'

'Our orders are to *follow* orders, not disobey them.' The Chief Tech turned from his console to stare out his junior officer. 'We *have* to do things by the schedule.'

'But this creature's quite small ... what if it does get out, sir?'

'That is someone else's problem, not mine,' the Chief Tech's tongue flicked in and out of his mouth as the spines on his head bristled. 'We are *not* here to question orders!' he said, slapping his fist into the palm of his hand.

* * *

Dez couldn't believe his luck. They weren't in deep space, and the Väds were opening the doors for him. All he had to do was get through them unseen. *All he had to do!* He nearly laughed out loud; the three metres between him and the outside world were fraught with the danger of discovery.

He looked over at the two Väds, who were deep in conversation and not looking his way. Gripping the laser pistol, Dez counted to ten and then crept out from behind the crate.

Eyes peeled for anything that would make a noise and give him away, his progress was painfully slow. He'd gone just over a metre when the whine of the motors stopped. The door must be fully open, thought Dez, risking a quick glance in the direction of the Väds; they still seemed to be unaware of his presence. He moved on, but he forgot to look first.

Dez's foot snagged on a thin bundle of cables snaking across the floor between gaps in the crates and boxes and, because he was moving in a crouch, he overbalanced and tipped forward. As he landed on the ground, letting out a grunt, he heard the simultaneous slapping of hands and the voices behind him raised in a harsh cackle.

Dez lay on the cold, gritty metal, not daring to move. And then he realized the two Väds were still talking, not moving his way. He didn't believe in guardian angels, but *something* was very definitely on his side right now. Little by little he got up.

Only a metre and a half to go.

His heart was racing, pounding so hard and so fast he thought it might burst. With one last look over his shoulder he moved out into the open, no boxes giving cover now. Each step was filled with panic, his body screaming for him to *run, run, run!* and his head saying *wait, slow down, we'll get there.*

And then he was jumping off the door lip and plummeting to the ground. Dez hadn't bothered to look before he leapt, but no matter how far it was, nothing would have stopped him; he'd come too far, been through too much not to go through with it now. He landed with a thump on the dusty earth and the jarring pain in his legs had never felt so good.

He looked up behind him. The Väd ship was obviously cloaked, touchable (he could feel its cool surface) but invisible – and there, suspended in mid-air, was the opening to the cargo bay. It looked like a large TV screen showing a very dull movie.

From where he was kneeling he couldn't see the technicians as they talked in rapid-fire sentences to each other. And then he heard the sound of running feet and raised voices shouting orders. Above him the whirr of motors starting up came seconds before the bay door began to close. He'd made it just in time.

Looking away from the ship he could see, in the approaching dawn, some trees about a hundred metres away and a clump of bushes a bit nearer. He had to get as far as those bushes. But he also had to assume that the Väds, like the Tylurians, had equipment that would be scanning the surrounding area – although, if they thought he was still aboard the ship, would they be concentrating on finding him and not be so worried about stuff moving around outside? Would they credit him, a mere creature, with being able to escape? If he stayed where he was he'd never find out.

Dez was getting tired of running, but this last dash might be just that – his last. He got up off his knees, fastened his eyes on his destination and went for it, crouched and zig-zagging like he'd seen soldiers do in films. Dark shapes of birds that had been resting for the night woke and scattered as he ran near them. Half expecting to be pulverized at any moment, or at the very least paralysed like he'd been outside Treece's house, Dez suddenly found himself in a panting heap behind the bushes. Nothing had happened. He'd made it! Yes, yes, *yes!*

The bubble of his relief and happiness burst almost as soon as it was born. He'd made it, but he was stuck behind a bush in the middle of nowhere, with a whacking great huge Väd ship a hop, skip and a jump away. They must be going mad in there, thought Dez, half-smiling, tearing the place apart to find him. He wouldn't want to be the guard he'd left in the cell, or the ones in the cargo bay if it was ever discovered that was where he'd escaped from. He had an idea that, as he'd heard someone say once, hanging would be too good for them.

The sky was slowly changing colour to his left, the slate grey gaining a hot orange glow on the horizon. Dez knew he'd have to move fast or he wouldn't even have the bad light on his side any more. As he got up, one hand on his calf for support, he felt something in his shorts pocket. Reaching in he found the communicator Bess had made him take as a safety precaution when he'd left the van.

Somehow in all the terror he'd forgotten he had it with him, and the Väds, never bothering to search him, hadn't found it either. He took it out and turned it over. Triff, he thought: a communicator. But how the heck did he communicate with it? Dez had seen Yakob use his for all manner of things, including putting Treece to sleep, but he never paid much attention to what he was actually doing.

'Probably broken anyway,' Dez muttered to himself, squinting at the little black box. In the half light it was difficult to see which was the business side of its two flat surfaces, but it didn't look trashed.

He strained his eyes and eventually saw a series of small bumps on one of the sides, almost like Braille. Dez ran his fingers gently over them, hardly able to feel they were there, and wondered what they meant.

The orange glow on the horizon had grown and it now had a yolk-yellow centre. The sky was beginning to turn blue and in no time, Dez knew, it would be broad daylight. He had to do something, and fast.

He stabbed a finger at the communicator and punched

in a random pattern. All he could do now was wait and see if anything happened. If it didn't, he'd try again.

'There are no signs of him anywhere, sir,' reported the search squad leader. He didn't like bringing bad news to his commander, but there was no alternative.

'Go back and look again,' came the curt reply.

'It would help if we could turn all the surveillance equipment back on, sir.'

'It would help the Tylurians as well. Just turn this ship upside down instead. It can only be a matter of time before we find him.'

'Yes, sir!' The squad leader saluted.

'Has that over-zealous Chief Tech been told to keep *all* hatches shut until further notice?'

'He has, yes.'

'And there's no chance the creature got out?'

'None.'

'I do hope so.'

Chapter 25

'Alert! Alert! Alert!' screamed a voice from every speaker in the gun deck. 'We've picked up a scrambled data transmission – incoming craft expected. Fire on immediate visual pick-up!'

The three gunners on duty froze in their seats and then started frantically barking orders to their laser and photon platforms while they stared at vast arrays of holographic information streams racing across the surface of their visors.

'Anything?' yelled the senior gunner above the babble.

'No!'

'Not yet!'

'None, sir!'

Hands hovered over complex light panels; eyes strained to be the first to find what they all assumed would be a wing of Tylurian fighters, maybe even a battle cruiser.

The three gunners waited, like cats about to pounce...

Dez was about to punch another sequence into the communicator when he felt a definite change in the air pressure. It gave him a weird sense of *déjà vu* – it had happened before, but he couldn't quite remember where. And then it hit him. Up on the mountains when the Tylurian scout ship had arrived!

He spun round on his heels, looking about wildly, searching for a sign that *Stark* had materialized. As his eyes darted left and right the panic hit like a furious punch in the stomach – *Stark Revenge* was going to leap out of nowhere right in front of an angry hornets' nest, otherwise known as a heavily-armed Väd ship! Dez hadn't meant that to happen, he'd just been trying to send them a message, *talk* to them! He stuffed the communicator back in his pocket.

Anger and fear mixed together inside him, knotting his throat and giving everything he looked at a major significance; every leaf that twitched, every warm breath of wind could be a sign of where *Stark* was. Then, with a terrible slowness, he saw the tell-tale edge of a hidden space appear in the air not so far away to his right.

Stark's door was opening.

He shot a glance over to where he knew the Väd ship was and then turned to yell a warning to Yakob to get out, but he was too late.

An explosion of light erupted around him as deadly laser pulses raked the trees and turned the dusty ground into puddles of boiling glass; shattered wood burst into flame and a ragged flock of terrified birds rose into the air, many vaporizing in a lazy burst of feathers as the lasers tracked them. The early morning's delicate colours had been bleached out and washed away in a tidal wave of brilliant, diamond-sharp hysteria, too painful to look at. But in all the mind-numbing chaos there was no sound of gunfire, just Nature in uproar.

The spell that had held Dez rigid broke. He had to try and get to the van. At his feet he saw the hand gun he'd taken from the guard; snatching it up he flung himself to the ground by the side of the bush and saw the throbbing white heart of a laser platform some twelve metres above the ground.

Pointing the gun at it he pulled his trigger finger and held it, firing a stuttering series of light pulses; his eyes closed to a slit because the brightness was so intense. Dez was now on automatic; he didn't know what he was going to do next, but some part of his brain was in control and making the moves. He found himself rolling out into the open and firing again, then he got up and ran for *Stark*'s door as if the Devil was on his heels.

He saw Yakob staring at him through the narrow gap in the cloaking and his mind registered that his face was white. This didn't make any sense, but all Dez could think of was keeping his feet pounding the ground between him and the safety of the door. As he ran Dez half noticed two orangey-red circles appear at either side of where Yakob was, and as he reached *Stark* there was a high-pitched scream and they both turned an electric ultramarine.

Behind him Dez heard a series of sharp thuds, and

then, as the door opened wider to let him in, a wild shaft of blue-white light warped over his left shoulder and scythed through the folds of Yakob's T-shirt. Diving through the gap Dez didn't notice Yakob's face contort in pain, and the next thing he knew he was hitting the carpeted floor with his arms in front of him.

'Close it!' he heard Yakob shout. 'And get us out of here!'

There was a deep bass *WH-OOOMP!* as *Stark* hit hyper-drive and the stomach-churning G-force pinned Dez to the floor, his face pressed down so hard it felt like someone had their foot on his head. The floor began to compensate and mould itself to his shape to relieve the pressure, but Dez still couldn't get up.

All around him he could hear the insane chatter of the drone intelligences and then nothing. He felt the floor level out underneath him and realized he could now get up. With the laser pistol still firmly gripped in his hand he pushed himself off the carpet. A voice he didn't recognize broke the ominous silence.

'Are you OK?' it said.

'I'm fine,' replied Dez.

'Not you,' said the voice.

Dez looked round and saw a girl his age, dressed in a pink blouse and white shorts, bending over Yakob. The Tylurian was slumped on the floor. He didn't look white any more – he almost looked green and was clutching his side.

'Bess?' said Dez. 'Bess, what happened?'

Chapter 26

'We've been hit,' said Bess, her voice sounding strained and slightly edgy. 'Inside.'

'It's my fault,' said Dez, sitting back on his haunches. 'I brought you there by pressing those buttons on that box. I didn't know it was going to happen, honest! I was just trying to *talk* to you...'

'We know you didn't mean to do it,' said Yakob. 'I'd told Bess to put the scanners on high-gain, in case you were able to use the communicator, and when *Stark* picked up the signal we just came.'

Dez looked round and saw the girl – it had to be Treece – helping Yakob off the floor and on to one of the chairs. He stared at her.

'You must be Dez,' she said.

He nodded, lost for words.

'Yakob has sustained minor internal damage,' said Bess. 'And the same can be said for *Stark*. But, whereas Yakob's metabolism is capable of repairing him to a good 80 per cent efficiency in about thirty minutes, my recon bioware is going to be hard pushed to make the guidance drone serviceable in under two or three hours.'

'What does that mean, Bess?' asked Dez, getting up. 'You know, in simple English.'

'I got us up here – we're now geo-stationary 2.5 kliks over the Atlantic Ocean – but I can't take us anywhere else myself with the drone off-line and basically unusable,' Bess sighed. 'And we *really* need to move out pretty fast. I need a pilot.'

'But Yakob—'

'Yakob is going into temporary stasis,' said Bess. 'He'll be asleep while his body mends and we can't afford to wait. *You'll* have to do it, Dez.'

'Me? But I've never even driven a go-cart!'

'I'll tell you what to do,' said Bess. 'It's not difficult.'

'You say.' Dez felt as if he'd jumped out of a frying pan and straight into the fire. He wanted to relax, wind down, take it easy – *not* pilot a light-speed alien craft.

'You'll be fine,' Yakob sounded a bit slurred. Dez walked over to him, watching as the chair he was sitting on began to recline, its sides growing a lip that held Yakob in place. The Tylurian, his face deathly pale and drawn, took one of Dez's hands and gripped it. 'You'll be fine and I'll be fine,' he murmured, his eyes closing.

'I hope so,' Dez let Yakob's hand fall limply by his side. He looked up at Treece, who was standing the other side of the chair. 'Well,' he smiled weakly, 'here we go again ...'

'What happened to you?' asked Treece, tentatively reaching a hand out to him.

Dez was silent for a moment, then he took a deep breath and told Bess and Treece what happened after the Väd snatch squad had got him, right up to the battle he'd just been in.

'What happened out there, Bess?' he asked, when he'd finished talking. He felt completely drained. 'Did you record it?'

'Yes, I did,' said Bess. 'Do you want to see it?'

'Just tell him,' said Treece. '*I* don't want to look at it again, and I wasn't even out there.'

'I think I want to see it,' said Dez.

'It doesn't last long – less than a minute.'

'Really?' Dez's eyebrows rose. 'Seemed like for *ever*.'

A holo screen blinked open and Dez saw himself hiding behind the bush. Then a point in the grey morning sky suddenly exploded like a thunderflash, seemingly random stabs of throbbing laser pulses streaming out towards the camera.

'They knew we'd arrived,' said Bess, 'but they couldn't pin-point us, so they blanketed the area.'

'But why would they do that?' asked Dez, puzzled. 'I was told that plans had changed and they wanted us alive ... to take back to their planet.'

'I can only assume they thought we were a hostile scout ship,' replied Bess. 'Probably on high alert after that incident in France. Anyway, the Väds always prefer to shoot first and ask questions later.'

'Must've thought I was still on board the ship then.' Dez watched himself pick up the pistol and fire, then roll out into the open and fire again. To his utter amazement he saw a gout of hot redness erupt in the air and for an instant the entire shape of the Väd craft appeared and in a blink was gone again. Dez wasn't sure he'd really seen it at all.

'What was that?' he asked, seeing himself get up and turn to run for the van.

'A direct hit,' said Bess. 'You hit one of their gun pods and that seems to have momentarily shorted their cloaking – you basically gave yourself the time to get into *Stark*.'

'I did *that* with *this*?' Dez pointed at the laser.

'Couldn't have done better myself,' said Bess.

The screen showed Dez hurtling towards *Stark* and then an orangey glow appeared at either side of the picture. The speakers let out a high-pitched yowl and the glow went a deep blue. As his image disappeared from the screen Dez saw the air behind him, where he knew the Väd ship was, distort; it was like watching something being dropped into a pool of still water, ripples fanning out in time with a series of brittle thumps.

'My parting shot – a Cold Pulse cannon broadside,' commented Bess as the picture showed a twisting beam of blue-white light leaping towards the camera. Then the screen blanked. 'And that was what hit Yakob.'

'Can you freeze-frame the Väd ship? You know, when it appears for that second or two trick?' asked Dez.

'Certainly,' said Bess, and up on screen came a still picture of a dark, squat insect of a thing, with plates, like a stegosaurus, running down its back. The exploding gun pod looked like an angry burst boil.

'Nasty,' said Dez, his upper lip curling.

'Fighting craft rarely look pretty.' Bess closed down the screen.

'Did we trash them?'

'No, Dez, but we certainly put them out of action for a bit,' said Bess. 'As far as I can tell, they haven't moved. That's why I want to get us out of here before they do; our shielding can't take another battering like that.'

'S'pose we'd better get on with it,' sighed Dez, getting up. 'Coming?' he asked Treece.

'Where?'

'Up front – that's where you want me, isn't it, Bess?'

'In the driving seat.'

Dez let Treece go past him and then followed after her.

'Which seat shall I sit in?' she asked.

'The right hand one,' said Dez, moving left and sitting down. 'How much do you know?' he asked, looking at Treece.

'Everything,' she replied.

'Unbelievable, isn't it?'

'I freaked out when I woke up.' Treece smoothed the fabric of the chair with her thumb as she spoke. 'I thought I was dreaming.'

'I'm not surprised,' grinned Dez. 'This place doesn't look much like your bedroom!'

'Time to go to work,' said Bess, as the dashboard lit up like a Christmas tree. 'You two can catch up with each other later.'

'What do I have to do?' enquired Dez.

'*Exactly* what I tell you and *nothing* else.'

Dez watched as the steering wheel folded itself out of the dashboard and settled above his lap. 'I'm going to *drive*? No roads up here, Bess!'

'No, you're not going to drive. This only looks like a steering wheel, it's actually the Prime Interface Unit.'

'What's that?' asked Treece, leaning over to look.

'I can make a connection with Dez's nervous system through it, create a link between his brain and the intelligence pods controlling our flight capabilities. In effect,' said Bess, 'he becomes the guidance drone I'm trying to repair right now.'

'And I always thought drones were those bees that hung around the hive and didn't get up to much,' grinned Dez. 'So what do I do now?'

'Take hold of the wheel, like you were in a car,' instructed Bess. 'And grip it – not too hard. Fine, just right. Can you feel a slight tingle?'

Dez nodded.

'That's the neural connection being made,' said Bess. 'I've logged-on to your brain. I'm going to switch to direct communication mode now, and give you some practice instructions. OK, Dez?'

'Fine,' he replied. And then the weirdest thing happened. Inside his head – right inside, in the very centre – Bess began to talk to him.

Chapter 27

'Wow!' said Dez, sitting back in the seat, letting his hands fall from the wheel and breaking his connection with Bess. His eyes were wide and he had a silly grin on his face. 'That was *fantastic*!'

'What happened?' Treece was kneeling on her seat staring at him, fascinated. 'Your hair's all standing on end!'

'It was amazing! I had Bess *inside* my head, telling me what to do – and I could speak to her, too! I was looking at the dashboard, all those lights and stuff that've always puzzled the heck out of me, and I *understood*, I *knew* what they all meant! It was … it was … I don't know *what* it was like, Treece. Can't describe it.'

'You looked like a robot,' said Treece. 'Your voice sounded weird, too.'

'I spoke?'

'Gave all kinds of instructions.'

'He did well,' said Bess. 'Which is good because the repairs are taking longer than I anticipated, both mine and Yakob's.'

'Is he going to be all right?' asked Dez, looking over his shoulder at the sleeping form behind him. The lights were down and Yakob looked calm and very peaceful.

'He'll be fine,' said Bess. 'That laser blast had a particularly evil Viper core – poisonous light, if you like. The burn would have been bad enough on its own, but his body's having to deal with some nasty side-effects. Me too.'

'How come?' Treece got off her knees and sat back down.

'There are side-effects, it's like an infection, and it can spread.' Bess paused. 'If I don't stop it in the guidance drone it might get into something else and then we'll be in *real* trouble.'

'How many things can you do at once, Bess?' asked Treece.

'Never thought about it,' she said. 'Enough, I suppose.'

'Should we be going?' Dez stretched. 'You know, do it for real?'

'We should. Are you ready?'

'As I'll ever be.' Dez rubbed his hands together and took hold of the wheel again, feeling the log-on tingle. He waited.

'We have a problem,' Bess finally said inside him.

'What?' Dez thought.

'The Väd ship.'

'What about it?'

'It's on the move.'

'What are we going to do?'

'Nothing yet ... hold it, here they come.'

Four screens flickered on in front of Dez. He instantly knew they were showing him a complete sub-ether scan around *Stark*. In one he could see the Earth in strange negative colours, blue showing as green, green as red. A grid appeared and the outline of one of the squares went bright blue and flashed on and off. The picture jumped until that square filled the screen, and in it Dez could see a shape.

'The Väd ship,' he said. 'But how?'

'They're still cloaked, but we must have damaged their shielding enough so the scanners can pick them up,' replied Bess. 'At least we can see them now.'

'But they can't see us?'

'No, we're completely screened out.'

'What do you think they'll do?' Dez enquired, his eyes fixed on the schematic picture on the screen. It looked like a computer-generated wire frame illustration, a complex web of white lines on a black background making up an image of the Väd ship.

'They'll get out as fast as possible, I should think,' said Bess. 'If we can pick them up it means they must be in trouble.'

Dez watched the shape on the screen grow. It was a top view of the craft, and it looked huge – had to be, from his own experience of running around in it. Now he could see that its squat, ugly shell had two "arms" at the front and a series of pods at the rear. The large, bulging front end, with its cluster of antennae, completed the picture and made Dez think the ship looked like some kind of evil mutated beetle. He shivered and his hands broke connection with the wheel.

'Are you all right?' said Treece. 'You look so pale.'

Dez had almost forgotten she was there, his link-up with Bess had been so total. 'I was looking at the Väd ship,' he said.

'You mustn't lose contact when we're in flight, Dez, it could be disastrous.' Bess sounded ever so slightly miffed.

'Sorry, Bess; it won't happen again.' Dez reached out for the wheel. 'Do you want to go now?'

'No, we'll wait until they've gone. They're very near us now, max half a klik away, and if we hit light speed they'll know and they'll follow. We can't risk it.'

'How will they know?' asked Treece.

'Attaining light speed always leaves what we call a "ghost" signature; no one's ever found a way of disguising it,' explained Bess. 'Watch carefully and we should see theirs very soon.'

Nobody said a word for what seemed like hours. Everyone knew that out there in the cold vacuum of space loomed the invisible hulk of a deadly enemy; one wrong move on their part and it would strike like a venomous snake.

The silence continued almost as if, by being quiet, they'd make sure the Väds wouldn't hear them. Dez looked over at Treece. She was staring through her own reflection in the mirrored glass of the windscreen, nervously twisting her hair. He knew almost nothing about her, except that she was very like him in one important way: inside her she had the second part of the jigsaw puzzle that was the Tylurians' only way of defeating the Väd-Raatch. They were part of the same family, for better or worse.

'There!' said Bess.

'Where?' Dez jerked his head round to look at the screens. They were all blank, although one of them showed a faint after-image of the Väd ship.

'They've gone.' Bess seemed to sigh with relief. 'And I got a trace on them – they appear to have gone in the direction of your moon.'

'Great!' yelled Dez, relief flooding through him. Even though the Väds hadn't gone completely, they were no longer the *visible* threat they had been. A small difference, he knew, but enough to make him want to jump for joy.

'Time to burn some anti-matter, Dez,' said Bess. 'Log-on and let's go.'

Dez raised his eyebrows and glanced over at Treece. 'Full speed ahead,' he grinned nervously.

'You think you can do it?' she asked.

Dez took hold of the steering wheel. 'We'll find out …'

It was like entering another dimension. The short run-through Bess had given him hadn't really prepared Dez for connecting with the whole of *Stark*'s teeming network of intelligences. For a moment he felt like he had on the first day at real school: overawed by the sheer size of what he was in, aware of how little he knew and just a tiny bit frightened. Only now he had no mother's hand to hold, no home to run back to.

'Let me introduce you,' Bess said, and in his mind the "voices" of the drones, echoing very slightly, made themselves known.

They were extremely polite, each one informing him what they did: trajectory, speed, armament, supplies, environment – the list seemed endless, with only the guidance drone missing and sending its apologies. When it was over Dez's mind boggled at the realization of the authority he now wielded – as long as Bess told him what to do and when to do it.

Under her instruction he readied *Stark* for flight, and on the edge of his consciousness he was aware of Bess telling Treece how to prepare herself. And then his concentration became completely focused on what he was doing. There was no world except the one he was surrounded by, and that was a blaze of colours and full of demands, questions and action.

Bess fed him a list of co-ordinates, parameters, three-dimensional grid references, energy dissipation ratios and more. Much more. Dez channelled the information as he was told to and relayed queries back to Bess. It was like being in charge of the biggest train set in the universe, although the one thing he wasn't aware of was movement. Space and time had lost their meaning.

With his hands glued to the wheel and his mind in overdrive, Dez became part of a living machine, a fluid member of an intense, dedicated team. If knowledge was power he thought he knew what it must be like to be Zeus, standing on top of Mount Olympus, in control of all he saw.

'We're there now,' said Bess. 'You can let go.'

For a moment Dez didn't want to let go. He wanted this to carry on for ever, but a voice was calling from very, very far away and he knew he had to answer.

'OK, Bess,' he said, his hands slipping off the wheel and on to his lap.

'You did it!' said Treece, her excited voice suddenly very loud in his ear.

Dez looked round, almost surprised to see her there. 'Did I?' he smiled. 'What was it like?'

'Don't you know?'

'I know what it was like for me, but what did it really *look* like?'

'It was over so fast!' said Treece. 'Bess cleared the windscreen for me, but all I saw was a blur of lights. Look out of the window, though – you can see America!'

'Eh?' Dez pressed his head against the door window. 'Blimey!'

Far below him he could see the distinctive outline of the east coast of the United States, with the shape of the five Great Lakes clearly visible. Clumps of clouds strayed across them, and the view looked like the satellite weather pictures he'd seen on TV. Only better.

'I've always wanted to go to America,' said Treece.

'Me too.'

'Well,' said a voice behind him, 'you've both made it – nearly!'

'Yakob!' Dez turned in his seat and saw the Tylurian standing, hands on hips. 'But Bess said it'd take *ages* for you to get better!'

'You can't keep a good pilot down,' said Bess. 'He's made a remarkable recovery.'

Dez leapt out of his seat. 'Are you OK now?'

Yakob felt his left side, his eyes narrowing. 'Not bad … give me another hour or so and I'll be 100 per cent.'

'Me too,' chipped in Bess. 'I've got that infection on the run and guidance will be online very shortly.'

'You won't be needing me again then?' queried Dez.

'You never know.'

'Bess tells me you were a natural, Dez.' Yakob leaned over the seat and peered out of the window. 'Right on target!'

'It was incredible! Not me, I mean, but *being* there, being a part of *Stark*.'

'I know what you mean,' said Yakob. 'I've done many simulations, test runs training us for what to do in an emergency.'

'Have you ever done it for real?' queried Treece.

'Never.' Yakob smiled, reaching over and playfully punching Dez on the shoulder. 'You really came through for us!'

'What happens now?' asked Treece. 'How long do we stay up here?'

'Long enough to have a rest, eat some food and let you two get to know each other a bit better.' Yakob looked down at the hole in his burnt T-shirt. 'And I think I'm going to need a change of clothes before I can go in search of the last piece of this puzzle.'

'What do we know about him?' asked Dez.

'Or her.' Treece dug him in the ribs with her elbow. 'It could be a girl!'

'I have the same amount of information as I had for Treece,' said Bess. 'I have a name – Tyler; I have the age – eleven, of course; and I have a four-block area in which he – or she – lives.'

'Tyler sounds like a boy's name to me,' said Dez, making a "so there" face at Treece.

'We'll find out soon enough.' Yakob turned to go into the back of the craft.

'And then it'll all be over?' said Treece.

'The hard part'll be over,' Yakob said thoughtfully. 'Once I've got the three of you, all I have to do is get you back to *Tyson's Grip* and on to Priam, and who knows what can happen between here and there.'

'You really know how to make a person feel safe and secure,' commented Dez, nodding to himself. The future looked as perilous as it had since this whole thing started.

'It's one of his many talents,' said Bess. 'You should be used to it by now.'

'Yeah, right.'

'Cheer up! You're going to New York.' Bess's voice

was suddenly pure American. 'I hear it's one heck of a town!'

On the dark side of the solitary grey satellite moon orbiting the target planet a damaged craft lay hidden...

Battle wounds had to be tended; tempers defused.

Reports to a higher authority would have to be made. And they would be the most difficult of the tasks that needed completing.

The Commander ordered a communications circuit opened. He'd already had a second chance. He was about to find out if it had been his last...

Chapter 28

Dez couldn't make out exactly where New York was; his school atlas had got the state boundaries clearly marked and the towns had their names by them, but in real life it all looked confusingly similar – no names, no different-coloured areas, everything a mottled green. 'Looks amazing, doesn't it?'

Dez turned towards Treece. She was in the passenger seat next to him, staring at one of *Stark*'s screens. On it was an ultra-high definition picture showing an aerial view of Manhattan. Dez peered closer and found he could see cars moving on the streets. 'Unreal ...' he whispered. 'I wonder if she can get any closer?'

Before either of them had a chance to say anything the picture leapt forward and they found themselves looking at a pigeon pecking at a discarded hot dog in a gutter.

'Yeuchh! Not *that* close, Bess!' laughed Treece.

'Just doing an equipment test,' said Bess, as the picture on the screen zoomed back up to a large-scale view at a dizzying speed. 'That place down there looks like a concrete ants' nest, only less organized.'

'Sounds attractive,' said Dez. 'Just the sort of place you'd want to go on holiday.'

'Lucky this isn't a holiday then, isn't it?'

Dez looked round to find Yakob standing behind him, arms folded and chewing on his lower lip. 'Is it going to be dangerous?' he asked.

'Nowhere's safe with the Väds on your tail.' Yakob raised his eyebrows and took a deep breath. 'Well, there's no point in wasting any more time; have you completed all the checks, Bess?'

'All systems up and running,' she replied. 'The guidance drone is fully on-line and 98 per cent of all damage has been repaired; just a few minor glitches I can deal with later.'

'Is that acceptable?' asked Yakob, frowning.

'Under the circumstances it'll have to do.'

'Right.' Yakob beckoned for Dez to get out of the driving seat. 'We're going to Manhattan Island ...'

'Update, now,' said the voice, sounding as cold as the soul of an iceberg.

'We docked the ground craft for repairs some time ago. I anticipate ...'

'Facts are required, Commader, not possibilities – what happened to the creature?'

'It got away.'

'Don't state the obvious; where is it now? Did the Tylurian craft escape?'

'Yes.'

'And?'

'We were lucky. We had a second ship in orbit and it picked up the ghost when they finally warped out.'

'Where are they now?'

'We think somewhere on the east coast of the major land mass they call America.'

'Find them.'

The connection was terminated. The Commander sat back, relaxing slightly with the knowledge that he'd been given another chance. These must, he thought, be truly desperate times.

Chapter 29

Early morning light filtered through the trees, throwing down shafts of pale glass that shattered on the branches and fell in pieces onto the leaf-covered ground. It had rained the night before and the smell of damp earth filled the air along with the soft sounds of birds calling to each other. Distant traffic noise hummed and grumbled in the background like a tone-deaf old man, and under a nearby bush a large rat gnawed on a discarded chicken bone.

'Is this Central Park?' asked Dez.

'It is,' said Yakob as he got up out of his seat. 'Looks nice, doesn't it, until you look a bit closer.'

'Are we gonna be staying long?' Dez asked.

'Only as long as it takes to find Tyler, and not a moment longer.' Yakob walked to the rear of the van and sat down in front of one of the consoles. It trilled at him and he spoke a few words back. A moment later a 3D picture of a dense block of skyscrapers appeared beside him, hanging vertically in the air so that the buildings stuck out sideways.

'What's that?' Dez went over to have a closer look. 'Does Tyler live in there somewhere?' He peered at the aerial view, amazed at the detail the hologram contained. 'Quite a small area, really.'

'Some of those buildings are thirty storeys high,' said Yakob. 'Each one's like a small village.'

'Your sniffer thingy'll do the trick though, won't it?'

'Sniffer?' said Treece.

'They did something to us when they put the code in our DNA,' explained Dez. 'Apparently the three of us smell different from everyone else and he's got this little black box that can sniff out the niff from miles away.'

'I do not *smell*!'

'Don't worry, Treece; it's not a *real* smell, like rotten socks or anything,' said Dez. 'Right, Yakob?'

'Absolutely correct. Nothing to worry about.' Yakob stood back from the hologram, cocked his head sideways and muttered something. The picture turned into a snowstorm of coloured pixels and then instantly reformed to a smaller scale, this time including a green wooded area in its bottom right-hand corner.

'Is that where we are?' asked Dez, pointing at the trees.

'Don't you care?' said Treece angrily, before Yakob had a chance to reply.

'Me?' said Dez, looking mildly puzzled. 'Care about what?'

'Them,' she pointed at Yakob. 'Them messing about

with our lives, messing about with our *bodies*! I feel like I'm some kind of medical experiment, a some lab mouse …' Treece's voice trailed off as she bit her knuckle. A solitary tear blossomed in her eye and threw itself down her dark cheek. Dez didn't know what to do. Girls were one thing, crying girls quite another. Then Treece straightened her shoulders, wiping her eyes with the back of her hand. 'Sorry,' she said. 'I … I just feel so *alone*. I don't normally cry, honestly.'

'Nothing's normal right now, Treece.' Yakob put one hand on her shoulder and one on Dez's. 'We all get way out of our depth sometimes, even me, but with your help it'll all be over soon.'

'How can *we* help?' she asked.

'By not doing anything stupid while I'm away.' Yakob looked pointedly at Dez, who had the good grace to blush and play close attention to his trainers.

'OK, OK,' he said. 'No need to rub it in; we'll stay here until you get back. Promise.'

'Fine.' Yakob picked his sun-glasses up and put them on. 'Time to hit the streets.'

With nothing to do, and plenty of time to do it in, Dez and Treece started talking about each other.

'It's odd, you know,' Treece commented.

'What is?'

'Us both being adopted.'

'*You're* adopted!' Dez was stunned.

'When I was a baby.'

'Me too!' he almost yelled. 'This is *really* weird, Treece.'

'It gets weirder.'

'How?' said Dez, leaning forward in anticipation.

'I was born in England.'

Suddenly everything became unnaturally quiet, like the moment after an explosion. Dez stared at the girl opposite him, looking at her, searching for something in her face, some recognition that went beyond the short time he'd known her. She looked right back at him, eyebrows slightly raised, her face a question.

'What do you think it means?' she said.

'No idea.'

'Coincidence?'

'D'you know where you were born?'

'Yes.'

'Me too.' Dez nodded.

'Nottingham?'

'Nottingham.'

'Sounds less and less like a coincidence to me.' Bess's voice was thoughtful. 'I wouldn't mind betting we'll find a similar connection with Tyler.'

'*If* we find him, or her,' said Treece.

'You think we all came from one place, Bess?' asked Dez, looking at his skewed reflection in the windscreen.

'Looks likely, wouldn't you think? And it would seem logical that all three of you were operated on at the same time, rather than in different places. If it'd been me, that's what I'd have done, anyway.'

‘Blimey,’ Dez sat back in his chair and looked over at Treece; she wasn’t exactly his sister, but they shared something extremely important, which, under the circumstances, made her a pretty special person.

Before anyone could say another word an ear-piercing scream split the air. Four screens on the dashboard instantly blinked into life, showing images from the scanning cameras. One screen immediately started tracking left and right, as if searching like a hound for a scent, and then it zoomed through the undergrowth.

‘Someone’s being attacked!’ said Bess.

Chapter 30

'It's a woman!' yelled Treece, pointing at the screen.

Through a mesh of leaves Dez could see a figure with a blonde ponytail and dressed in jogging gear being pounded by a couple of greasy street types while three more young men looked on and laughed. 'It's a mugging!'

'Bess, we have to do something!' said Treece, as the two men wrestled the woman to the ground.

'It may look like a van, but this is a battle-equipped, front line combat craft,' said Bess tensely. 'Everything I have at my disposal is as lethal as a plague. I blow up star ships, not fire warning shots at people …'

'Well, *I* can't just sit around in this van and watch!' Treece whirled round, reaching for the door.

'It's locked,' said Bess. 'Yakob's orders.'

'So *un*lock it!' screamed Treece.

'We've got to help, Bess – listen to her!' pleaded Dez, the woman's screams for help ringing in his ears. 'Please!'

'What can the two of you do?'

'We can use that!' said Treece, pointing at the Väd-Raatch laser pistol Dez had escaped with. It was lying forgotten on the chair where he'd put it. He leaped up and grabbed it.

'I'm responsible for what happens to you two!'

'*We'll* be responsible for what happens to that woman if we don't do something!' Treece grabbed the gun and pointed it at the dashboard. 'Open the door, Bess – now!'

You could almost hear the electrons in Bess's circuitry tying themselves in knots as they attempted to deal with the dilemma of what to do in these extraordinary circumstances. 'All right,' Bess said, finally. 'Don't show yourselves; just scare them off and get back in here as quickly as possible. I'll be watching you.'

'Right!' Treece opened the door and jumped out, loudly whispering 'Ger-*ron*-imo!' as she went. Dez, still staggered by what she'd done, tumbled after her and the two of them ran pell-mell through the undergrowth towards the woman and her attackers.

'Couldn't make more noise if they tried,' muttered Bess as she directed one of the cameras at their disappearing backs.

Realizing they must sound like a herd of rampaging elephants, Dez waved at Treece and immediately slowed down. They both started to creep as quickly and quietly as they could over to some denser cover a few metres away from the unfolding scene.

‘What happens now?’ whispered Dez.

‘We frighten the living daylights out of those creeps, I hope,’ Treece waved the pistol.

‘Can you shoot that?’ Treece hesitated, looking at the laser in her hand. ‘Give it here,’ Dex grabbed it. ‘You got me into this, now I’ll just have to try and get us out of it …’

‘They’re going to hurt her!’ hissed Treece. ‘*Do* something *now*!’

‘Give me a chance!’ said Dez, desperately searching for something to fire at to create the kind of panic that would scare the gang away. Then he saw it. One of the men was holding a large bottle in one hand, his arm hanging loosely by his side, and from the way he was acting it didn’t have mountain fresh spring water in it. The bottle looked to be almost full and Dez held his breath as he took aim and fired.

A bolt of pure light sizzled from the tip of the barrel and the bottle erupted in the man’s hand; the liquid it contained burst into a vivid sheet of blue-white flame that leapt, enveloping the man. He started screaming, much louder than the woman his friends were attacking, and flung himself to the ground, writhing as if he was possessed by demons and beating himself in an attempt to douse the fire.

‘You genius!’ grinned Treece, watching as the man’s four companions momentarily forgot what they were doing and watched, dumbstruck, as their friend rolled in the dirt, ablaze. The acrid smell of burning hair cut the air.

'No, just lucky …' Dez took the opportunity to fire twice more at the frozen statues in front of him. His first shot vaporized the can of beer one of them was holding, showering a molten spray on its owner, and the second zapped the knife blade in another's hand. It vanished, leaving the man clutching only a super-heated handle.

The spell broke and four of the men turned and ran, leaving the fifth lying on the ground, groaning and smouldering. The woman sat dishevelled on the ground, mascara tears ran down her face, and it was obvious she was in a state of shock.

'Job done; we'd better get back to *Stark*,' whispered Dez.

Treece was up off the ground before Dez could stop her. 'Can't just leave her there,' she said, running round the bushes. 'Got to see if she's all right.'

Dez glanced over his shoulder at where he knew the van was; Bess, watching their every move, must be going nuts, but what could he do? He got up and went after Treece, shoving the laser pistol into the back of his jeans. He was so preoccupied he didn't notice the distant siren wail.

Dez found Treece on her knees by the woman's side, one arm round her shoulders and using her sleeve to wipe away tear-smudged make-up.

'Treece?'

'Wait, I want to make sure she's OK.' She smoothed the woman's hair off her forehead. 'Can you stand up?'

The woman nodded and stood up a little unsteadily,

turning as she heard the moans of the man on the ground and twisting back again at the approaching sound of clattering footsteps. 'Are they coming back?' she said in a small, frightened voice. 'Those men?'

'No, don't think so …' Dez's heart sank as he saw the blue uniform of a New York cop come thundering into view. A moment later a second policeman followed and he knew they were sunk; he and Treece were well and truly involved and the chances of them slipping away and back to *Stark* were slimmer than a stick of chewing gum.

'What took you so long?' asked the woman, still holding on to Treece as if she was a crutch, but not sounding so small and frightened any more. 'I was breaking *windows* screaming for help and two *kids* get here first!'

'We got the call a coupla minutes ago, ma'am.' The first cop was panting, sweat pouring off his forehead. A name patch on his shirt told the world he was called Zuchowsky. 'What the heck happened here?' he pointed at the singed man.

'I got attacked by a bunch of sleazeballs,' said the woman, 'and as bad was just about to get much worse all hell broke loose. He,' she jerked a thumb at the man on the ground, 'burst into flames and weird stuff happened to the two creeps being real nasty to me.'

The second cop bent over the mugger. 'Looks like flash burns, nothing too serious. What was he doing, trying to flambé himself?'

'We didn't see anything,' said Dez, before Treece could

open her mouth. 'We just heard this lady yelling and came to help. We found them both on the ground.'

Officer Zuchowsky looked from Dez to Treece and back at Dez. 'You two English?'

As Dez said 'Yes', Treece was saying the opposite. They fell silent.

'Get your stories straight while I call this lady an ambulance,' said Zuchowsky, unhitching a radio from his belt. 'Your parents know where you are?' He glanced down at the mugger. 'This ain't really the place for kids to go wandering.'

'We took a wrong turning,' said Dez. 'But I'm sure I know where we are now, so if you don't mind, we'd better be getting back or our parents'll start worrying.'

'You two ain't going nowhere,' said Officer Zuchowsky, ''cept back to the station with us ...'

In the sun-dappled clearing the fully cloaked Tylurian craft *Stark Revenge* sat, invisible, in its hiding place. Through the external cameras Bess watched, powerless, as her two charges were led off down a wooded path.

It was all very well being cleverer than a room full of geniuses, she thought to herself, aware that neither child had left the craft with a homing device, but there are certain circumstances where a pair of legs would be a distinct advantage.

Lacking the means to go after Treece and Dez herself, Bess did the next best thing and launched a tiny remote surveillance unit. It was risky, but what else could she do?

Chapter 31

'Is the squad prepared?'

'Yes, sir!' The armourer saluted the Commander like a machine. 'Fully equipped and briefed, sir!'

'Flight Control!' The Commander shouted at the console. 'Are *you* ready?'

'Programming complete, jump sequence loaded,' came the reply. 'We're ready if they are, sir.'

'Get them land-side – *NOW!*'

'So,' said Yakob, wearily massaging his temples, 'what happened and where are they?'

Bess didn't say a word, just ran the edited highlights of the events that led up to Dez and Treece being taken away by two New York policeman.

'I had no choice,' she said when the screen closed down. 'And they were doing fine until the police showed up.'

'Is the remote still with them?'

'Yes.'

'I don't blame you, I just don't understand how they

can be so irrational …' Yakob re-ran the section where Dez exploded the tequila bottle and scared the wits out of the other two men. 'That boy can really think on his feet, shoot straight too.'

'He's still got the laser with him; how's he going to talk his way out of that one? Not many kids round here have Väd-Raatch hand-held supra-heats for toys.'

'Thankfully.' Yakob stood up. 'Patch in the remote and give me its position on the schematic. I want to see where they are.'

A screen lit up with a picture of Dez and Treece sitting in a small cramped room. A policewoman was with them and no one looked particularly happy about the situation. Yakob walked over to the holo-map; one building and the park were in full colour, the rest had been faded back and the quickest route from the van to the building was marked in red.

'Problem,' said Bess as Yakob bent down to examine the map.

'What?'

'I think I've picked up an overflight.'

'The Väds?'

'Unless current Earth tech has made a sudden, inexplicable leap forward.'

'No need to be sarcastic, Bess,' said Yakob. 'Close down the remote and bring it home.'

'It's on its way.'

'You're so fast you'll meet yourself coming back.'

'I wish.'

'So,' mused Yakob, standing up. 'The kids are in police custody, along with a potentially devastating laser weapon, and we face the distinct possibility of a Väd strike squad joining us out there on the street.'

'Isn't life fun on the outer edges of the civilized universe?'

'I'd better go and get those kids,' said Yakob. 'I'm going to need some assistance. I hope you're feeling artistic.'

'Sounds interesting,' said Bess. 'But before we start, any news about Tyler? Did you find him?'

'I found where he lives, but now I've got to go and make a personal appearance at a police station with a convincing explanation of why those two were on the loose – let's get to work, I want a life-size holo of Dez's head, and be quick about it!'

'Patching through message from landside, Commander.'

'I've got it.' The Commander swung round to look at his holo-screen. 'What do you want?'

'We've picked up a trace transmission, sir. It was very short, but we got a position.'

'So?'

'Confirming our moves, as per orders.'

'I don't want the details, I want results! I want those creatures and I don't care how you do it!' The Commander leant towards the console. 'And remember, if this fails I take full responsibility ... but you take the blame.'

'I am fully aware of that, sir.'

'I do hope so. I hate losing good officers.'

Chapter 32

The police station was totally depressing. Inside it had been painted two shades of puke green and there was the smell of disinfectant; sort of like school, but without the kids.

'What d'you think they're going to do with us?'

'Ask us for our parents' phone numbers, probably.' Lying next to him on the bench Dez saw a newspaper. He picked it up and began turning the pages as nonchalantly as possible.

'How can you read a *paper* at a time like this!'

'I'm not reading it. I'm looking for a phone number – *any* phone number – to give them.'

'Oh … good idea.' Treece looked over Dez's shoulder as he began riffling through the pages. All she could see were ads for discount computer shops and pages of supermarket money-off coupons.

'A-ha …' Dez flicked a glance at Officer Zuchowsky, whose cell phone had just buzzed, then looked back at the half-page advertisement for a hotel chain. Smiling to himself he folded the paper and put it back on the bench.

'Did you find one?' asked Treece.

'Yes and no.' Dez watched as the big cop walked towards them.

'Someone wants to have a little chat with you two,' he said. 'Follow me.'

Ushering them in front of him Zuchowsky took them past the front desk, up some stairs and along a dingy corridor. Half-way down it he told them to stop and then opened a door, pointing for them to go in and closing the door behind him.

'Yakob's going to go mad when he finds out we left *Stark*, isn't he?' Treece sat down on one of the metal chairs.

'*Yakob*'s going to go mad? You wait till Bess starts having a go at you for pulling a gun on her!' Dez sat down. 'You're certifiable, you are …'

'I *had* to something!' Treece turned away. 'That policeman didn't lock the door, you know.'

'So?'

'So let's make a break for it!' Treece stood up.

'We should stay put.'

'Why?' Treece looked round the small room. 'Why stay here?'

'Because there's an outside chance Yakob might find us. On the street we'd just be lost – I've no idea where we are.'

Neither of them looked at each other, nor did they

notice the tiny remote unit clinging to the ceiling by the window, and then the door opened and a slightly flustered man walked in and sat down opposite them

'My names's Lieutenant Esterhaus ... so what's the story?'

Nobody spoke.

'You kids mutes or am I suddenly a deaf person?' The lieutenant sat forward. 'Cut the cute stuff. I don't care what you were doing in the Park, so just give me your folks' numbers, they come down here, you leave the premises, end of story. Unless you're runaways – you ain't runaways, are you? Zuchowsky told me you were from England, a difficult place to run away from at your age.'

Dez opened his mouth to reply, but was interrupted by the lieutenant.

'You two scared what your parents might do when they get their mitts on you? Don't worry, I'll square things. You wanna drink or something?'

Dez shook his head. 'No, and I don't know the number of the hotel our families are staying at.'

'You speak? Great – I thought for a moment I was going to have to get a mime artist to come in and help out here!'

Dez ignored the sarcasm and went on: 'I know the name, though. It's the Marriott.'

'Which one?'

The question caught Dez off his guard; he'd been expecting to be asked for his and Treece's surnames. 'Which one?'

'Yeah, there are a number.'

'It's … um … it's quite near the Park,' said Dez, beginning to wish he'd never started lying.

'I'll call them all,' sighed the lieutenant. 'What're your family names?'

'Oh … um … Windsor,' said Dez. It was the only really English name he could think of on the spur of the moment.

The lieutenant looked enquiringly at Treece. 'Castle,' she replied, a silly grin on her face.

'Windsor, and Castle,' said the lieutenant, pointing at each of them. 'Really – what are you two, some kind of double act? Stop wasting my time and spill, kids.'

Dez's mouth felt as dry as old toast and knew he must look totally guilty; he glanced at Treece, wondering what on earth to do next, but before either of them could say anything the phone on the wall behind the lieutenant rang. Saved by the bell …

'What?' The lieutenant listened, glancing over at Dez and Treece and then put the phone down. 'OK, Jack Danby, your father's out front; come on …'

Ten minutes later the three of them were at a table in a small diner a block away from the police station. Dez and Treece were sitting opposite each other drinking glasses of milk and eating hamburgers and Yakob – who had morphed his face so there could be no doubt whose father he was – was letting a cup of coffee cool in front of him.

'What *I* want to know,' said Dez, sitting back and pushing his plate away from him, 'is how you knew where to find us.'

'You were being tracked by a remote,' explained Yakob. 'I saw everything right up until the lieutenant came.'

'Did the remote break down?' asked Treece.

'No, I had to pull it back.'

'Why?'

'Bess picked up a scan.'

'What does that mean?'

'The Väds,' said Dez. 'They're here.'

'Yes, the Väds.' Yakob finished his coffee, shaking his head at the waitress as she started to come over to refill it. 'And no, they haven't found us ... but they know we're here, somewhere.'

'What are we going to do?' said Dez.

'Get Tyler,' Yakob put some money on the table and stood up. 'Come on, time to make tracks.'

Chapter 33

Standing on the pavement outside the diner, Yakob hailed a cab and hurried Dez and Treece into it.

'Where are we going?' asked Treece, who was sitting in the middle. 'Park and 78th,' said Yakob.

Dez was staring at the driver's picture on his licence, which made him look like an axe-murderer, when, with an awful sense of *déjà vu*, he saw a large van accelerate out of a side turning only metres ahead of the cab. Instantly he was flashed back to the road in France; he could almost see his father as he jammed on the brakes, too late to stop their car smashing into the huge truck in front of them. And here it was, all happening again. Instinctively he reached for the door.

'No! This side!' Yakob grabbed Treece as the cab slewed sideways, its tyres screeching.

'What?' Dez yelled.

'Get out *this* side!' Yakob flung the right-hand door open. 'And keep down!'

As he got out of the cab Dez saw the driver, who was fighting with his air bag. 'What about him?'

'The Väds don't want him – have you still got that laser pistol?'

'Yeah, but ...' As a large hole boiled in the glass of the cab's rear window, Dez realised that the horror really was repeating itself.

Yakob pulled Dez out on to the street. 'No buts – *move!*'

The normal hubbub of early afternoon Manhattan rose to a deafening crescendo as the traffic in the street ground to a halt, horns blasted and people yelled. And then the yells turned to screams as a stuttering laser blast from the driver of the van ate a hole in the cab door and hit the petrol tank of a car behind it.

The confusion caused by the resulting explosion allowed Yakob to drag Treece and Dez across the pavement and into the safety of a shop doorway. 'Give me the pistol,' he said, snapping his fingers.

Out on the street everything was chaos. Oily black smoke billowed up from the burning car and frightened people ran around like chickens. Yakob, who had pushed Dez and Treece behind him, was inching forward to try and see what the Väds were up to when there was an ear-splitting shriek followed by the sound of shattering glass.

Dez leant forward to see what was happening, then a man lumbered out of nowhere, a black leatherette bag over his shoulder, and tumbled into the doorway to join them. The thing that Dez fixed on was that he was wearing bright red cowboy boots

'They makin' a movie or sumthin'?' the man said, reaching into his bag and bringing out a small video camera. 'I thought they only did this kind of thing in studios – these special effects are *incredible,* ain't they?'

'Get back!' Yakob shouted over his shoulder as the very unlaser-like *KRAKK!* of a hand gun rang out. 'The police have arrived and it's going to get very messy!'

'You actors?' said the man, swinging the camera round to look at Dez and Treece. 'You actually *in* this movie?'

'It's not a film, it's *real*!' Treece ducked down as the window in the shop front disintegrated, showering the pavement with an avalanche of glass hailstones. 'Those people are *aliens* and they're trying to kill us!'

'You say!' grinned the man. He seemed to be really enjoying himself. 'You been watchin' *way* too much TV. This don't happen in real life, and it sure as heck don't happen in Tuscaloosa.'

There was a ragged volley as more hand gun shots echoed in the brick canyon, and a voice on a loud-hailer shouted something Dez couldn't understand. Once again the horrible sense of having been there before washed over him; huddled in a confined space, with the world exploding around him, this was almost exactly like that night up in the Alps. Was everything that had happened going to repeat itself, and did that then mean capture was inevitable? 'What's going on? Where are the Väds now?' he yelled above the racket.

'Out on the street, as far as I can see,' said Yakob. 'Their van's been blocked in and it looks like they can't move it!'

'Great!' Dez ducked as bullets thudded into the wall outside. 'But how do *we* get out of here without them seeing us?'

The street was a war zone, and with the kind of firepower they had Dez was sure it wouldn't be long before the Väds tried to get at them again. He was staring at the back of the man with the video camera, frantically worrying about everything, when Treece spoke up.

'How about the back entrance to this shop?'

Both Yakob and Dez looked at Treece and then at the door behind her.

'It's just a thought,' she said.

Yakob put the pistol in his pocket and swiftly hustled Dez and Treece into the shop. On a normal day it did a brisk trade in discount shoes, but now the place was empty, smoke from the burning car drifting in through its shattered front window.

'What's going on?' said a small, scared voice. It belonged to the head that poked out of a dimly lit back room.

'They're making a movie,' said Dez.

'Well, no one told *us* they were going to trash the place!' The shop assistant peered further out of the shadows. 'That's a coupla thousand dollars of plate glass they're gonna havta pay for and one movie *I* won't be queueing up to see!'

'Is there a way out through the back?' asked Yakob.

'We're late for an appointment and we'll never make it if we have to wait for them to finish out there.'

'Yeah, well, I suppose there is.' The man beckoned to them. 'Mrs Klein, take these folks out back while I keep a watch so no one steals anything from the window.'

Walking quickly into what turned out to be a cluttered store room, the three of them followed a middle-aged lady past ceiling-high stacks of cardboard boxes and out into a narrow alleyway.

'Mind the dog mess,' she said, pulling the door closed. 'And have a nice day.'

It was weirdly peaceful in the alley, almost as if what they'd just witnessed had been a bad dream. But back through the shop, a few brick walls away, were people who seemed prepared to risk everything to get them. A thought struck Dez and he frowned.

'They can shape-change too, can't they,' he said quietly. 'Just like you.'

'Yes,' said Yakob.

'What do you really look like?'

'You'll find out soon enough, but we've got to get Tyler first.' Yakob had the kind of look on his face that said any more questions would be pointless. Dez watched him scan the alley. 'We'd better go that way.' He pointed to his left and began to walk.

'How did they know where to find us?' asked Treece.

'I'd like it to have been luck,' said Yakob, 'but I don't really think it was. Anyway, however they did it, this town's getting far too dangerous.'

'This *planet's* getting far too dangerous,' muttered Dez, and then his foot sank into something soft, brown and squidgy. 'Oh, *perfect*!' he groaned, searching to see somewhere to wipe his trainer.

'You were warned!' grinned Treece.

Chapter 34

Getting away turned out to be simplicity itself as every policemen they met seemed to have only one thing in mind – evacuating as many people as possible from the surrounding area as fast as they could.

This, of course, suited Yakob down to the ground; a virtual armed escort took them a block or two away from the disturbance, where they picked up another cab and soon found themselves outside a large apartment building on 78th Street. The relief was immense, but Dez was beginning to feel more than a little disoriented by the speed at which things were progressing; an ominous feeling of dread, accompanied by major butterflies, kept him tense and on edge.

'Is this where Tyler lives?' he shaded his eyes and craned his neck as he looked up at the thirty storeys stacked in front of him.

'This is the place,' said Yakob. 'Apartment 12 on the fourteenth floor. His or her name's Robinson – Tyler Robinson.'

'How'd you find that out?' said Treece.

Yakob took the small black box out of his pocket. 'My little sniffer picked up a trace on 1412's letter box, and the name on the box was "Robinson",' he said, closing his fist round it.

'So what happens now?' asked Treece.

'We go in and …' Yakob stopped mid-sentence. Somewhere they could all hear a muffled bleeping and Yakob slowly opened his hand. A tiny light was flashing on the black box.

'Tyler?' said Dez.

'Where?' said Treece, spinning round.

Yakob turned and looked over his shoulder and then back at the winking light. 'In the foyer of the apartment block, I think …'

'I can't see any kids,' said Dez, searching everywhere, 'just that woman taking her dog for a walk.'

'That's who it is.' Yakob put the box in his pocket and shook his head.

'Who?' Dez frowned.

'It's the dog?' Treece almost yelped.

'The dog it is,' Yakob nodded. 'And I think I can safely say he's a boy.'

The dog was a feisty-looking Jack Russell terrier, all of thirty centimetres high, who seemed hell-bent on dragging his owner's arm off in his enthusiasm to get going. Dez could hardly believe it; he was going to have to add dognapping to the list of criminal activities he'd been involved in since he'd met Yakob.

'Why a dog?' said Treece, breaking into Dez's thoughts. 'Why'd they choose to put that valuable information in a dog? They don't live *that* long!'

'He's probably had his DNA tweaked to extend his lifespan,' explained Yakob. 'He could live as long as you do.'

'It's as good a place as any, I suppose,' mused Treece, 'if you think about it.'

'He's seventy-seven years old now,' Dez told no one in particular. 'Seven dog years for every human one. Doesn't look like a pensioner, though. I wonder if he bites?'

'We'll no doubt find out,' said Yakob.

They followed the woman, who was basically following the dog, east for five blocks. Tyler seemed to know exactly where he was going, and to be in no little hurry to get there. His chosen destination turned out to be a small park overlooking the East River and the island in the middle of it.

Sitting on a bench they watched as Tyler chased birds, fetched anything that was thrown for him and generally had the time of his life. It occurred to Dez that the phrase 'it's a dog's life', which usually meant things weren't up to much, didn't apply to Tyler Robinson. 'What if he doesn't want to come with us, Yakob?'

'What if his *owner* doesn't want us to take him, more like!' said Treece.

'Come with me,' Yakob stood up. The three of them

walked along a path that led behind a big thick clump of tall bushes, and when they could no longer see Tyler and his mistress, Yakob suddenly pushed his way into the shrubbery and beckoned for Treece and Dez to come with him.

'Have you spotted something?' whispered Dez. 'More Väds?'

'Nothing like that,' Yakob squatted down.

'What then?'

Yakob let out a series of high-pitched barks in reply. He barked once more, ignoring Treece and Dez's questioning faces, and then from the other side of the bushes they heard the yip of a response; moments later there were scrabbling noises as Tyler pushed through the low branches and looked enquiringly up at them, his stubby tail wagging furiously.

'How did he do that?' said Treece, her voice a loud, squeaky whisper.

'I should've known!' Dez slapped his hand on his forehead. 'He can talk *dog* – I saw him do it outside your house! He made friends with that set of teeth on legs you've got in no time at all.'

'Quiet, you two!' said Yakob, patting Tyler, who had come over to sit right next to him. 'This is going to be the tricky bit.'

'Trickier than getting out of Treece's house?' Dez put his hand out and let Tyler sniff it.

'In its way,' said Yakob. 'Dez, I want you to come with me.'

'What am *I* going to do?' said Treece.

'Stay here with Tyler and don't make a sound.'

'But what if he runs away?' Treece looked over her shoulder as they heard a woman's voice calling Tyler's name. The dog looked up at Yakob, who shook his head.

'He'll stay with you, don't worry.' Yakob got up and began to move towards the path. 'Come on, Dez, we've got to help Mrs Robinson find her dog.'

Shaking his head, Dez went after him. They walked round the bushes, back the way they'd come, the sound of Tyler's name being called getting louder with each step.

'Just agree with everything I say,' said Yakob, as they turned the corner and saw a perplexed Mrs Robinson, stick in hand, looking their way.

'Excuse me,' she called over to them, 'but have you seen a small dog?'

'Black and white?' said Yakob.

'That's right.'

'Well, yes we did; he came tearing through the bushes and ran off in that direction.' Yakob indicated away over to the right of the park. 'He seemed to be chasing something, didn't he?' he continued, looking at Dez.

'Yes ... yes, he did.' Dez found he couldn't look directly at the woman. 'Went like a rocket.'

'If he's seen a squirrel he's going to take some getting back!' she said, and then stared at Dez. 'Are you English?'

'Ah, yes ... from Nottingham, actually.' He didn't know why he said it, the words simply tumbled from his lips.

'What a coincidence!' the woman smiled briefly and then looked in the direction Yakob had pointed. 'That's where I lived, before I came back here. Sorry I can't stay and chat – must go and find my dog ...'

'Hope you find him,' said Yakob. But Mrs Robinson, like her dog, was running off and didn't hear him.

'Well, there you go,' said Dez.

'What?'

'We're all from the same town – Treece, Tyler and me.'

'Bess told me about that ... makes sense.'

'About the only thing that does.' Dez pointed at the bushes. 'Can they come out now?'

Yakob knelt down and gave a short, sharp whistle. There was a frantic rustling and Tyler launched himself out of the bushes at them. 'Treece?' Yakob called.

'Yes?' came the muffled reply.

'Come round and meet us, quickly!'

Picking Tyler up, Yakob set off at a brisk pace towards the pathway.

'Why are you carrying him?' asked Dez, almost running to keep up.

'Less noticeable this way,' he replied as Treece caught them up.

'*Carrying* a dog is less noticeable than walking one?' Dez looked puzzled. 'Is this Tylurian logic or am I going bonkers?'

'What he means,' said Treece, 'is that Mrs Robinson'll ask people if they saw a small black and white dog running round, and this way they won't have.'

'Oh ...' said Dez, wondering why he hadn't thought of that.

Chapter 35

In the late afternoon there weren't many people in Central Park. The lunchtime crowds had gone and there were just a few rollerbladers skimming the tarmac like multi-coloured low-flying birds, swooping and twirling with an effortless grace.

Turning off the main pathway Yakob led Dez and Treece in the direction of the dense mass of trees and shrubbery where *Stark* was waiting, Tyler at their heels.

Up ahead Dez spotted a policeman in conversation with a scruffily dressed woman.

Her arms were waving, making jerky semaphore signals as she nodded and shook her head in an intense, angry way. He could hear their voices but not what they were saying, but as they got closer he began to pick up words and then sentences.

'It's there, I tell you! Something's there!' the woman was saying.

'Calm down, Missy,' said the cop, 'you're just seeing

things that ain't there. Now come on, let me take to you back to your pitch.'

'Will you listen! I'm as sober as you are, ain't had a drop all day!' The woman waved a grubby hand up the path. 'It's like a big glass wall. I walked straight into the damn thing – look!' She pointed to a nasty bruise on her forehead.

'I see it, Missy, I see it. Are you angling for a trip to the Emergency Room or something? Cos all you gotta do is say you fell over – no need to make up goofy stories about glass walls in the middle of nowhere.'

Dez nudged Yakob. 'Hear that?'

'Every word.'

'Lucky for us it was her and not someone more believable,' said Treece.

'It's not some goofy story, you big lunk!' Missy's rasping voice followed them as they started to walk faster down the path. 'You come with me, I'll *show* you!'

'I ain't got time to go on no wild goose chases,' said the cop. 'Now, d'you wanna go to the hospital or what?'

Missy's reply was lost in the distance and all they could hear was her angry rattle and the cop's gruff but calm rumble in reply.

'What if she persuades him to go and have a look?' asked Dez, following Yakob as he struck off the pathway and into the undergrowth.

'The moment we get on board we're out of here.' Yakob ducked under a low branch and strode on. 'I'm not going to stay here a moment longer than it takes

Bess to check the systems, do a quick scan and then get us in orbit so we can warp to the edge of your system. *If* they come looking, we'll be long gone.'

'Won't the Väds be looking for us too?' Dez asked as he followed Yakob.

'They'll be waiting for us, but we'll have the element of surprise on our side.' Yakob held some branches back to let Treece and Dez through into a small clearing.

'We're here, aren't we?' said Dez, stopping.

There was a soft hissing noise and on the other side of the clearing, like the entrance to Alice's Wonderland, a door opened up in the air. Tyler growled, his ears lying back flat against his head. Inside the door the lights of *Stark*'s consoles winked a colourful greeting. With a swift look over his shoulder, Yakob loped across the carpet of dead leaves and jumped up into the van.

'Hey! Wait for us!' yelled Dez, as the three of them stampeded after him through the door.

'Well, *hasn't* it been an interesting day!' said Bess, as the door closed with a soft click behind Dez. 'I've been following your progress through the city and I get the feeling the good people of New York aren't going to forget your little visit for quite some time.'

'Hello, Bess,' Dez mumbled.

Treece started to apologise. 'Sorry, Bess ...'

'Did you know that your profile, thankfully in shadow, has been on *every* TV station? I've been checking the broadcasts; so much for an undercover operation ...'

'It was my fault, Bess,' said Treece, 'and I apologize.'

'*And* I've been stuck here for hours with a mad woman thundering around and throwing things at me …' Bess stopped in mid-flow. 'What's that with you?'

Dez knelt down. 'This is Tyler; he's a dog.'

There was a moment's silence and then Tyler barked, his tail, what there was of it, wagging like mad.

'I hope he likes our menu,' said Bess. 'I didn't stock up with dog food for this trip.'

'If everyone's now fully acquainted,' Yakob turned in his seat, 'I think we should strap in and move on out. Bess, update me on what's happening out there.'

'You don't want to know,' she replied. 'There's so much scanning activity you could fry plakk in the microwave transmissions. We move, they'll know about it.'

'Not much we can do about that,' shrugged Yakob. 'How's the shielding?'

'Fine. Just a couple of dents where that oddball lady threw stones at me.'

'How can you joke at a time like this?' demanded Treece.

'Better a smile than a tear,' said Bess.

'And better get strapped in,' added Yakob, pulling a seat-belt over his shoulder and locking it tight. 'Dez, make sure you keep hold of Tyler; this is going to be a rough ride at best.'

'And at worst?' asked Dez.

'At worst? A very short one.'

'But I thought the reason they didn't kill Dez when

they had the chance was that the Väds wanted us alive?' said Treece. 'They won't try and blow us up, right?'

'Logically, you're absolutely correct,' said Yakob, pulling the steering column interface towards him and making contact with *Stark*'s flight intelligence units. 'But where the Väds are concerned, logic has nothing to do with anything and I'd be mad to assume they won't do something stupid, like launch an all-out attack on us. I'm going to be like the Väds and shoot first, ask questions later. I can't let them capture you.'

'But what if it looks like they're going to?' asked Dez, not really wanting to know the answer but having to ask the question. 'What then?'

Yakob shook his head, staring at the windscreen as he spoke. 'I don't know,' he said. 'I'll do my best, that's all I can promise you.'

Dez looked at Treece and then down at Tyler, lying curled up on his lap. He hadn't known either of them very long, Tyler hardly at all, but they were bound together by the strange circumstance surrounding their birth. It seemed unlikely that he'd ever find out the whole truth, but it didn't really matter now – what good was the truth if you were going to die?

The interior of the van suddenly darkened, the only illumination coming from the eerie dancing lights of the consoles as they trilled and warbled instructions and information. In the driving seat Yakob had lapsed back into Tylurian and then fell silent as *Stark* echoed with the high-pitched whine that Dez recognized as the beginning of the warp cycle. On his lap he felt Tyler shiver, letting out a soulful whimper and burrowing his head into the crook of his arm. On the chair opposite him Treece sat, gripping the seat with both hands. He smiled at her, but felt that all he was really doing was showing his teeth.

There was a stomach-churning jolt and the van was filled with a chaotic babble. Glancing at Yakob, Dez saw him sitting, arms rigid in front of him, knuckles white as his hands gripped the wheel. He knew what was happening: Yakob's mind was linked directly to the complex intelligence pods, it was ablaze with information, a place where the thought processes of dozens of computers threw uncountable gigabytes of data at him and he responded. He was part of the machine.

Only once you'd actually done it was it possible to understand what that meant; in the world Dez had grown up in machines were slaves, and even if people sometimes liked to think of them as having lives of their own only a human had true control. And then everything stopped.

Silence.

Darkness.

Nothing.

Had it happened? Was he dead? How do you know if you aren't alive any more? There was a plaintive whine from the small furry ball he'd forgotten was on his lap. If he was dead, at least he had company.

'Have you ever been to Disney World?' said a small voice in the deep gloom. It belonged to Treece.

'No,' he said, glad that, wherever he was, he could speak.

'The person who designed the Space Mountain ride would've appreciated what we just did.'

Chapter 36

The lights inside *Stark* came up very slowly and Dez could see Yakob, slumped back in his chair almost as if he was asleep. 'Bess?' he asked, 'is Yakob all right?'

'He's OK, but a few of his synapses got fried on the way. The medic pod is flooding him with a neuron enhancer; he'll be with us in a minute or two.'

'Where are we, Bess?' Dez got up and gave Tyler to Treece. 'I can't see anything out there.'

'Come up front.'

Dez sat down next to Yakob, still deep in recovery mode. 'What am I supposed to be looking at?'

'What I gather you call Pluto,' said Bess. 'It's right in front of you.'

'Where?' Dez saw only an immense star-spotted blackness in front of him, an intense lack of colour that seemed to want to suck him through the glass and absorb him completely.

'Look for where the stars aren't,' said Bess. 'Can you see it now?'

Staring hard Dez eventually found he could make out the edge of a blacker starless circle. 'What's the bulge on its side?'

'Pluto's moon, Charon,' Bess told him.

'It's so dark, I can hardly make it out at all.'

'Probably something to do with being over six million kliks from your Sun,' said Yakob, sitting up and rubbing his face. 'Boy, that was a tough one.'

'Yakob!' Dez's face split with a huge grin. 'Are you OK now? What happened when we warped out? Did the Väds spot us?'

'Slow down! My brain's still limping!' Yakob leaned forward to check the console displays in front of him. 'It looks like I bought us some time back there, although it was a pretty close run thing at one point.'

'You flew like you were on fire,' said Bess. 'They didn't have a chance.'

'They had a few, but I was just that bit quicker.'

'I particularly liked the quark turn you did; it was …' she stopped mid-sentence. 'Ten degrees, low quadrant, thousand kliks and closing … four – no, five hostiles, at least half a fighter wing. It's battle stations, Captain Pell.'

'Where the hell's *Tyson's Grip*?' grunted Yakob, grabbing the interface and barking a stream of commands that made the dashboard heave with colour. 'They were supposed to be here to meet us!'

Stark suddenly spun round, the starscape whirling madly in front of them; on the screens Dez could see views of the approaching Väd fighters, hunched, menacing and deadly insects that grew bigger by the second.

'Don't give me a warning then!' Treece called out from the back of the van. 'I'll just sit on the floor if that's all right with you lot.'

'He didn't know,' Dez yelled back, the sides of his seat gripping him as tight as he was holding on to it. 'We're under attack!'

The words had hardly left his lips when there was shattering blast of light to his right and he was thrown sideways. A second barrage of photo-sonic clusters ripped the dark apart, tossing *Stark* about with the ease of a cat toying with a dying bird. It was like watching TV with the sound turned down; the silent violence lost all its meaning and nothing made any sense.

'They're trying to kill us!' screamed Dez.

'No … no, they're not.' Bess's voice sounded strained and edgy. 'If they wanted to do that we'd be dead by now; they're containing us, forcing us to fly in the direction they want.'

'Why?'

'They want to catch us, Dez; there can be no other reason.'

Dez glanced at Yakob. His face was contorted, almost as if he was in pain, and deep frowning grooves ran down his forehead; he looked like an animal at bay, lips drawn back in an ugly snarl, teeth clenched and the strain of keeping control evident in every move he made.

Dragging his eyes away from the the view out of the windscreen, Dez craned his neck and strained to see what had happened to Treece and Tyler. They were still on the floor, at the back of the van; Treece had wedged herself under one of the consoles, feet jammed against the base to stop her from moving. Tyler was gripped tight in her arms.

'Are you OK?' he yelled.

'Yeah, just about!'

'How's Tyler?'

A loud howling bark came in reply, but before Dez had a chance to smile *Stark* did something completely gut-wrenching that almost instantly put it on a collision course with one of the chasing Väd fighters, turning it from prey into hunter.

'Got to fight back, can't keep on running ...' Yakob was talking like a robot. 'Going to find a target ... *hold tight*!'

Dez was eternally grateful he hadn't eaten for some time.

'Range!' yelled Yakob.

'1,500!' said Bess. 'Target locked!'

'Fire!' Yakob wrenched the wheel to his left and the Väd fighter disappeared from view as *Stark* powered away from it; on one of the screens Dez saw the craft disintegrate in a vicious red gash.

'You got it!' he punched the air. 'One down, four to go!'

'That's going to change the game a bit,' muttered

Yakob, looping and twisting *Stark* through a hail of potentially devastating photon blasts.

'Newcomer,' said Bess. 'A big one too; could be their mother ship.'

'Where?' said Yakob.

'Upper quadrant, in our path … now!'

Into their field of vision came a huge beetle-like craft with massive twin vanes running down its back and four big arms reaching out from the front. It took a moment, but then Dez realized where he'd seen something similar – it was like the Väd craft he'd escaped from, but with one difference: it was much, much bigger.

'Someone sound a little unhappy,' said Bess. 'I'm getting a blanket message on all frequencies … it says we have no chance of escape.'

Horribly fascinated, Dez watched six, seven, eight more fighters burst out of the belly of the Väd craft, wasps leaving their nest. That meant there were twelve hunters after them. In a chess game someone would now be sitting back with a smirk on their face, about to say "Checkmate!" as they fatally trapped the King. The fight was over; there was nowhere for *Stark* to go.

'Something's gone very wrong,' muttered Yakob as he brought *Stark* to rest and the vast shroud of space seemed to start closing in, getting ready to smother them.

'What do you mean?' said Dez.

'We've been signalling our arrival from the moment we came out of the warp, and the *Grip* should've come here to meet us straight away.'

'Uh-hum …' Bess gave every indication of clearing a throat she didn't have.

'What?' said Yakob.

'I've just discovered something.'

'Go on.'

'Remember I told you we were back to 98 per cent efficiency after the firefight outside Lagos?' Yakob nodded and Bess went on, 'Well, those glitches I said I could deal with later included a communications breakdown caused by that rogue two per cent and …'

' … the message never got sent,' said Yakob, finishing off her sentence.

'No, I'd've noticed that.'

'What then?'

'It went on the wrong frequency.'

'Change it!' said Yakob.

'What d'you think I've been *trying* to do? It's locked in by a software sub-routine that's so scrambled I can't access the core data to reroute it. Everything looked fine when I checked it after the battle, it just went haywire when the program ran. I can't understand it.'

'Sounds like a virus,' said Yakob. 'It wouldn't surprise me at all if it hasn't been there since we left Priam.'

'The spy?'

'Who else?'

Dez stared out of the windscreen at the Väd forces lined up against them and thought about the useless message being broadcast, like a misdialled telephone number ringing a phone in an empty house – even if someone was there to answer it they'd be the wrong person, unable to help. What a cruel joke, to have made it this far, only to be stymied by a mangled bit of software code.

'They don't know we're here, do they.' Treece didn't pose it as a question but a statement of fact. She was standing, Tyler in her arms, behind Dez's seat. 'I can't believe it.'

Tyler let out a short humphing sigh and everyone aboard *Stark Revenge* knew exactly how he felt. Gutted.

'We have them!'

'On board?'

'No, surrounded and with no escape route.'

'Then you don't have them except in your sights. Stop wasting time and bring them in – they may override the virus at any moment!'

'Yes, sir!'

'And remember, an animal is at its most dangerous when cornered. As I gather you have already found out.'

Chapter 37

'Why aren't they doing anything?' asked Treece, bending down to look out at the Väd ships.

'They're waiting for us to acknowledge their message and reply,' said Yakob.

'And then?' Dez couldn't bear to watch any more and was staring blankly at the dashboard, its screens showing images of varying enlargements of the Väd mother ship.

'And then, no doubt, those fighters behind us will escort *Stark* down to a docking bay and we will become prisoners of war.'

'You might, but what about us?' said Treece. 'Prisoners of war get sent home, but they aren't going to give *us* three back, are they? Not in a million years.'

Dez swallowed. He'd had first-hand experience of how the Väds treated prisoners; pictures flashed through his mind, especially the moment when the Väd commander had taken his helmet off and he'd seen for the first time what they looked like.

Dez's eyes blinked open with the image of a dark red

forked tongue flicking through two rows of tiny sharp teeth and he felt cold all over. He couldn't focus for a moment; the screen he was still staring at was a blur in front of him, and when he looked up he saw that they were moving very slowly towards the Väd mother ship. This is it then, he thought; *finito la musica* as his dad used to say when a film on TV was over.

No one said a word as *Stark* fell through the blackness, but the silence spoke volumes and you could almost feel the sadness and defeat in the cool air. To their left and right Dez could see Väd fighters guiding them in, sheepdogs worrying the last of the flock into the fold at night. Or wolves loping in for the kill.

Dez had an awful feeling of finality, that what he was experiencing was the last full stop in the story of Jack Danby, Beatrice Okonkwo and Tyler Robinson.

The mother ship grew in size until it filled the windscreen and there was nothing else to see. In front of them Dez saw a large circle of red lights come on. The circle then blinked smaller and smaller until it reached a square bright hole in the hull, hypnotically repeating the pattern over and over again as they got closer.

'The docking bay they want us to use,' said Yakob, breaking the heavy silence.

'Scanners are picking up a lot of hardware in there,' said Bess. 'Quite a welcoming party waiting for us, I'd say.'

'They're not taking any chances, are they?' commented Dez.

'Not with our escape record.' Yakob leaned back and took his hands off the controls. 'I'll let you take us in, Bess. I'd better go and put my uniform on so I can at least surrender in style.'

'I'd prefer it if you'd stay where you are, Yakob.'

The Tylurian stiffened in his seat, reaching out and grabbing back the controls. 'What are you planning?' he said, frowning. 'If you've got any little surprises in store for the Väds I'd like to know sooner rather than later.'

'Just stay where you are,' Bess said, sounding distracted and a bit mysterious. 'You'll know what to do when – and if – whatever it is happens.'

'Bess ... you tell me *now* exactly what it is you're planning!'

There was no reply.

'She can't have *gone* anywhere,' said Dez, 'so what's she up to?'

'I have no idea,' sighed Yakob. 'She's a law unto herself, that one, and we're just going to have to wait and see. I've tried losing my temper with these intelligences before and it's simply a waste of energy.'

'Well, whatever she's up to I hope it happens soon,' Treece pointed ahead. 'Look.'

Tyler struggled out of her arms and jumped on to Dez's lap, ears to attention, tail up and quivering. They were now only about a couple of hundred metres from the docking bay entrance, itself about fifty metres wide and some twenty tall. A flashing line of red lights running down the centre of an area almost the size of a football pitch showed where the Väds wanted them to come in to land. Dez could see clumps of armed men lining the sides. Once they'd touched down in that floodlit space there'd be no turning back. No exit.

The two fighters flying next to them came in closer and Dez could see *Stark* reflected in the pilots' visors, the single mirrored eyes observing their progress. Tyler looked round at the fighter to his right and growled. Dez patted him and felt the little dog shivering. Was it fear or anger? He didn't know which of the two emotions he was feeling, so the dog probably didn't either.

A hundred metres to go. What was Bess up to? thought Dez, chewing the inside of his cheek so hard it hurt and he had to stop. Tyler jumped off his lap and trotted to the back of the van.

Fifty metres. The warm salty taste of blood seeped across his tongue and his cheek ached. He looked round at Treece sitting on the nearest chair and the ghost of a smile crossed her face. He couldn't see Tyler.

Twenty metres. He could make out details on the uniforms of the nearest group of Väd soldiers, their laser rifles held at the ready. Some of them looked almost as nervous as he felt, their hands flexing and gripping their rifles.

Stark's metallic nose appeared to grow incandescent as it reflected the brilliant white light from the array of intense spotlights along the top edge of the bay door. Dez put a hand up to shade his eyes and in a couple of the rear view screens he saw four or five more of the fighter escort, white smudges against the dark backdrop of space. And then the blackness turned light blue.

Light *blue*? Dez didn't have a chance to digest the bizarre sight ...

'*FULL REVERSE POWER! FIRING COLD PULSE STRAFE AND SIDE SALVOES!*' Bess's voice boomed out of nowhere and *Stark* shot backwards so fast that Dez's seat didn't have a chance to grip him and he cannoned into the dashboard and was then flung backwards. '*TILT-SPIN AND DIVE! DROPPING PLASMA CHAFF!*'

With Bess's orders echoing in his head, Dez scrambled to pull out his seat-belt and strap himself in. His last sight of the Väd mothership, before *Stark* dropped like a stone, was a series of vibrant mushrooming clouds erupting from the docking bay. What sort of plan was this? he wondered, his mind spinning. A last-minute suicide mission? And then he remembered the sight of deep space turning light blue on the rear view screen. Was he going mad, or had he really seen that?

The answer to his question came seconds later when the whole of the windscreen filled with the same faded denim colour, smooth yet rippled – like some huge vertical sand dune.

'What is *that*?' he said, his voice a hushed whisper.

'That,' said Yakob, 'is *Tyson's Grip*.'

'How ... ?'

'I finally trashed that sucker of a virus,' said Bess.

'You spend a day in New York and you sound like you were born there!' grinned Dez. 'How'd you do it?'

'I'm a genius under pressure.'

'Treece, come and look!' yelled Dez. 'It's *enormous*!'

'Oh, my!' she gasped. 'But what happened to all the Väds?'

Yakob pointed at the dashboard screens. On three of them they could see Väd fighters with their photon cannons blazing; one moment they were there and the next, like shattering lightbulbs, they were gone. The fourth screen showed the mothership, a great rip in its hull from which hung a jagged cloud of debris. Its guns were silent. If a thing could look forlorn, dejected and beaten, it did.

'They've given up!' said Treece. 'We've won!'

'They have and we did.' Yakob had a relieved smile on his face.

'What'll happen to them?'

'The *Grip* will send a boarding party to take control and they'll bring the ship back to Priam,' said Yakob. 'Which is better than they deserve, considering what they've put us through.'

'Message coming through from the *Grip*,' said Bess. 'Want me to put it up on screen?'

'Patch it through,' said Yakob.

The whole windscreen blanked and then cleared to reveal a woman in uniform, sitting in a chair. She was in a glass-walled room, but the glass was very dark and obscured what was on the other side. It was, Dez realized, the woman whose hologram had spoken to him when he'd first set foot in *Stark*. Tor Kobal, Wing Leader of the T-class StarJumper *Tyson's Grip*, didn't say anything for a moment or two, just smiled and nodded at them.

'Whatever happened to "contact Wing Leader immediately on arrival at pick-up"?' she asked. 'Or did you have a different set of orders to mine, Captain Pell?'

'There was a virus in the communications lobe.' Yakob sat bolt upright in his seat. 'Bess can confirm.'

'Bess?' frowned Tor Kobal.

'I'm sorry ...' Yakob looked flustered and embarrassed. 'I mean B-SI 96774/XA can confirm the details of the infection that stopped us sending co-ordinates.'

'Bee Ess Eye nine-whatever?' said Treece, whispering in Dez's ear.

'Bio-Syntonic Intelligence,' Dez whispered back. 'That's what she's called.'

'Permission to dock?' asked Yakob.

'Permission granted. You do have all *three* subjects on board?'

'We do.'

'Good work. You will come in to secure dock 12-700 and go straight into isolation. No one on the *Grip*, apart from myself, knows why we're here,' said Tor, looking over her shoulder at the blacked-out glass behind her. 'And only a handful of personnel will know you're on board. I've over-ridden all communications systems, and we're not even telling Command Centre on Priam what's happened.'

'They haven't caught the spy yet?' queried Yakob.

'No,' frowned Tor. 'Still on the loose and making life incredibly difficult. I'll see you all in the Iso-unit.'

The screen blanked and then cleared to reveal the great blue wave that was the side of *Tyson's Grip*. Dez could see no windows, and nothing that looked even remotely like a docking bay.

'How big is that thing?' he said, bending over to see how much more of it there was. At the top of the windscreen he could just make out the upper edge of the *Grip*, where blue met black and the stars began again.

'One and a half kliks long, with a crew of some 30,000,' said Bess. 'Big enough.'

'And they're going to stick us in an isolation unit when we get there.' Treece picked up Tyler, who was sitting by her feet, and tickled his ears. 'Not going to be much different from being on board that Väd ship, is it, Tyler?'

'What's going on?' the Väd-Raatch Quadrant Marshall thumped his console angrily. 'I can't get any reply. Has some idiot broken the link?'

'No, sir ... at least not from this end,' replied his second-in-command. 'I'm checking, but it seems the problem is on the assault craft.'

'How could there be a problem now? They were just docking the Tylurian – I *saw* it happening with my own eyes!'

'We can get no response, sir. Do you want to authorize another craft to warp to those co-ordinates?'

'I have a feeling it would be a waste of time,' said the Quadrant Marshall, suddenly aware of how bitter the taste of failure was.

Chapter 38

Leaving Bess to guide *Stark* into the secure bay, Yakob went back to change into his uniform. Treece, with Tyler on her lap, sat in his seat and all three of them watched, fascinated, as they approached *Tyson's Grip*.

'What do you look like, Bess?' said Dez.

Bess didn't reply for a moment and then she laughed. 'Good question! And one I'm sure no B-SI has ever been asked before.' She paused, as if unsure of what to say next. 'I don't have an answer, Dez, although I am, in almost every way, alive – just like you. I come from a culture that accepts us for what we are … essential yet invisible. I suppose I look like *Stark*, because that's where I am.'

'Right,' Dez nodded. 'I kind of understand. Hope you didn't mind me asking.'

'Not at all,' said Bess. 'And look, in case we don't meet again I just want to say that, even if I've been a bit tough on you at times, I wouldn't have missed meeting you three for the world.'

Stark banked slightly and swooped down towards a pattern of lights, similar to those on the Väd ship, that had lit up around a brilliant white oblong. The docking bay entrance. Unlike the one they'd so recently exited with Cold Pulse cannons blazing, this one was almost deserted, with only a small isolated group of people waiting at the far end.

'Aren't you coming back to Priam with us?' asked Dez.

'Yes, but I'm part of a military operation,' she said. 'I have no control over what happens to me or where I'll be.'

As *Stark* levelled out and flew into the bay, Yakob came back up front. He was now wearing a smart light grey one-piece uniform which had bright red markings on the shoulder and the breast pocket. Hanging from his belt was a holster with a laser pistol in it.

'OK, Bess,' he said. 'Take us down.'

'Better stop calling me that, Captain Pell; they'll think you've gone mad.'

'It's going to take some time for me to get used to the old ways,' said Yakob. 'I've rather enjoyed being able to do things how I want to.'

'Why should it change?' said Treece, holding on to Tyler as he strained forward, quivering as he looked at the half-dozen or so people waiting for them.

'I'm back in uniform,' he replied, 'and under orders. Now I have to do as I'm told.'

'Yakob ...' Dez tapped his arm. 'Yakob, why are they all wearing visored helmets?'

'Standard Iso-unit gear,' he said.

Bess brought *Stark* down like a feather and, for what he thought was probably the last time, Dez watched its stubby wings melt seamlessly away.

'Let's go,' said Yakob, patting Treece and Dez on their shoulders. 'Mustn't keep security waiting.'

Dez looked round the bland grey and white Iso-unit. It was a series of some half a dozen rooms that were sealed off from the rest of *Tyson's Grip* and under heavy guard. What spooked him was that the guards were on the inside, still wearing their full-face helmets. Yakob had gone off into one of the rooms with the squad leader, leaving the three of them alone.

'These *are* the good guys, aren't they?' said Treece after a while.

'Don't ask me stuff like that,' said Dez, watching Tyler sniffing his way round the room and paying close attention to the guard by the door. 'Why are you so suspicious?'

'Why are we locked up?'

'They said it was for our own safety, so the spy wouldn't know anything about us.'

'Well, they would, wouldn't they?'

Yakob walked out of the room he'd been in and Tyler stopped investigating the guard's boots and ran over to him, leaping up on his spring-loaded legs. He looked like a crazed jack-in-a-box.

'There's something I have to say, or rather show you,'

Yakob said, bending to catch Tyler in mid-leap and letting him lick his hand. 'It's a secret I had to keep until now …'

'You *are* the bad guys – I knew it!' Treece moved away from Yakob and closer to Dez. 'What are you going to do to us?'

'Hold on, Treece … let him finish,' said Dez, standing up. A thought had surfaced in his mind – more a collection of random events and unconnected sentences that were only now beginning to make sense. 'I think I know what he's going to show us. Do it, Yakob.'

'Do what?' said Treece, frowning.

'Look at him.'

They both looked. Of all the weird, strange things Dez had seen, this just about topped the list: as if someone was pouring water on to his head, colour began to run down Yakob's face, making it look like a painting left out in a rain storm. His hair disappeared, revealing instead short dark spines; pale skin washed away, leaving behind shiny light green scales, hooded dark green eyes and a thin mouth. Tyler lay rigid in his arms, his ears flat back on his head.

'You guessed,' he said, a blue forked tongue flicking through his sharp teeth. His voice, unlike his appearance, hadn't changed one bit. 'When?'

'Just now,' said Dez, aware that the guard by the door had lifted the visor on his helmet. He felt a bit light-headed and sat down very slowly.

'How?'

'Dunno,' he said. 'Lots of little things ... they just sort of added up.'

'He ... they look like ... *lizards*!' Treece came and sat right next to him, very close.

'They look like the Väds,' Dez corrected her. 'But why, Yakob?'

'Why did I hide what I really looked like from you?' Yakob put Tyler down and he ran behind Dez's legs. 'How would you have reacted if *this*,' he pointed at his face, 'was what you'd seen when we first met?'

Dez was silent. Yakob was right, of course; if he'd come to after being thrown from his parents' car to find himself staring at someone who looked like a talking reptile there was no telling what he'd have done. The deception had, he realized, been a vital one. It was still a deception though.

'Why didn't you tell me, you know, later, when things had calmed down?'

'They never did calm down; it was one crisis after another,' Yakob said. 'And then you got captured by the Väds. After that there was no way I could tell you; you'd never have believed in me once you knew the truth.'

'*I* still don't,' said Treece.

'Why?' Yakob walked over and sat on a chair opposite them, ignoring Tyler's growling. 'Because we look the same? We come from the same planet, originally, so is it so odd we are similar? I know it's hard, but think about yourselves – so alike but so different. It's what's underneath the skin, not the colour of that skin, that counts, and I think I've proved the kind of person I really am, underneath.'

'"Don't judge people by what they look like, they aren't always what they seem." Isn't that what you said?' asked Dez, getting up.

'I think I did.'

'Can I touch you?'

'Go ahead, I don't bite,' said Yakob, extending his right hand.

'Unlike Tyler!' grinned Dez, taking Yakob's hand and shaking it. 'Cool and soft,' he said.

'That's me.'

Dez heard a snuffling noise and looked down to see Tyler gingerly examining Yakob's legs, ears still back and ready to make a run for it. He bent down and picked him up. Yakob put his hand out and let the dog sniff it.

'Still me,' he said, tickling him behind the ear. 'What about you, Treece? How do you feel about me now?'

'Confused ... how do we know it's not just another trick?'

Yakob looked over at the guard by the door and then at the squad leader who'd come out of the room they'd both been in. 'We're all the same,' he said. 'And what would be the point of lying to you now?'

'I don't know the point of *anything* any more,' Treece shrugged. 'Do you lot lay eggs, then? The lizards where I come from do.'

'Amazing! From total distrust to highly personal questions in one easy bound!' Yakob laughed out loud, showing off all the many sharp teeth in his disconcertingly wide mouth and clapping his hands.

'Do I take it that the shock wasn't too much for them, Captain Pell?'

Dez hadn't noticed the guard let someone into the Iso-unit. The newcomer stood by the door, hands on hips, and looked at them, head on one side in an almost bird-like fashion. 'Aren't you going to introduce me?'

Yakob stiffened noticeably. 'Wing Leader! I didn't hear you come in.' He nodded curtly. 'Dez, Treece and, er, Tyler, this is Tor Kobal, Commander of *Tyson's Grip*.'

'Happy to make your acquaintance,' said Tor, shaking Dez and Treece by the hand and patting Tyler's head. 'Our course is plotted and we should be leaving for the Cygnus Rift very shortly, just as soon as the co-ordinates match. I'm sorry that we have to keep you locked away, but do let me know if there's anything you want.'

'I've got a question,' said Dez.

Tor Kobal's tongue flicked in and out. 'What?'

'Are you, like, *female*? Or …'

'Or was I pretending?' Tor showed some teeth. 'I am female, and to answer the previous question,' she looked at Treece, 'I do lay eggs, but only in private.'

With that she left the room, and it was quite some time before anyone could think of what to say.

Chapter 39

T-class StarJumpers, like *Tyson's Grip*, never landed anywhere. They were built off-planet and stayed there, ships in a dark sea with no port to call home. The vast, seemingly endless wastes of deep space were what these enormous fortresses were made to journey through. And, like old medieval cities, they were entirely self sufficient and had no needs they couldn't supply themselves.

The journey from Pluto orbit to Priam would be over almost the instant it began, but in the time they had to wait for warp alignment, Yakob, using holo-displays and wall-sized screens, took Dez and Treece on a short guided tour of the vessel.

If *Stark Revenge* had seemed to be an Aladdin's cave of near-magical technology, *Tyson's Grip* made it look like a toy. This gargantuan construction, with its tree-lined walkways and seasonal micro-climate, its factory levels and leisure facilities, was too vast to be run by a single intelligence and Yakob explained that it was controlled by a panel of B-SIs, like Bess. A sort of Board of Directors who cooperated in the joint venture of keeping all the complex systems running smoothly.

Timing, when it came to 300,000 light year jumps of the sort they were about to make, was of paramount importance. The screen they were looking at showed the control deck. It was tense and silent and of the hundred or so people there not one spoke. Sitting at a relatively small desk Dez could see Tor Kobal, her hands poised above its consoles, looking like a statue. She was waiting for the word from the intelligences, for the go-ahead to warp out.

'Don't we have to strap ourselves in or anything?' asked Dez, remembering the sickening heave the simple jumps out of Earth orbit had brought with them.

'A ship this size has all sorts of compensating equipment, and it's also in zero gravity, so, no, we don't,' said Yakob.

In the moment that Dez glanced away from the screen to see what Tyler was up to something must have happened, because when he looked back the control deck was a hive of activity and he could feel, rather than hear, the tell-tale whine of a warp drive kicking in.

'We're off!' yelled Treece, jumping up and down.

'We're there,' said Yakob. He spoke softly to the screen's console and the picture changed. Instead of the control deck it now showed a starscape, but not one that Dez recognized, except maybe that it looked like the cover of the sci-fi books his friend Tim liked to read.

In the top right-hand corner two white circles, one

larger than the other, were burned into a purply-black curtain. But, centre stage, was the thing that made Dez and Treece gasp, both putting their hands to their faces in the comic-strip way of showing amazement. A huge blue-red planet, with random patterns of white cloud swirling across it, almost filled the screen. Around it spun a glittering multicoloured belt that rippled like a river.

'Wha-?' sputtered Dez.

'Home,' said Yakob. 'May I present Priam in all its glory.'

'It's like Saturn,' whispered Treece, 'but prettier.'

'True, but nowhere near as big,' said Yakob. 'It's very like your planet in many respects, although nearly twice the size.'

'The rings are beautiful.'

'They're what's left of the half dozen or so moons that used to orbit us millions of years ago. You should see them from land-side.' Yakob stopped talking and looked at the guard who'd called his name. 'And it seems you'll be able to do that very soon. We have to prepare to go; they've got a shuttle waiting for us.'

'What happens next?' said Dez, picking Tyler up.

'Downloading.'

'No, I meant *after* we get down.'

'That's what I mean,' said Yakob, walking towards the door. 'They're going to go into your DNA and download the information you three have been so carefully looking after for us.'

Treece turned away from the screen. 'This is it, then.'

'This is the next "it",' smiled Yakob, ushering them out of the Iso-unit. 'There are a lot of people who want to meet you after that's over.'

'Life is full of "its",' said Dez.

'It is, isn't it?' replied Treece, following him into the corridor.

It was a weird experience being hurried through sealed-off maintenance corridors, away from prying eyes. Like mice under the floorboards, they saw no one until they got on board the shuttle craft, where they found Tor Kobal waiting for them. Once everyone was seated she took off and jumped the cloaked shuttle down into Priam's upper atmosphere, piloting it through dense clouds and out into the brilliant light of the twin suns.

Before Dez and Treece had had a chance to take in this extraordinary sight the shuttle dipped into another cloud level, where it stayed for most of the rest of their journey. When it finally came out into the open they were flying low over a vast, trackless desert of reddish-brown sand littered with huge boulders. Dez could just make out a cluster of white domes on the far horizon.

'Even they don't know we're coming,' said Yakob, leaning over and pointing at the glistening domes.

'Who?'

'The people at that bio-facility.'

'If you can't trust anybody round here,' Dez looked

around at Yakob, Tor Kobal and the guards, 'how come *you're* in the know?'

'Some people have to be, but the fewer the better,' said Tor, taking the shuttle down even closer to the ground. 'It was agreed at the planning stages of this mission that once we'd got you, not even the President himself would be told.'

The domes were now much nearer and Dez could see that they didn't cover a very wide area.

'Not a very big place, is it, Yakob?' said Treece.

'It's like an iceberg; most of it's underground, away from prying eyes.'

The shuttle banked sharply, circled the scattered domes and then sank slowly to the ground. Dust was still billowing round the cloaked shuttle, giving it a strange, ghostly outline, when half the guards were outside it and in combat positions.

'Quickly!' said Tor, who now, Dez noticed, had a laser pistol in her hand. 'Get them below ground!'

They were rushed from the wide open desert into the tight claustrophobic confines of a box that began to plummet down at a terrifying rate. As soon as the lift doors opened Tor strode out and Dez could tell by her tone of voice that she was taking control, demanding action, issuing orders at a machine-gun rate and generally bossing the heck out of everyone.

'Glad she's not my mum,' Dez muttered to no one in particular.

Once the bio-facility had calmed down and Tor was satisfied it was secure, Dez, Treece and Tyler were led into a gleaming laboratory that smelled so clean it made your nose wrinkle. Everyone there wore white coveralls and talked in hushed voices.

Dez was getting used to the fact that the three of them were the odd ones out – that here on Priam green skin, of varying shades, was normal and having hair on your head was not. Being looked at, like an animal in a zoo, was harder to take, and as they walked through the lab he was aware they were the centre of attention.

They went through to a smaller room where a Tylurian sat behind a desk. He was big and the skin on his face was loose, a large fold hanging from his chin, and the spines on his head were a yellowy colour. Dez got the strong impression that he was old.

'This is Parak Coulter, Director of this facility,' said Tor. 'He will be in charge of taking the code out. He doesn't have your language, so Yakob will stay with you to translate.' She spoke to the director and listened to his gruff reply. 'He tells me the whole process will not take long and to follow him. I'll see you all later.'

With that Tor left the room; Parak Coulter looked at each of them in turn, leaning over his desk to peer at Tyler, and then spoke to Yakob.

'What did he say?' asked Treece nervously.

'He said they chose a very strange hiding place,' said Yakob.

Parak Coulter, it turned out, wasn't very big on conversation, so Yakob didn't have much to translate. He went with Treece, Dez and Tyler as they followed the director into a long, narrow room stuffed full of equipment that hummed, buzzed and danced with multicoloured flashing lights. The place somehow managed to look festive and surgical at the same time – frightening and friendly, thought Dez. At the very end he could see what looked like a large, softly curved black dentist's chair.

'He's not going to take a tooth out, is he?'

'No,' said Yakob, 'just two tissue samples and some blood from each of you. I've suggested we do Tyler first. Who wants to hold him?'

'I will,' said Dez. 'I've done this before … you know, with my dog at home.'

He bent down and picked the little Jack Russell up, stroking him behind the ears, watching Parak Coulter as he went over to a shiny metal worktop and opened a case that sat on it. Dez tensed when he saw him take out what appeared to be a chromed pistol with three clawed spikes curving to a point from the tip of its barrel.

Tyler, his sharp, beady eyes fixed on the shambling Tylurian, stiffened and a low growl rumbled in his throat.

'This could be tricky.' Dez looked over at Yakob. 'Can't you say something to him? Calm him down? Like you did with Treece's dog?'

Yakob came over and stood by Dez, stroking Tyler's

head with one hand and slowly bringing his other one up in front of him. Dez watched as the dog looked at the small black box Yakob was holding, and he almost missed the multiple throb of light it emitted. He couldn't miss the fact that Tyler was now spark out in his arms.

'Are you going to hypno-pulse us as well?' he asked.

'Only if you want me to.'

Dez looked at Treece. She shook her head, frowning.

'No,' she said. 'I want to be awake. I don't want any more stuff happening to me that I don't know about.'

Before Dez could reply, Parak Coulter said something to Yakob and walked over to the chair, the shiny gun glinting in his hand. It looked ready to bite.

'Bring Tyler and sit with him on your lap.' Yakob patted Dez on the shoulder. 'It'll be fine, he won't feel a thing.'

With Treece standing right next to him, Dez, cradling Tyler in his arms, watched as the Tylurian parted the fur on the dog's back leg, placed the silver instrument firmly over the exposed skin and pulled the trigger. There was a soft *TH-TEW!-TH-TEW!-TH-TEW!* sound and Parak Coulter took the gun away, repeating the operation on Tyler's neck.

Smoothing the dog's fur and gently patting him, he walked away and, with his back to them, did something at a work bench. Dez could feel the tension gripping his body; this was what it all came down to – this moment in a windowless room, deep underground on a planet unimaginably far from Earth.

His mind teemed with thoughts, like a pond full of frantic tadpoles. Everything that had happened to him had been leading up to an incident as horribly normal as having a 'flu jab at school. Dez found himself feeling disappointed, expecting more, wanting there to be a real sense of occasion. They were saving a world, for heaven's sake! Shouldn't that mean something? It was all too … well, ordinary.

'Want to go next?'

Dez looked up at Yakob. 'Sorry? I was miles away,' he said.

'I'll hold Tyler,' Yakob said, holding his hands out. Dez saw Parak Coulter turning back towards them; he was fitting a new spiked head on the gun as he spoke to Yakob.

'Sit back in the chair and roll up both your sleeves,' said Yakob.

Dez looked down at his arm, concentrating on the tiny blond hairs. Then Parak Coulter's cool, scaly hand touched him and he jumped. He looked up into the slightly sagging face of the old Tylurian and then down again as he felt the cool metal spikes on his skin.

This was it.

He held his breath and waited. The gun sighed as Parak pulled the trigger and Dez felt something sharp dart into his arm … once … twice … three times. 'What's that thing do?' asked Dez, as Parak went behind him.

'Basically, it grabs minute tissue and blood samples, three at a time,' explained Yakob. 'He does it twice and then does a cross-match to check he's got everything he needs to extract the information.'

Dez felt the spikes on his other arm, and seconds later it was all over. He got off the chair and rolled his sleeves down.

'You OK?' asked Treece, as she took his place.

'S'pose so,' Dez made a face.

'What's the matter?'

'I don't know … I expected more.'

'More what?'

'I dunno, more machinery,' said Dez, 'more pain, more *something*!'

'I'd have thought you would have had enough excitement to last you for a long time,' Yakob said.

'Maybe.' Dez went over to look at Tyler. 'Maybe I've just got used to living on the edge.'

Chapter 40

They were now back in the shuttle, the bio-facility somewhere over the horizon behind them and the desert rushing by only metres below.

'All that fuss for a couple of minutes in a fancy dentist's chair!' said Treece.

'The hard work is only just beginning,' said Tor. 'Parak Coulter has to decode the information and recreate the matrix. He'll have to work alone and it could take him some time. Your job is over, but his has just started.'

'Are we safe now?' said Treece. 'Can we go back to Earth? Back home?'

'Not yet,' Tor continued. 'Although we've got you now, the Väds still think you have the code in your DNA and may try and grab you back.'

'We *don't* still have the code?' Dez leaned forward in his seat.

'No,' said Yakob. 'Parak injected a "seek-and-destroy" anti-gene into you all at the same time as he took the samples; it's wiping the extra matter from your DNA right now … it should have finished doing its job before we get to the Kapitol.'

'Can't feel anything,' said Dez.

'You didn't know it was there and you won't know when it's gone,' grinned Yakob.

'Is this positively the last time you lot are going to mess about with us?' Treece sounded ready for an argument. 'Because I don't know about Dez, but I'm *totally* fed up with it.'

'A major apology is coming your way, all of you,' said Tor. 'Elat Yeriaf, our President, will deliver it himself.'

'Does he know we're coming now?' asked Dez.

'He knows the operation's been a success, but that's all.'

'Talk about cloak and dagger!' Dez was about to say something to Treece when a flurry of messages erupted from the speakers in the cockpit and Tor began issuing commands. The guards, who had been relaxing after a job well done, all made a grab for their weapons. 'What the heck … ?'

'Planet-wide alarm,' muttered Yakob. 'Väd attack!'

'Blanket missile attack,' Tor said over her shoulder. 'We're going to land and wait this out.'

The landing was abrupt, the shuttle juddering and shaking as it touched down. For a couple of seconds no one said anything, then Tor spoke to the craft's Bio-Syntonic Intelligence and the windscreen darkened and threw up a holo-image of Priam. Hundreds of red lines snaked and twisted towards it from space.

'I'm getting a feed direct from Central Command,'

said Tor. 'We should see our defences kicking in about now.'

As she spoke, vivid blue lines shot up from the planet's surface and, where they connected with the incoming red ones, brilliant purple globes blossomed and died. A small number of red attackers evaded the Tylurian counter-attack and pulsating circles on Priam's surface showed where they'd hit.

A high-pitched siren suddenly bellowed inside the shuttle and Yakob yelled above the racket: 'Escaper in our quadrant – everyone down!'

A sound that Dez recognized echoed inside the shuttle as they hit the floor. Tor was blasting away with the shuttle's battery of Cold Pulse cannon. 'How do they know we're here?' he shouted to Yakob.

'They don't know *where* you are,' he yelled back. 'This is a pure revenge attack.'

'Just our luck if they hit us,' said Treece, grabbing Dez as the shuttle bucked. 'What was *that*?'

'The Väd missile exploding – we got it before it made the ground,' Tor called back.

The incoming missile trails on the holo-image suddenly stopped appearing and everyone watched as the last of the red lines bloomed and faded. 'Our hunters must've found their attack fleet,' said Tor. 'Looks like it's over.'

For now, thought Dez, as the shuttle lifted off. But would it ever really be over? Giving up wasn't something the Väds seemed capable of doing, and the idea that the rest of his life might be spent hiding from them was just too depressing. He forced the notion away to the very back of his mind and went to look out of a window.

Below him he could see the red grass and trees, the small villages and towns, and the roads weaving their way between them. In an odd sort of way it looked vaguely familiar, people carrying on their daily lives unaware of his existence. Just like on Earth.

Flying into the Kapitol, the shuttle, with its military insignia, was just another craft with the necessary electronic clearance code coming in to land on the vast roof of the Tylurian High Command's flat-topped pyramid tower. No one took much notice of it until a dozen or so nervously efficient guards silently ushered three strange-looking creatures across the landing pad.

The first the High Command's security chief knew about it was when Tor Kobal walked straight into his office unannounced and told him to seal the building and not let anyone in or out.

'This is completely unreal,' said Treece, as they stood surrounded by guards whose eyes never stopped moving, checking, observing.

'I think I must be getting used to it,' Dez nodded to himself. 'I mean, after what we've seen and done in the last few days, how much more unreal can it get?'

Tor came out of the security chief's office, issuing a stream of commands to the guards. 'Right,' she said.

'We're going straight to the Council Chamber, they're in session now!'

'Is that good?' Dez asked Yakob as he hurried along beside him and out into a corridor.

'It means everyone who matters on Priam will hear the news at the same time and Elat Yeriaf can contact the Väd-Raatch and negotiate a cease-fire immediately,' he replied. 'It could all be over within hours.'

Spearing their way through a maze of wide corridors, ignoring the amazed stares and rising babble of voices, the guards burst into a brightly-lit circular anteroom, forming two lines through which Tor led Yakob and his three Earthlings.

She stopped and demanded something of the fifty or so people standing in small groups in the room. Someone spoke up in one of the groups nearest her, stepping forward as he did so.

'What's happening?' Treece asked Yakob.

'She wants to know where Elat Yeriaf is, and that councillor told her he'd be here any minute now.'

Dez had been gawping at the room when he noticed Tyler wandering through the guards' legs, sniffing the carpet. He trotted over to the Tylurian standing next to the one who'd been speaking to Tor and sat down to scratch his ear. The sight of the strange little creature broke the tension in the room and everyone laughed. Tyler got up and wagged his tail.

The Tylurian bent down to pat him and said something which Treece again asked Yakob to translate. Dez heard him whisper: 'He said, "So this is what a dog looks like," although he used the word "biter", which is the nearest to dog we have in Tylurian.'

For a moment Dez just stood where he was, his mind locked in a tumble of recurring questions to which there was only one possible answer. He pushed past two of the guards and walked over to the man.

'What did you say?' he asked, trying to sound as polite as possible.

The Tylurian looked puzzled and shook his head.

'He doesn't speak English, Dez,' Yakob called out.

Dez turned his back to the councillor. 'You told Treece he said that *this*,' he pointed to Tyler, 'is what a dog looks like, didn't you?'

Yakob nodded.

'Well, how did he know?' asked Dez.

'Know what?' said Tor, frowning.

'How did he know there'd be a dog when nobody else did? We all thought Tyler was going to be another kid until we found him ...' Dez's voice died away. Everyone in the room was staring past him, as though he was invisible. Only then did he realize the full meaning of what he'd said.

He stood and waited, listening to the sound of Tyler panting, and then he saw Treece pointing, a silent scream on her lips, but her warning came too late. A soft ribbed hand grabbed him by the throat and he nearly fell as he was pulled backwards.

'I'm afraid Captain Pell is wrong,' said a voice behind

him. 'I do speak your language, and his accurate translation of what I stupidly said about that creature has rather spoiled my carefully laid plans.'

'You can't escape, Councillor Berow,' said Tor, her laser pistol pointed their way. 'The whole building is sealed off and you are surrounded.'

'I have a one-way ticket.' Dez felt something cold and hard against his forehead. 'And I will have no hesitation in destroying it if anyone comes anywhere near me.' Dez felt the hand on his neck tighten its grip. 'I want a clear path to the roof and transport when I get there. I want a safe passage off-planet, or Jack Danby ceases to exist.'

From where Dez stood he could see a bristling array of weaponry aimed in his general direction and he cursed himself for not engaging brain before he spoke. How many times had his dad told him to do that? Millions, probably.

If he'd kept his mouth shut and quietly told Yakob the meaning of what he'd heard the spy say – because that was what Councillor Berow was without a doubt – he wouldn't have a deadly laser at his head right now.

He was staggered at the stupid things a mind could start doing when panic set in; he found himself trying to count the buttons on the nearest guard's uniform, and his whole head filled with the insistent drum-beat of his heart … one button, two buttons, three buttons.

'Tell your guards to move, Wing Leader!' barked the councillor, his angry voice jerking Dez back to reality. 'Now!'

'No one tells *anyone* to do *anything* except me, Sarke Berow,' boomed a voice Dez hadn't heard before. 'And I'm telling you to put down that gun and let the boy go.'

'Not a chance, Elat,' sneered Berow. 'I don't want to spend the rest of my life in some festering prison cell – I'd rather die!'

'That can be arranged with no trouble at all,' said the newcomer, an imposing figure dressed in black who now stood beside Tor.

'I die, he dies,' said Berow, jabbing the gun at Dez, 'and you lose the weapon. Can you afford to do that, when your enemy is the Väd-Raatch?'

Dez watched Tor whisper something in Elat Yeriaf's ear. He smiled and nodded. 'We have the weapon already, Sarke; we have the code and it's been wiped from their DNA ... you're too late.'

'I don't believe you! You're bluffing!' Berow angrily waved the gun at the guards. 'Move them!' he yelled. And then he let out an agonized howl, his other hand letting go of Dez's neck.

'Get down!' shouted Yakob, and as Dez threw himself sideways he saw a small white and black dog trying his level best to kill Councillor Sarke Berow's arm.

'We all forgot about Tyler,' Yakob said, checking the bruises on Dez's neck. They were standing behind a line of guards, watching Councillor Berow being taken out of the anteroom. He was spitting insults at everyone, his tongue quivering between his teeth.

'Lucky for me Sarke Berow had forgotten about him,' said Dez. 'How did he do it?'

'He just jumped,' said Treece, who had Tyler in her arms. 'Didn't you, boy? He was like a guided missile ... flew through the air and zapped him! I thought he was going to tear his arm off.'

'It took three of us to get him to let go.' Yakob leaned over and stroked Tyler's head. 'He's lethal, this one. I'm glad he's on my side!'

'We all are,' said a voice. Dez looked up and saw the black-clad figure of Elat Yeriaf standing by them, the scales of his very dark green skin glistening. 'Would you like to come with us into the Council Chamber? We're going to open channels to Anavrin and lay our cards on the negotiating table with the Väd-Raatch – and it's all thanks to you three that we have an unbeatable hand.'

Chapter 41

Even if they hadn't been given tiny ear plug translation units Dez was sure he'd have been able to understand most of what was going on. Sitting high up at the back of the Council Chamber together with Yakob and Treece, with Tyler asleep next to them, he'd watched as the comms-link opened between Priam and Anavrin.

The Väd-Raatch leader, General Garel, flanked by six others also in battle uniform, said nothing while Elat told them the bare facts of how things now stood.

'All your efforts have been in vain, Garel,' he said. 'We found the three and got them back safely to Priam – at no small cost to you, I gather.' A low murmur rippled through the Council Chamber and then Elat continued: 'So, it is with some sadness that I have to tell you we are reconstructing the bacteria.'

He paused, waiting to see what the Väd leader would say, but he remained silent.

'We have always said it was there as a threat, no more, no less, and not one we ever wanted to use. Until the coup that brought you to power our two planets had held a truce, uneasy though it may have been, for longer than I can remember …'

'A truce is merely a coward's way to end a fight.' Garel's harsh voice echoed round the Council Chamber. 'A fight should end with the blood of the vanquished in the victor's cup, no more, no less.'

'We don't want your blood; we want peace, but on *our* terms!' Elat slammed his fist down on the desk in front of him. 'Ours! You have forced us to do this, Garel, and we will make sure the whole of Anavrin knows that. We *will* use the weapon if you attack us again. And in case you had forgotten what that will mean, let me show you.' He signalled to someone and to his left a screen flickered into life. 'Watch,' he said, 'and remember.'

A voice in Dez's ear told him that he was watching a controlled experiment in which a mutated and genetically reconstructed bacteria was introduced into a hermetically sealed environment. On the screen he saw some kind of vivarium, like they'd had in his school's science lab; a variety of small furry creatures skittered about and what appeared to be tiny winged snakes flew erratically around.

One cubic millimetre of the *Exaer bacillus*, said the voice, was released into a unit containing twelve and a half cubic metres of atmospheric air. Dez saw some digits racing away in the bottom right-hand corner of the screen and within seconds every living thing in the vivarium was dead and there was a thick blue growth crawling down two sides of the glass. Seconds after that the growth had turned a light brown and stopped growing.

The disembodied voice in Dez's head said that the entire oxygen content had been devoured by the microscopic plant-like *bacillus* in approximately 0.268 seconds, and 0.317 seconds later the bacteria had bloomed out of control and the colony itself was dead.

'It wouldn't take long for Anavrin to be suffocated,' said Elat, the image on the screen frozen on the dead animals strewn about the floor of the glass box. 'Once this particular cage door is opened there is no getting the beast back in.'

Dez saw the Väd leader listen as the person next to him whispered in his ear. He clenched and unclenched his fists and finally spoke: 'We agree to stand down our forces,' he said, not looking directly at the camera.

'And to return all captured territory and personnel?'

'If you do.'

'Agreed,' said Elat. 'Your spy will be with the first contingent. We don't want him.'

Garel's teeth bared momentarily. 'Our spy?'

'Sarke Berow. You see, Garel, it really *is* all over.'

Dez sat at the head of the longest table he'd ever seen in his whole life. It was loaded with all manner of strange delights and stretched the full length of the massive room they were in. Yakob was to his right with Tor Kobal next to him, and Treece was two seats to his left. They were either side of Elat Yeriaf, who now stood to address the members of the Council gathered to celebrate the end of the war and congratulate the three young aliens who had made it all possible. The third "young alien" was asleep under Dez's chair.

Elat apologized profusely for the trouble his guests had been put through, continuing that there was really nothing he could say or do to make up for the torment and danger they, the Tylurian race, had caused them. They would, he said, be returned to Earth immediately – in fact *Tyson's Grip* was waiting in orbit to do just that. Treece looked happier than Dez had ever seen her, but for some reason he couldn't put his finger on, he didn't feel the same way at all.

When everything was over, Dez found himself alone with Yakob, sitting in one of the room's many alcoves.

'What's wrong, Dez?'

'How d'you know anything is?' Dez looked away and saw Tyler trotting over to them, tail wagging lazily and stomach bulging. He'd eaten a lot of something, that was for sure.

'I know you well enough to know when something's not right. Want to talk about it?'

'I would if I knew what to say, but it's really just a feeling and I can't seem to put it into words.'

'Aren't you pleased to be going home?' asked Yakob, as Tyler jumped up on to Dez's lap and licked his chin.

It took a moment to sink in, but Dez suddenly realized what the matter was. 'That's the problem, Yakob,' he sighed, hugging the dog. 'I don't *have* a home any more. My parents are dead, I've got no family – you and Bess and Treece are the only people who really know who I am now.' He felt a weight of sadness push down on him unlike anything he'd ever experienced. 'What have I got to go back to?' he said. 'What have I got to go back *for*?'

Yakob sat and looked at him thoughtfully. 'It's where you belong; it's your place,' he said.

'If I go back to England what will I tell them? I can't tell the truth; they'd think I was mad. I'd probably get put in some home, 'cos no one wants to adopt kids my age, and it'll be a nightmare.' Dez leant forward and put his head on his hand.

'Got a headache or something?'

Dez looked up and saw Treece had joined them. 'In more ways than one,' he said.

'I'm sure they've got something to cure it, haven't you, Yakob?'

'Not this one,' he replied.

'I don't want to go back to Earth,' mumbled Dez, not looking at her.

'What? Why not?'

'It's different for you; you've got a home and a family, friends and everything. I'm on my own now, *really* on my own.'

'You could live with me,' said Treece.

'You're going to find it hard enough explaining your sudden disappearance without turning up with me in tow.' Dez glanced at Yakob. 'How *is* she going to explain that?'

'The wonders of hyper-light drive, combined with the complex nature of the curved universe, mean that she will be back in Lagos just over twenty-four hours after she left.'

'How?' interrupted Dez. 'That's not possible – we've been away *far* longer than that!'

'Well, time is an odd thing; it stretches and it contracts,' continued Yakob. 'I even showed you how it could be reversed, if only slightly. With the right co-ordinates we can have Treece home the day before yesterday.'

'And her excuse when she walks through the front door?' said Dez.

'I'll say I was kidnapped,' said Treece.

'But that's what happened!'

'Yeah, but I won't say it was by *aliens*, silly!' laughed Treece. 'As long as they don't think I ran away to get out of summer school I'll be all right.'

'But why would anyone want to kidnap you?'

'My dad works for a bank; it's happened before to people like us. Why d'you think we have an alarm and the big dog?'

'Fat lot of good they did,' said Dez.

'They weren't expecting someone like me,' said Yakob. 'So what do *you* think Dez should do?'

Treece went to the table and picked up a piece of green and white striped fruit. 'I think he should stay,' she said, biting into it.

'Why?'

'He can always go back later, when he's ready.'

'Yeah!' said Dez, suddenly feeling a whole lot better. 'When I'm eighteen I can go back and do what I like – live on my own, get a job, anything!'

'Come and visit me,' grinned Treece, wiping juice from her lips. 'Tell me all the news from Priam.'

'And what about Tyler?' asked Yakob.

Tyler was asleep on Dez's lap and looked about as content as a dog could be.

'He'll be my connection, you know, with Earth,' said Dez.

It was dawn when the shuttle left the landing pad on the roof of the High Command building. The twin suns rose slowly above the skyline, one after the other, bleeding light across the horizon like a double wound. It was cold on the roof and the air felt damp; Dez shivered inside the thick coat he'd been given and huddled close to Yakob as they watched Tor Kobal in the cockpit window.

When Treece joined her they both waved. The shuttle lifted off, silent as a leaf blown by an autumn wind, and then they were gone, quickly becoming a mere speck in the dark blue sky. Finally they disappeared and Dez realized dawn had broken on his first real day on Priam.

Tyler poked his head out of Dez's coat and yawned. He felt like a hot water bottle and just as comforting.

'Are you sure you've made the right decision?' asked Yakob, turning to go back inside. 'It's not too late to change your mind.'

'If it's OK to stay, I'm staying.'

'The Council were unanimous,' said Yakob, calling a lift to take them down. 'They said it was the least we could do to offer you a place to stay for as long as you liked. How do you feel about my suggestion you live with my family?'

'How do *they* feel about it?' Dez watched the lift doors close.

'Can't wait to meet you!' said Yakob.

'It's going to be odd being the only one of a kind, but I'm sure everyone'll get used to me after a while.'

'I have another suggestion to make about that,' said Yakob. 'Come with me.'

The lift stopped and Dez, Tyler at his heels, followed him down a corridor and into a room. 'I'm told there's no reason this shouldn't work,' said Yakob, looking rather pleased with himself. 'I've just had to get the techs to make a few adjustments for cell structure.'

'What are you going on about?' Dez couldn't see anything special, just a room full of consoles twittering to each other.

'Wait there,' said Yakob, sitting in front of a console and giving some instructions. 'This will only take a moment.'

Dez waited. Then he felt his skin tingle, almost heat up, and a twitch ran through him. Looking down he saw Tyler staring back at him, his hackles up. 'What's going on?' he said, his tongue feeling really weird.

‘Look in the mirror,’ Yakob pointed at the wall behind him. ‘Go on.’

Dez walked over to it and stopped dead. Looking back at him was a young, green-skinned Tylurian, mouth open and the spines on his head standing up.

‘How did you *do* that?’ said Dez, eyes riveted on the full set of very sharp teeth in his lipless mouth.

‘I’ve morphed you!’ grinned Yakob. ‘Now you’re one of us – or not, if you don’t want to be. We can switch it off any time you like.’

Dez stared at himself, or rather at the person he’d become. If he was going to stay on an alien planet, a quarter of a million light years from Earth, looking the part was half the battle. ‘I like it,’ he laughed, fascinated by his new reflection. ‘White boy really *does* speak with forked tongue!’

‘What’s that?’

‘Oh, nothing,’ he said, turning away from the mirror. ‘Let’s go home.’

Look out for two other exciting books
by Graham Marks published by Catnip.

TAKEDOWN

One teenage boy, seven days to save the world.

It's 2667 and time is running out for the human race. The safety of the world is in the hands of one man, a soldier more used to taking life than saving it. In turn, he has to rely on a sixteen-year old boy. The two are going to get closer than ever they thought possible.

'A dark, paranoid thriller – I loved it' Philip Reeve

Shortlisted for the Coventry Inspiration Book Awards and The John Lewis Solihull Children's Book Award.

FAULTLINE

Jamie's all that's standing between civilization and outright chaos.

In California the one thing you can be sure of is the past. At least, that's what Jamie Delgado's always thought. Until the day a pack of dinosaurs causes bloody mayhem in a quiet park. Someone, somewhere, has learnt to use history as a weapon. And the result is going to be destruction on a massive scale. Unless Jamie can stop them.

'A pacy, page-turning sci-fi adventure' Philip Reeve